MUR[illegible]

[illegible]

C[illegible]GE

A totally grip[illegible] British crime mystery

BRIAN BATTISON

Detective Jim Ashworth Book 4

Originally published as *The Witch's Familiar*

JOFFE BOOKS

Revised edition 2021
Joffe Books, London
www.joffebooks.com

First published in Great Britain in 1996
as *The Witch's Familiar*

Cover art by Nina Kicul

ISBN: 978-1-78931-756-5

To my mother-in-law
Violet Bowker
for making me feel a part of her happy, loving family

PROLOGUE

Monotonous sounds of a repetitive drumbeat filled the cool night air with an awesome resonance, and alerted Isobel Perkins.

The good folk of Bridgetown were coming for her.

She rushed to the window of her cottage and watched as a torchlight procession wound its way slowly through fields where corn had swayed in a warm breeze just weeks before.

Sparks leapt towards the night sky as that single line of flame reached a bridge spanning the river. More than two hundred torches burned. So, nearly all of them had turned against her.

Although the procession was still a mile away, the smell of burning wood was rich in her nostrils, and still that drumbeat assaulted her ears.

Isobel's first thought was of flight. She hastened to the door of the cottage and flung it open. Then, hampered by her flowing skirts, she made for the manor house at the top of a sharp incline, her long red hair streaming behind as she stumbled along. The night was now cold but the sweat of fear held her clothing fast to her body.

A jet-black cat appeared in the cottage doorway. It stretched and yawned languidly before fixing brilliant green eyes on the slow-moving column of spluttering, flickering light advancing towards it.

As the drumbeat echoed ever louder, the cat set off in pursuit of its mistress, its legs and underbelly soon saturated by the long wet grass.

By the time she reached the manor, Isobel was breathless. She sank to her knees and took large draughts of welcome air into her bursting lungs.

As soon as she was able, Isobel tested the windows, but all were tightly shuttered; and fresh waves of panic swept across her as a new noise rose up to accompany the drumbeat: it was the sound of many voices raised in the chant of 'witch'.

She pulled herself upright and pounded on the door. 'In the name of God, grant me entrance,' she screamed.

The drumbeat reverberated, and the wail of 'witch' increased as the crowd moved closer.

But no sound, no movement came from within the house. In desperation, Isobel looked around for a place to hide.

The line of fire was now snaking past her cottage. So close. She could make out the vague outlines of those carrying the torches, could see the hatred on their faces illuminated in circles of light.

An icy wind came from nowhere and tousled her flame-coloured hair and dried the perspiration on her face.

She scurried down the wide stone steps of the manor like a frightened rabbit and staggered to the building's rear to take sanctuary in a barn.

The cat viewed the advancing horde, its back arched, its teeth bared; and it let out a vengeful spat before following its mistress.

Isobel huddled behind bales of hay in a corner of the barn. Her heart was pounding loudly, rivalling the drumbeat.

The cat settled uneasily on wooden rafters criss-crossing the inner roof, invisible but for its eyes glowing green in the darkness.

Isobel, her voice hoarse and panic-filled, whispered, 'Sathan, conceal thyself.' Immediately, the cat leapt down and burrowed in the hay.

Paralysed by fright, it was a long time before Isobel could move, and her lips spoke a silent prayer as she peered over the bales.

All around was blackness, making it impossible to distinguish shape or form. Only the heavenly cloud-shrouded moon was visible through the open doors. Presently, Isobel crawled towards them, the cold of the stone floor piercing her thick garments.

She had perhaps covered half the distance when a shuffling sound began, and then many boots were stamping on the floor.

'No,' she cried, rising to her feet and trying to run.

Six torches were ignited, their crackling light bringing to life the interior of the barn. Many folk were standing around the sides, still beating their feet with an ominous fury. More appeared in the doorway, crowding, jostling, as they pushed towards her, chanting 'witch' in their dull monotone.

Isobel turned in desperate flight, uttering gibberish as she scrambled upon the hay bales.

But escape was impossible.

And as she made a futile attempt to scale the sheer wall of the barn, rough hands grabbed her, pulled at her ankles and legs until she toppled over and crashed into her attackers.

She landed on the floor, screaming, as clothing was torn from her body, and cold air rushed between her legs. She kicked and screeched, bit and clawed at her assailants, but was overpowered by their sheer numbers, and very soon Isobel was flat on her back, her legs held apart.

A man appeared above her, his wild eyes gleaming, his tongue flicking hungrily as he lowered his breeches. He knelt down quickly and mounted her.

The excited throng pushed forward and cheered as they watched the man enjoying his carnal pleasure.

Isobel lay still and, as coarse fingernails dug into her thighs, she prayed that once he had had his way, they might let her go.

But the rabble became frenzied, brayed for more as the man's seed shot into her. In all, seven men emptied themselves into Isobel before the mood of the onlookers changed.

At last the dead weight of the final violator lifted from her. 'Torch,' he commanded breathlessly, standing over her slight form.

A torch was passed over the heads of the crowd.

'Isobel Perkins,' the man began solemnly. 'I, Jed Collins, Alderman of Bridgetown, do pronounce you a witch, guilty of sorcery and blasphemy in the face of God. Tonight, the good people of this town have witnessed how you can make animals out of upright men.' A murmur of approval circulated around the confined space.

Isobel's breath caught in her throat as heat from the torch neared her legs, and its smoke made her cough and retch.

'No, no,' she implored. 'Please show me mercy. Please . . . please show me mercy.'

But already the flaming torch was moving between her legs. The pain was unbearable and Isobel cried out, struggled, but firm hands held her.

The torch was thrust forward, setting alight her red pubic hair; and Isobel's tortured screams touched all corners of the barn as an excruciating pain racked her body.

Although the flame was extinguished as the torch entered her vagina, its tip remained white hot as it nudged the entrance to her womb.

Isobel was barely conscious now, but she managed to struggle to her feet as the implement was withdrawn.

The crowd jeered in triumph and pushed her from side to side, to and fro, as she staggered, crying out in torment.

Again the dreaded heat came as her frock was set ablaze. Then her head was on fire; her hair, a mass of flame.

'I curse you all,' she yelled, 'and all your future issue.'

Her steps were laboured as she emerged from the barn, the cat close behind, howling its protests at the fire assailing its mistress's back.

Light rain hissed as it touched Isobel's burning body, and she travelled but a few yards before collapsing on to the ground, writhing in agony.

'Kill them, Sathan. Kill them all,' was her choking cry as a soothing balm enveloped her, and the last breath left her body.

* * *

William Martin stood up and staggered. Even for a hard drinker such as he, eight pints of strong ale were more than sufficient to blur the vision and affect the coordination of the limbs.

The alehouse was crowded, but all fellow drinkers stood aside to let him pass, patting his back and speaking in friendly terms.

Yet all the time there was fear in their eyes, for William Martin was one of the seven aldermen of Bridgetown. It was he who had ordered the execution of Isobel Perkins. And those good townsfolk knew only too well that any soul who did not fit in, or caused the committee the slightest displeasure, could suffer the same fate.

Outside, William Martin took one step forward, three steps back, then lurched to his left, colliding heavily with the stone wall of the alehouse.

He righted himself, took a deep breath, and wove an uncertain course along a rutted cart track towards the lights of the town. The frost-covered earth crunched underfoot and the money, which he had saved due to others' generosity, jangled in his pouch.

Rounding a corner near the manor house, he descended the hill which led to the witch's cottage. The sight of it brought a pleasure to his loins, such as he had experienced when taking Isobel. His drunken mind dwelt on it, built excitement within, until he knew he must have a wench that night.

It was then that he noticed the lantern light emanating from within the cottage. It drew him steadily along the path, but his step faltered when the door was opened by Isobel.

'I knew you would come, Will,' she whispered, running a brush through her thick red hair.

'But you . . . you are dead,' he stammered, staggering back. 'We did burn you.'

'Dead?' Isobel laughed. 'Then perhaps I am a spirit, returned to haunt you.'

'No,' he whimpered.

William Martin tried to turn away but found himself rooted to the spot; and then she was beside him, taking his hand, rubbing it over her breasts.

'Is this not of the flesh?' she asked, taking the hand down to her stomach, and on further to the cleft between her legs. 'Is this not a thing of substance that can bring pleasure to a man?'

She stole back into the cottage and waited in the hall. 'Come, Will,' she tempted, removing her long frock.

William's mind was too befuddled, his body too excited for rational thought; he watched, spellbound, as Isobel deposited her frock on the floor to stand before him in long white drawers and clinging bodice.

He stumbled forward but before he was upon her, Isobel had darted into the room and he saw her seated on a wooden settle, the bodice now removed to reveal her large firm breasts.

William came towards her with an ungainly gait, but she simply laughed and side-stepped, causing him to pitch forward and collide with the hard wood of the settle before crashing to the ground.

Dazed, ignoring the pain in his shoulder, William rose to his feet, and Isobel giggled lightly as she vanished through a doorway.

'Come, Will,' she called as her steps sounded on the stairs. 'Come.'

Candlelight flickered from the bedroom. William, his breath now coming in ragged gasps, stopped in the doorway, his eyes wide.

Isobel was standing by the window, a smile playing around her lips. She reached down, her hands pushing the drawers along with them; every movement slow, designed to excite, while the candlelight flickered.

'Enter, Will,' she coaxed as his eyes swept over her now naked body. 'And close the door.'

Bewitched, he obeyed.

When the door banged shut, she started towards him. As she neared, William put out a hand to touch her and an icy blast swept through the room, cutting through his clothing, raising goose-flesh beneath.

Isobel did not stop, did not falter, and he braced himself for a collision.

But it did not happen. And he could only watch as she passed through his body.

Alarmed, he turned quickly to see her standing by the door, her image fading into a hazy mass until only her mocking laughter remained.

Suddenly sober, panic-stricken, and fearing witchcraft, William rushed to the door and flung it open.

Green eyes flashed on the staircase and padded paws began to ascend.

'God, grant me thy protection,' William howled as the panther tossed its head to catch his scent before bounding up the stairs.

With uncontrollable screams of terror, William fled back into the bedroom, slamming the door at the moment the big cat sprang. Unperturbed, it launched itself at the door, smashing it open.

William had no time to cry out. He felt the hot contents of his bowels fill his breeches, and then the black shape was upon him.

CHAPTER 1

'You've lost her?'

Malcolm Headlands thrust the receiver away from his ear and winced at the loudness of the question.

'Only temporarily,' he said, keeping the telephone at a tentative distance for fear of another explosion.

But all that came back was a laugh. 'Find her, Malc. Joyce Regent may only be page five news today, but if she's done a runner, that means she's got something to hide.'

'She moved house,' Headlands explained. 'No "For Sale" board; no advertising in the paper. But I've dug out the names of the estate agent and her solicitor.'

'Find her, Malc, she's worth a lot of money to you.' The line went dead.

'Editors,' Headlands muttered, replacing the receiver. 'But what I didn't tell you', he said to himself, 'is that neither the estate agent nor the solicitor would let on where she's gone. So now what do I do?'

Malcolm Headlands was in his late twenties, tall, slim, and well-proportioned; his dark hair was slick with gel, and a frown spoilt his handsome face.

But he did not pause in thought for very long; as a freelance journalist, Headlands had developed the ability to think on his feet. News was only news for so long, and the tabloids' thirst for dishing the dirt had to be quenched if he was to eat.

Invading people's privacy, even ruining their lives, did not trouble his conscience overmuch; he had been educated at the school of hard knocks, and any finer feelings he might have possessed had long since departed.

Headlands made his way through the small London flat to his study and took a book entitled *Revenge of the Bridgetown Witch* from his large bookcase.

'Yes, worth a try,' he said, flicking through the pages.

He noted the publishers' name and looked up their number in the directory. Dialling from the telephone on his desk, Headlands crossed his fingers as the last digit was punched out.

'Campbell and Shoeturn. Can I help you?' a pleasant female voice answered.

'Good morning, yes, can I speak to the editor handling Joyce Regent's books?'

'That's Gillian Rolands—'

'Of course, Gillian Rolands,' he cut in. 'I'm just looking through my notes.'

'Who shall I say is calling?'

'Dominic Masters,' he lied effortlessly. 'I handle the artwork on Ms Regent's books.'

'Hold the line, please.'

As he listened to an irritating metallic noise passing itself off as a tune, Headlands looked again at a letter from his ex-girlfriend, the mother of his one-year-old child, and blew out air through pursed lips.

Paying maintenance for the kid wasn't enough to satisfy that girl. She wanted him to visit, actually expected him to help in bringing up his son.

'Poor cow,' he laughed, screwing up the letter and taking a straight aim at the wastepaper basket.

Then a voice was in his ear. 'Hello? Jackie speaking. Sorry I kept you waiting.'

‘That’s all right, Jackie. Can I speak to Gillian Rolands, please?’

‘Sorry, she’s in a meeting all morning. Can I help?’

Headlands smiled and mouthed ‘Thank God’ at the ceiling. ‘Yes, I think so, Dominic Masters here. I do all the artwork for Joyce Regent’s books. As you know, she’s moved house and I’ve lost her new address. You couldn’t take a peep for me, could you? I’ve got some designs I must get off to her this morning.’

‘Hold the line, please.’

After thirty seconds, Jackie was back. ‘Right, got it. Actually, it’s a very apt address. It’s Witch’s Cottage, Manor Lane, Bridgetown.’

Headlands scribbled the address on his notepad, and rudely dropped the receiver back in its cradle without further speech. He sat studying the address.

‘OK, Ms Regent, you’re going to be all over the front of the papers again,’ he said, grinning.

* * *

Chief Inspector Jim Ashworth was driving his Sierra along Manor Lane when he passed Joyce Regent, but she made little impression on him. As a man who avoided the tabloid newspapers at all costs, he was unaware that her face had been all over them for weeks.

In any case, his active mind had a more pressing matter to worry over: as from today the very equilibrium of his working life was set to change.

Until recently, Bridgetown Police Station had been run on an outdated system, with the chief constable in residence, and Ashworth directly answerable to him. Now that arrangement was to be altered as relatively rural parts of the Midlands were up-dated.

Ken Savage, the chief constable, was now stationed in Bridgenorton, a town some twenty miles away, and Ashworth was to be responsible to the new superintendent, John Newton.

This bothered Ashworth. He was of an age when change was not welcome, and his methods of detection could be unorthodox to say the least when viewed from a position of authority.

He was now following the exact route taken by Isobel Perkins's executioners almost four hundred years ago, only now the rutted track was a dual carriageway which linked the centre of Bridgetown with estates that had sprung up around it in recent years.

As he crossed the bridge over the River Thane, Malcolm Headlands's car was advancing towards him, heading for Manor Lane.

Ashworth drove along the High Street in which many of the former cottages were now shops, but little else had changed since Isobel Perkins's time. And direct descendants of the witch-hunters still lived in many of the cottages around the town centre.

They, unlike Ashworth, were well aware of the identity of Joyce Regent; and their general opinion was that the aldermen group would be far from happy with the return of the witch.

And the return of the curse.

* * *

After parking his Sierra at the rear of the station, Ashworth bounded up the steps with the energy of a man half his age. A combination of diet and exercise kept him outstandingly fit for a man in his fifties; and his large but firm frame, his thick black hair and youthful, if somewhat lined, face belied his years.

Sergeant Martin Dutton, with panic adding a redness to his bald head, was manning front reception.

'Morning, Jim,' he called.

'Good morning, Martin. What's the news from on high?'

'Well, he's in,' Dutton replied, his homely face creasing into an uncertain smile. 'He's prowled around the station but said very little. I think he's waiting to see you first.'

'Right, let's get it over with, then.' He stopped at the stairs and turned back. 'First impressions, Martin?'

Dutton frowned. 'Difficult to say. Seems a bit stuffy . . . rigid—'

'Inflexible?' Ashworth suggested.

'Yes, that's the word, inflexible.'

'Just what I need.'

He took the stairs two at a time and was still breathing normally after climbing the three flights to the new superintendent's office. He made his knock assertive.

'Come in,' the man commanded.

John Newton rose from his seat as Ashworth entered. By police standards he was a small man at five foot nine, with a slim build. He was forty-three years old, and his brown hair was carefully styled to conceal the fact that it was thinning. The silver buttons shone out from his immaculate uniform, and his humourless face was set in a stern expression. He took a moment to appraise Ashworth.

'Chief Inspect—'

'I know who you are, Chief Inspector,' Newton said briskly. 'Your reputation precedes you.'

As Ashworth came to a halt before the desk, he searched for some trace of humour in the remark but, alas, there was none to be found.

'Take a seat,' Newton ordered, as he resumed his own.

Ashworth settled his bulk in the chair, aware that the office still carried the unpleasant aroma of Ken Savage's chain-smoking habit. Better the devil you know, he thought.

'Right,' Newton began in a crusty tone, 'I know my manner of taking up this post is unusual — not going around the station to meet all personnel — but that is deliberate. I see the major part of my job as delegation. You, Chief Inspector, are head of CID and I will not be superimposing myself upon you.'

'Good,' Ashworth responded quietly.

'As long as things are running efficiently, that is.'

The remark held an insulting ring which angered Ashworth, and he locked eyes with Newton who seemed determined not to avert his gaze.

After a moment, though, the superintendent did lower his eyes, saying, 'I see my job as a public relations man on behalf of the force, and it seems to me that the image of the force needs a polish. The people of this town need to feel safe to walk the streets, park their cars knowing they'll still be there when they get back; not to mention the fact that the councillors need to know everything's shipshape and Bristol-fashion.'

Ashworth remained silent, and Newton began to feel uncomfortable under his hostile stare.

'So, that's it,' he said. 'I don't want to meet your officers because I intend to remain aloof, detached. Familiarity breeds contempt, Chief Inspector, I'm a great believer in that, and I intend to run a tight ship.'

'Right.' Ashworth got to his feet, assuming the interview was over.

'Oh, there is one other thing, Chief Inspector, I'm a stickler for discipline and I've already noticed a distinct lack of it at this station. With that in mind I shall be addressed as "sir" at all times. I shall address all fellow officers by their ranks, and I expect you to follow my example.'

'Yes.' Ashworth paused. 'Sir.'

'Good.' A grave smile touched Newton's lips. 'Remember, with a steady hand at the helm, the crew behave.'

'I'll keep that to the forefront of my mind, sir,' Ashworth said. Then, almost tempted to salute, he turned on his heel and left the office.

Newton stared at the door long after it had closed, his expression stormy. His assessment of the chief inspector was in complete agreement with that of Ken Savage: beneath the polite manner, the countrified air, lurked a volatile nature, a dislike of authority and protocol; the man was obviously so entrenched in his ways as to resemble an immovable object.

'Well, Ashworth, meet an irresistible force,' Newton muttered, as he adjusted a picture of his wife and son until it stood at precisely the right angle on his desk.

* * *

Mick Wright steered his transit van into a loading area behind the newsagent's run by old Mrs Shallet.

Switching off the engine, he was suddenly overtaken by a fit of coughing; deep, rasping hacks that hurt his chest and left him gasping for breath. When he had more or less recovered, Wright clambered across the seat to retrieve a bundle of magazines from the back of the van.

A tall, extremely thin man in his late forties, with fine wispy grey hair, he earned his living delivering morning papers to the newsagents in the area. The magazines were the last drop of a shift which started at 2 a.m. and finished at 10 a.m.

Although it was a warm day at the beginning of September, Wright shivered as he jumped down from the van. The fifty magazines weighed heavy, and he was glad to reach the front of the shop in Bridgetown High Street.

Ma Shallet, as she was known locally, glanced up when he walked in. 'You look rough, Mick,' she croaked with typical candour.

'It's this cough, it's getting worse,' he said, breathing heavily as the magazines were deposited on the counter. 'I'm not getting any sleep, and nothing I get from the chemist touches it.'

'I see,' Ma said, with a sympathetic smile.

She had kept the shop for as long as anyone could remember, and her white hair, wizened face and bent frame suggested great age.

'Give me twenty Bensons,' Wright said, his breathing easier now.

'They won't do you any good,' Ma chided, as she hobbled on her stick to the cigarettes rack.

'You sound just like my missus,' he said, digging into his pocket for some change.

Ma passed across the cigarettes with apparent reluctance but was quick to take his money. 'Have you heard the news?' she asked ominously.

'What news?' Wright sounded uninterested as he tore at the Cellophane on the packet.

'Somebody's taken up residence in Witch's Cottage.'

Wright stopped dead, the colour draining from his face. 'Who?' he demanded shrilly.

Leaning heavily on her stick, Ma told him, 'A Mrs Regent.'

'But it's impossible,' Wright spluttered, bringing on his cough. 'The cottage can only be lived in—'

'By a direct descendant of Isobel Perkins,' Ma interjected. Then, with a mysterious look, 'Which is what this Mrs Regent is. Not only that, but she writes books about the occult, and that means she's a witch.'

'My God,' Wright blustered. 'Can I use your phone, Ma?'

'Through the back,' she said, lifting a flap in the counter.

Mick Wright pushed past and found the telephone in a small room behind the shop. He quickly dialled a number.

'Come on, come on,' he urged, listening impatiently to the dull ring.

There was a click on the line. 'Hello?'

'Edith, it's Mick. Have you heard about Witch's Cottage?'

'Yes, Mick, I have,' she admitted reluctantly.

'But—'

'Now don't panic. I've rung the others and they're coming round tonight so we can decide what to do about it.'

'How long's she been there?'

There was a long pause before Edith answered. Finally, she said, 'Three days.'

'Three days? Oh Christ, that's when this cough started getting bad.'

'Don't panic, Mick, it's probably a coincidence, that's all. Come home, eh?'

'Yes . . . all right.'

He stayed by the telephone for sometime before returning to the shop. Then, without a word, he picked up the cigarettes and left.

Ma Shallet watched him fumbling with the packet on the pavement, and as soon as the cigarette was lit, he doubled over in a spasm of coughing.

'The chickens are coming home to roost, Mick,' she rasped. 'And you've forgotten your change.' She opened the till and let the coins drop.

* * *

Ashworth strode into the CID office, peered at the glass wall with his usual distaste, and sank heavily into his seat.

'Morning, guv,' Holly Bedford and Josh Abraham chorused after he had completed this daily ritual.

'Good day, Detective Sergeant Bedford, and to you Detective Constable Abraham.'

'You all right, guv?' Holly asked with a puzzled frown. 'You haven't been at the Sanatogen wine again, have you?'

Ashworth's laugh was good-natured. 'No,' he said, 'I've just met our new superintendent, and he's ordered that all officers are to be addressed by their ranks.'

Josh wrenched his attention away from the computer, and turned in his chair, grimacing. 'He's as bad as that, is he?'

'Yes, Josh, he is as bad as that. Now, if anyone in this office stops calling me Guv, I'll hit them with my truncheon,' Ashworth warned.

'I can't wait,' Holly whispered, suppressing a laugh.

She was twenty-seven years old and had, at long last, managed to put on some weight, filling out her figure so that it was more in keeping with her five foot nine frame. Although not beautiful, Holly was attractive in an off-beat way, and regular attention from the hairdresser had helped to soften her features.

‘How’d it go?’ she asked.

Ashworth leant back in his chair, hands behind his head. ‘The man kept going on about everything being shipshape and Bristol-fashion, tight ships, crews — I don’t know if he thinks we’re in the Navy.’

His tone informed them clearly that the interview had not gone well; it was obvious that he was not taken with his new commanding officer so stormy seas ahead were a distinct possibility. They were relieved when he changed the subject.

‘What’s come in?’

‘Our local celebrity, Joyce Regent, is being pestered by a reporter,’ Holly informed him.

Ashworth appeared puzzled. ‘Who’s she?’

‘Joyce Regent,’ Holly repeated more clearly.

‘Yes, I’ve got the name, but who is she?’

Holly looked at Josh and laughed. ‘Which paper do you read?’

‘The *Daily Telegraph*. Why?’

‘Well, Miss Regent is a very well-known author,’ Holly explained. ‘She’s in her forties, and she has an unfortunate liking for very young boys. Some of the papers have been running stories about her for weeks. It seems some of these lads have been as young as sixteen. She moved from London a few days ago, and one of the reporters has followed her here.’

‘Why can’t uniformed deal with it?’ Ashworth wanted to know.

Holly studied her notes. ‘Central control sent PC Adams and PC Samuels, but this reporter told them to go and play with themselves.’

‘Did he, now?’ Ashworth intoned. ‘Well, as we’ve time to spare, perhaps we should go and have a word with him, Holly, and introduce ourselves to this famous author at the same time.’

And so CID started the day. An unlikely team headed by strait-laced, conservative Jim Ashworth; while Josh — despite his utterly masculine frame, now encased in casual manly clothes — was a non-practising homosexual.

And Holly, having suffered more than her fair share of tragedy in the love stakes, was at last finding herself. Unfortunately, this voyage of self-discovery was revealing a healthy sexual appetite, and Holly was finding it difficult to resist changing partners frequently. She was fast building a reputation for 'putting it about'; and that unsavoury judgement was greatly enhanced by her latest affair with a married PC.

Nevertheless, both officers had Ashworth's trust, and for almost the first time in his career he felt he had a team he could work with.

* * *

Superintendent Newton was at his window, making a mental note to complain about the grimy state of the glass, when Ashworth crossed the car park sharing a joke with Holly. He watched them with hostile interest until their car pulled away, and then he telephoned his wife.

'Mary,' he snapped as soon as she answered. It was obvious from his tone that his home was run on the same lines as those he intended for the police station: the iron fist in the stone glove. 'The boy has gone to school, I take it?'

'Yes, John,' she replied tersely, 'Jamie has gone to college.'

'Now look, Mary, I want you on board for this.' He was not a man to tolerate dissent, however slight.

'I always go along with what you say, John, but I really am worried about Jamie.'

'There's nothing at all to worry about. The boy just needs discipline, that's all.'

'But he's creative, you know that.'

'Creative, my foot,' Newton exploded, angered by her pleading tone. 'The world is full of shirkers claiming to be artistic. The boy needs guidance. If he had the backbone, I'd have him in the force with me. Computers, Mary, that's the thing of the future. He'll thank me for it in a few years' time. The important thing is that we stick together or he'll play us off one against the other.'

'Yes, dear,' Mary said, obedient once more.

'Good, I knew I could rely on you to see sense.'

CHAPTER 2

Ashworth's Sierra came to a stop behind Malcolm Headlands's red Volvo. The reporter, leaning against the car, a camera dangling from his neck, hardly looked up as Ashworth clambered from the driver's seat, but he did a quick double take when Holly emerged. His eyes raked over the close-fitting dark-blue suit which highlighted her curves, and Holly's green eyes sparkled in acknowledgement of his interest.

Ashworth produced his warrant card as he approached the reporter. 'Chief Inspector Ashworth, Bridgetown CID, and this is—'

'Plod,' Headlands sighed.

'No . . . Ashworth.'

Ignoring the humour, Headlands said, 'Some of your people dropped by earlier and I explained there's nothing in the law that stops me collecting news.'

Ashworth glanced around; beyond Witch's Cottage the road still rose steeply to where the manor house had once stood, before snaking off into the distance to join the motorway. The road on which they talked was no more than a winding lane which linked two dual carriageways and would no doubt have been scrapped years ago had it not been the only access to the cottage of the dead witch.

Headlands interpreted the chief inspector's silence as a victory, and there was a smug smile on his face as he turned to Holly. 'I'm from the big city. We know our rights there.'

'See that bend in the road?' Ashworth asked, pointing to his right.

'Yes,' Headlands said, following his finger.

'And the one to my left?'

'What are you getting at?' the reporter asked, looking decidedly bored.

'Your car's causing an obstruction.'

Headlands laughed. 'But no other vehicles use this road.'

'You don't think it was put here just for you to park on, do you? Move it.'

'OK, I'll move the car, but you can't stop me standing here.'

'Have you heard of loitering with intent?' Ashworth asked with a smile.

'You've got to be joking . . .'

'Son, I don't want a dispute with you, unless you're really keen on having one.'

Headlands seemed about to make a retort but Ashworth's expression changed his mind. 'All right, I'll move up there,' he said, pointing to the top of the rise. 'There's a lay-by. I'll watch the house from up there. You can't stop me gathering the news, you know.'

Ashworth remained stony-faced until Headlands had turned the Volvo and sped up the hill. 'No, but I'll put every possible obstacle in your way.'

* * *

Jamie Newton felt uncomfortable as he gazed around the noisy college canteen. Most of the students seemed to have made friends, and although this was the first morning for many of them, they were already laughing and fooling as if they had known each other for years.

He was painfully aware of his body as he queued for a cup of tea; every movement he made was clumsy, awkward. When his turn came, Jamie picked up the plastic cup and knocked over a sugar basin.

His embarrassment soared when the woman behind the counter shooed him away with exasperation; and, certain that everyone was watching, a blush still lingered on his pale cheeks as he paid the cashier.

A few of the more boisterous youths were already viewing him as a potential target, but being bullied was nothing new to Jamie; he had suffered it since primary school.

He was five foot ten and reasonably well-developed for his age, but his good-looking, slightly effeminate features always attracted hostility from other boys and, with his gentle, sensitive nature, Jamie found it difficult to reply in kind.

He pushed a hand through his unruly brown hair, willed the other holding the cup to stop shaking, and looked around for an empty table.

* * *

Ashworth studied, to the point of rudeness, the woman who opened the door to Witch's Cottage.

She had a pretty face, made more so by deep laughter lines travelling from the sides of her pert little nose to the corners of her full lips. Her glossy brown hair was tied back with an elastic band, and she wore a denim shirt and jeans which were well-cut and expensive-looking.

'Yes?' she queried after several seconds.

'Sorry,' Ashworth said, delving into his pocket for his warrant card. 'We're from Bridgetown CID. Your unwelcome guest has moved a hundred yards up the road. Best we could do, I'm afraid.'

Joyce Regent glanced at the detectives' credentials, then smiled. 'Thank you, I'm grateful for that. Thank you very much.'

She was ready to close the door when Ashworth said, 'I wonder if we could come in and have a word.'

'Well . . .' She seemed reluctant. 'Oh, come on in, I suppose it'll be all right.'

Two teenagers were framed in the kitchen doorway as they entered the hall.

'These are my daughters,' Joyce announced. 'There's Katie, my eldest, and Tanya.'

'Hello,' Ashworth said. Holly just smiled.

They were dressed in ill-fitting T-shirts and jeans. Katie was tall and gangling, with attractive chiselled features and shoulder-length fair hair; around eighteen, Holly surmised.

Tanya, in contrast, was a short dumpy girl, about fifteen, and fleshed out with puppy fat; but her dark hair and attractive face promised that she would grow into a beauty.

Their 'hellos' were hardly eager, after which Katie pushed past them, motioning to Tanya, and mumbling, 'Could you excuse us? We have to go upstairs.'

Katie was obviously the leader, and Tanya followed without question. When they were half-way up the stairs a black cat appeared; it darted past them and stood with back arched, spitting at the elder.

'Sathan,' Joyce called. 'Behave.'

Then the cat caught sight of Ashworth; immediately its hackles rose again, its green eyes shining with malice, and its mouth opening to reveal tiny white teeth.

'Sathan,' Joyce scolded, when it seemed ready to spring.

The cat looked up the stairs, then again at Ashworth, and dashed into the kitchen.

Joyce gave him an apologetic smile. 'Sorry about that.'

'The witch's familiar,' Ashworth remarked.

'Ah, I detect an understanding of witchcraft,' she observed.

'A slight one,' he admitted. 'The witch's familiar is a low-ranking demon. Its most common form is a black cat, but it could be a dog, an owl, or indeed any animal or insect.'

'Spot on,' Joyce smiled. 'Would you like to come through to the lounge?'

The room was gloomy with much dark wood: oak timbers showed on the ceiling; and the floor was carpetless, its boards stained black. The large open fireplace had a neglected look, as if it had not been used for years. A floral-patterned settee stood under the front window, but its matching chairs were stacked one on top of the other. Packing cases littered the room.

'Children,' Joyce said. 'Katie came home when this all started, and she's taken over my life. She insists on calling me Joyce now.' She laughed. 'Sometimes I feel like the child. Look, can I apologize for the girls? I know they were rude, but they've taken what's happened with the press quite badly and they're beginning to distrust all strangers.'

'That's understandable,' Ashworth said, as he studied his surroundings. 'May I take a look in the garden? If you're about to be besieged by reporters again, I'd like to spy out the grounds.'

A look of horror clouded Joyce's face. 'You don't think that's likely, do you?'

'I hope not,' Ashworth sighed, 'but I always prepare for the worst while hoping for the best.'

Joyce bit anxiously on her thumbnail. 'Yes, all right,' she said, 'it's through the kitchen. Oh, and mind the cat.'

Ashworth's soothing sounds did little to pacify the creature which spat and growled until he had closed the back door behind him.

'It doesn't intend to become familiar with my guv'nor, does it?' Holly joked.

The author's smile was condescending. 'Please sit down. I'm sorry about the mess.'

'It's OK, don't worry.'

Holly set about removing wrapping paper from the settee and made herself comfortable. 'And I wouldn't worry too much about reporters. The chief inspector only used that as an excuse to get out of the room. He felt you might be more relaxed with him out of the way as this is, well, a rather delicate matter.'

'That was sweet of him,' Joyce said, taking a packet of cigarettes from the mantelpiece. She lit one and fixed Holly with a defiant look. 'Well, now you've met the wicked woman.'

'Look, I'm not here to make any moral judgements,' Holly put in quickly. 'As far as we know you haven't broken the law. We just want to make sure you're not bothered.'

Joyce let out a bitter laugh. 'Have you ever had your life spread all over the newspapers?'

'No, but—'

'It comes as quite a shock, I can tell you. What seemed normal at the time . . .' She demolished the hardly smoked cigarette in an ashtray and shrugged. 'Oh, I don't know, they made it sound so dirty and sordid.'

'Well, as far as I'm concerned it's the dirty, sordid bits that make sex fun,' Holly said with a lewd chuckle.

The remark was meant to relax the woman, but Joyce continued to stare into space as if she had not heard.

'I never thought of them as boys,' she said suddenly. 'They were young men. But I've been made to look like some sex-crazed, dirty old woman.'

'Joyce,' Holly cut in, 'you don't have to justify yourself to me.'

'Don't I?' She shook her head. 'Sorry, I suppose I just need someone to talk to.'

'Talk to me, by all means,' Holly said, tapping the seat beside herself.

Joyce wandered over and sat down. 'Do you know what the press did? They dug up most of the young men I'd been with and paid them to tell what went on between the sheets. Half of it was untrue, but my lawyers say there's nothing I can do about it, it's just my word against the boys.' Her laugh was scornful. 'The boys — that's just how they put it, my own lawyers. Anyway, I've learned my lesson, realized how old I am. Now I just want the press to leave me alone.'

'If you don't give them any further grounds . . .' Holly ventured.

'Oh, don't worry, I won't do that,' Joyce assured her. 'My agent and publishers have told me, any more scandal and I'm finished.'

'As you said, all this must have affected your daughters.'

'Yes,' Joyce sighed. 'It's Tanya I feel sorry for. Sometimes I see her looking at me as if to say: How could my mother have done those things? I'm beginning to think she hates me.'

'I'm sure that in a few months' time all this will be forgotten,' Holly said, getting to her feet. 'By then the press will be after someone else.'

'I hope you're right,' Joyce said.

'What do you write about?'

'Crime fiction about the occult. My hero, Jess Oliver, is a white witch.'

'So, this cottage is aptly named for you.'

'Yes, very. Actually, I began my career writing about the woman who lived in this cottage,' Joyce said as she crossed to one of the tea-chests.

Holly watched as she riffled through some books. 'The chief inspector told me something about her on the way here.'

'Ah, here it is.' Joyce offered her the book. 'Take it with you, read it.'

'Thank you, I will.'

Holly collected Ashworth from the garden and steered him past the cat, and after they had said their farewells to Joyce Regent they sat in the Sierra.

'Well, guv, the woman's a mess, but then the press have crucified her.'

'Price of fame, I suppose,' Ashworth commented, as he opened the window to let in air. 'If she was just an ordinary housewife, I doubt if anybody would be interested.' He noticed the book. 'What's that?'

'It's the story of the witch who lived in the cottage. Do you want to read it?'

'But she loaned it to you.'

Holly's affair with the married PC Bruce Donegan was still in its early stages, and therefore when together they found it difficult to keep their hands off each other or their clothes on.

'I'm a bit busy at the moment,' she said, hiding a grin.

* * *

Malcolm Headlands was glad when the Sierra pulled away. From his vantage point in the lay-by, he had a good view of the cottage.

He trained the telescopic lens of his camera on to the windows.

'Come on, come on,' he muttered. 'If you don't do something soon, I'll have to make it happen. Time's money, girl.'

* * *

Superintendent John Newton glanced at the clock and smiled contentedly. It was 4.55 p.m. Nine to five were the hours he intended to work, so his day was over. He neatly replaced his pen in the desk-tidy whose angle was then adjusted until it stood correctly aligned with the blotter and looked again at his notes.

Clean up the streets — officers back on the beat.
Crackdown on drugs and pornography.
A little get-together with the local councillors — cheese and wine?

He stood up and gave a satisfied sigh. Yes, the councillors were the people to impress. Show a good efficient station, keep the yob element off the streets, and clean up the town.

Then, when Ken Savage's job came up for grabs . . .

* * *

Mick Wright's terraced cottage stood in a picturesque back lane. Late summer flowers still tumbled fragrantly from hanging baskets beside the front door, and although the narrow lane was only a stone's throw from the bustling high street, it seemed a world away.

But neither evening birdsong nor the heady smell of summer blooms were noticed by those within the Wrights' residence. Mick Wright sat at the head of the kitchen table. Beside him was his wife, Edith, a small, hawk-like woman; she wore a plain pinafore dress and toyed constantly with her mousy brown hair.

'It will work, Mick,' Ronald Curtis urged from the other end of the table. 'Just give it time.' He flashed Wright a superior smile which made his startlingly blue eyes sparkle.

'I may not have time,' Wright moaned after another coughing seizure.

His wife cast him a worried look and nodded towards the cough-medicine bottle on the draining-board.

Beside Ronald Curtis sat John Dempsey, whose wide floral tie added a touch of flamboyance to his well-dressed appearance. Both men were a good ten years younger than the Wrights, and both looked out of place in the dowdy kitchen.

Dempsey now said, 'I agree with Ronald. And from what I've been reading about Joyce Regent, the press could help to move her along.'

'It's all too slow,' Wright complained.

'We'll start it tonight,' Dempsey assured him. 'And go to the doctor's with that cough, Mick, put your mind at rest.'

'This cough's part of the curse, we all know that.'

'We don't,' Curtis argued. 'You're overreacting.'

Wright flared, 'Overreacting, am I? I can feel it right down in my lungs.' Suddenly he slumped back in his chair. 'God knows, I've been waiting all my life for this to happen.'

'And that's probably what's brought it on,' Curtis retorted.

'I've heard enough of this,' Edith declared, striking the table with the flat of her hand. 'I know you're both better educated than me and Mick, but you just look at your family trees, then tell us we're imagining it. Believe me,' she said, pointing a scrawny finger, 'it'll get us all, 'cause it has done down the ages.'

A shamefaced Ronald Curtis sat studying the tabletop. 'I'm as frightened as any of you,' he said. 'This thing's just come out of the blue. I mean, we thought it had been dead for over a hundred years. My wife didn't even know about the curse that was put on the family until I told her yesterday.'

'We've agreed on a course of action,' John Dempsey said, 'and we'll feel better once we've got it under way.'

Mick Wright looked at the kitchen clock. 'It'll have to do, I suppose. Anyway, I've got to go to work.'

'But you can't go, Mick,' Edith said. 'Not with that cough.'

'It's important that I go tonight, woman, so stop nagging. I'll take my medicine with me.'

* * *

Joyce Regent leant on the front garden gate. With the reporter gone, she felt more able to relax.

Dusk was falling, and the lights of Bridgetown glowed orange in the distance. It was then that she caught sight of two figures approaching.

Straightaway she tensed and was about to turn tail back into the cottage, when through the gloom she could just make out the shape of a Labrador with a stick clenched firmly between its teeth; following behind was a man with a boy of around sixteen.

'Good evening,' Joyce said warmly as they drew level. 'And a nice one for walking the dog.'

'Hello there,' the man replied. 'Are you living here?'

'Yes, that's right.' She found her eyes straying to the boy with his fair hair and slim body.

'Well, I never thought I'd see anybody living here in my lifetime.'

‘They say it’s haunted,’ Joyce remarked casually.

The man looked towards the shaft of yellow light escaping from the open door, and said darkly, ‘I know it is.’

They exchanged pleasantries for a few minutes and then the man called to his dog, but it failed to materialize so he went off in search of it.

Joyce looked at the boy. ‘What’s your name?’

‘Lee.’

‘Lee. That’s a nice name. I’ll use it in a book I’m writing.’

Joyce questioned him for a while, all the time hoping that the dog would be hard to catch. But then she turned to see Katie standing in the doorway.

‘Oh God,’ she muttered, hurrying along the path. ‘See you,’ she called to the boy.

Katie fixed her with a baleful glare.

‘He was with his father,’ Joyce explained hurriedly. ‘They were walking a dog.’

Katie said nothing, simply looked at her accusingly.

‘He was, for Christ’s sake. His father had just walked off.’

The front door slammed behind her, but their angry voices could still be heard in the lane.

CHAPTER 3

Ashworth arrived back at his four-bedroomed detached house eager to start reading Joyce Regent's book.

He was met at the door by his wife, Sarah, a handsome woman in her early fifties. She was wearing a tweed skirt and a blue silk shirt; a single row of pearls added a touch of elegance.

Sarah, like her husband, did not lower her standard of dress when at home; indeed Ashworth would remove the jacket to his suit, but only on occasions would he perhaps loosen his tie.

In the dining room, throughout a meal of pork chops and vegetables, Ashworth kept eyeing the book. In fact, such was his eagerness to start reading that Sarah was forced to warn him of the dangers in bolting his food.

When Sarah took the dishes into the kitchen, Ashworth retired with it to the lounge, a large comfortable room with deep-pile Wilton carpet and expensive furnishings accumulated over thirty years of marriage.

Peanuts, their Jack Russell, trotted after him with tail wagging. She had taken to sleeping on his slippers, which was fine when her lord and master had vacated them, but rather uncomfortable when he had them on. So Ashworth bowed to the inevitable and they were placed by his favourite chair while he padded about in his socks. As the dog curled up, Ashworth settled into his chair and opened the book.

The washing-up now done, Sarah looked into the lounge to find her husband totally absorbed, so rather than disturb him by watching television she returned to the kitchen and busied herself with some baking. Soon the house was filled with the tempting aroma of apple-and-blackberry pies.

At nine thirty she was in the dining room, catching up on family correspondence, when Ashworth appeared with a glass of sherry which was placed in front of her.

'Thank you, dear,' she said, smiling at his preoccupied look.

Every evening at nine thirty Ashworth poured a sherry for Sarah and a Scotch and soda for himself; it had become a reflex action over the years, and whatever he was doing the time never varied.

The sherry finished, Sarah joined her husband in the lounge. He was still in his armchair, bathed in the glow from the standard lamp. The book lay closed on his lap, and he was drumming his fingers on its cover. His eyes looked tired from the marathon reading session.

'Good book, dear?' Sarah asked, as she sat in the chair facing his.

'Yes,' he said, reaching for his glass. 'It's by Joyce Regent.'

'Is that the woman I've been hearing tittle-tattle about? Young boys, and all that?'

'The very same.' He sipped his drink. 'She's moved into Witch's Cottage. Holly and I were there today. She's being bothered by a reporter.'

'What's that got to do with the book?'

'She loaned it to me.' He drained his glass and pointed to Sarah's. 'Do you know the legend?'

'Of course,' Sarah said, handing him her glass. 'Isobel Perkins was declared a witch and killed. Then her seven executioners were all slain by a huge black cat, or dog, or whatever.'

'Yes,' Ashworth said, 'Isobel Perkins was raped and murdered by seven of the town's aldermen. Before she died, she ordered her familiar — the cat, Sathan — to kill them. The legend has it that the cat turned into a panther and despatched the seven to the hereafter within days.'

He passed her the sherry then resumed his seat. 'But Isobel also put a curse on all future issue of the seven men. Now, there were no more attacks by the big cat, but a catalogue of disasters befell those families: accidents, illnesses, all sorts of things. According to the book, at least two of them buried their newborn babies in sacrifice to the Devil, hoping to lift the curse. This went on right up to the middle of the last century.' He paused to take a drink.

'So why did it stop then?'

'Apparently the families sought the help of an exorcist. The story goes that after several hours the man emerged from the cottage covered in sweat, totally exhausted and close to collapse. All that time he'd been engaged in a battle with the spirit of Isobel Perkins.

'Finally he drove her out, but as she departed Isobel vowed that one day the witch would return, and with her the curse. She also promised that her own impotent spirit would remain there for ever.'

'It all sounds a bit far-fetched to me, Jim.'

'My first reaction too, I must confess. But I've been sitting here thinking. I remember when I was a lad, about twelve or thirteen. I used to play around the cottage with some friends. Even then people were frightened, thought it was haunted.

'Well, one day there were about half a dozen of us up there and we dared this lad to go inside. I can't for the life of me remember his name, but he had ginger hair. Anyway he went in, and about ten minutes later he came back out, as white as a sheet. His story — and he swore this on the Bible — was that the shadowy figure of a woman with long red hair had chased him all over the cottage, shouting, "Get out of my house".'

Sarah laughed. 'Oh, Jim, you must have been frightened to death.'

'Not really,' Ashworth chuckled. 'We'd bought a packet of cigarettes that day, and we just thought that the Woodbine smoke must have rotted his brain. Isn't it funny the explanations you come up with when you're young?'

'Jim, Peanuts hasn't been out for her walk.'

Upon hearing her name, the dog jumped up, ears pricked, tail wagging, and trotted off to return seconds later with the lead in her mouth.

* * *

Tall flames shot skyward, illuminating the dark night; sparks crackled, and the air was thick with the stench of burning rubber and upholstery.

A group of youngsters huddled together, walking backwards, eyes fixed on the fiery spectacle; all of them anticipating the excitement to come when the petrol tank finally blew. Seconds later it happened, and a crimson ball of flame lit up the deserted country lane as the group cheered.

They watched, spellbound, as the car windows exploded, showering the area with thousands of tiny splinters.

Then they turned and ran, but without any great haste. They were streetwise enough to know just how long it would take the police to respond when a stolen car was set ablaze.

Their youthful energy allowed them to run for a mile before the natural leader of the gang called a halt.

'Yeh,' Craig Summers shouted, 'that was great.'

The others stopped and waited for his lead. Craig was a slim youth, dressed in jeans and a grey hooded sweatshirt. He dropped to his knees laughing and attempted to get his breath.

'Who's got the grass?' he asked after a time, his attractive face grimy from the fire.

The group crowded around him.

'I have,' Rod Calway said.

He felt into the pocket of his denim jacket and withdrew a tin and some cigarette papers. His dark features were a mask of concentration as he poured cannabis along the thin paper. The others watched expectantly as he finished rolling the joint.

A third youth, Carl Chown, flicked the lighter and held it out to Calway. As the expertly constructed cigarette was passed around, the two girls, Sharon Cotton and Laurie Walton, waited for their turns.

The tip of the cigarette glowed brightly in the darkness as it was handed to Laurie, and she was only too aware of the boys' eyes on her when she drew on it. Her large breasts rose and fell beneath her black T-shirt as she passed the joint to Sharon. Then she dug her hands into the pockets of her blue jeans and tossed her shock of fluffed blonde hair while smoke poured from her mouth and nostrils.

'Wicked,' she enthused.

Sharon made her turn no less of a ritual. At five foot four she was two inches shorter than her friend, and the body beneath leather miniskirt and grey top was not as curvaceous as Laurie's, but it was still inviting enough for the boys to eye it hungrily. She exhaled, her devil-may-care face alive with pleasure.

'Nice one,' she gasped.

The joint was smoked until it burned their fingers, and they set off, light-headed, across the fields towards Bridgetown.

Craig was a magnet for the two girls who walked either side of him.

'You know weirdo at college?' he asked no one in particular.

'Jamie Newton,' they chorused.

'Right. Well I've found out that weirdo's old man is pure pig.'

'That's why he's thick,' Rod Calway said.

'But not just ordinary pig,' Craig went on. 'He's the top pig.'

'Death to the filth. Death to the filth,' Carl Chown chanted as he danced around in a circle. He was shorter, more stockily built than the other youths; and his first reaction to any situation was invariably one of violence.

When his war dance was over and the laughter had subsided, he said, 'Why don't we duff him up?'

'Not a good game plan,' Craig replied.

They stopped at the edge of a field of ripening corn.

'No, what I think we should do is take him under our wing.'

'Craig, you're out of your tiny mind,' Rod jeered. 'The guy's a dickhead.'

'Agreed.' Craig grinned. 'But think about getting the leader of the pigs' son into trouble.'

'How do we do that?' Sharon asked. 'The creep doesn't talk to anybody.'

Craig smiled slyly. 'Get you or Laurie to be nice to him.'

'I'm not having anything to do with that creep,' Laurie protested.

'Let's just duff him up,' Carl shouted.

'I'll do it,' Sharon said softly.

The others stared at her; Laurie looked horrified.

'Good girl,' Craig said. 'That'll give me time to make plans. Now, follow me.'

He led them across the field, deliberately flattening the corn as he went. They ran in large circles, stamping on the crop, whooping and shouting.

* * *

Joyce Regent slid her hands over the muscular young body. Her warm fingers glided over satin smooth skin to reach his waist and lingered for a moment, gripping, her fingers digging into flesh as his flat hard stomach hit her own with a slippery slap.

Unable to remain still, Joyce grasped his buttocks firmly, her hands demanding that he increase his pace; and the youth uttered low grunts of pleasure as he obeyed.

'Oh, yes, yes,' she panted, oblivious to all but her own fulfilment.

Through the thick stone wall of the cottage, Tanya Regent could hear her mother urging the boy on.

Blind hatred welled up inside her as she pulled the pillow over her head, sobbing, 'No, don't. Stop it. Please stop it.'

Joyce's moans increased as she approached and reached her climax. And although the sounds were now familiar to Tanya, she still found them hard to bear.

'Don't do it anymore,' she cried into the pillow. 'I don't want you to do it anymore.'

* * *

'He's a prat,' Sergeant Dutton announced. 'A twenty-four carat prat.'

Chief Inspector Ashworth, with nothing more pressing on his mind than clearing up the garden ready for autumn, wandered over to the reception desk.

'Good morning, Martin,' he said, smiling. 'And I must say, that's rather strong language coming from you. I take it you're talking about the one on high.'

Dutton took to tidying the already neat desk, too annoyed to answer. But Bobby Adams, a recently recruited PC with a short-back-and-sides haircut and a healthy respect for Ashworth's temper, felt the question required a reply.

'Superintendent Newton, sir,' he said shyly.

'All right, Bobby, I can speak for myself,' Dutton snapped.

'Steady, Martin,' Ashworth cautioned amiably.

Dutton drew in a deep breath and said, 'Sorry, Bobby,' before turning his attention back to Ashworth. 'He's driving us potty, Jim.'

'Calm down,' Ashworth said, leaning on the desk.

'Calm down?' Dutton threw up his hands. 'Do you know what he did last night? He put nearly every copper in the nick on the beat. Said it would reassure the public. All the lads had to walk the streets, chatting to people. The local kids had a field day: eight cars stolen; twelve break-ins; Solomon's newsagent's ransacked. Nobody was close enough to respond when the calls came in.'

'Have you had a word with him?' Ashworth asked.

'Had a word with him?' Dutton's colour rose with his voice. 'The pompous prat said we've got to anticipate likely trouble spots and deploy our resources to them.'

'Anything else?'

'Oh yes, there's plenty more,' Dutton blustered. 'He's having a cheese and wine buffet for the councillors this afternoon, and he wants three WPCs to act as waitresses. I'm not kidding, Jim, much more from him and I'll bump him one.'

Ashworth studied him for a few seconds, then asked mock-seriously, 'Now I want you to be honest about this, Martin — don't you like the man?'

For a moment it looked as if Dutton would blow, but with most of his anger already released his kindly face broke into a smile. 'It's all right for you to take one, Jim, but I could have a mutiny on my hands.'

'I'll have a word with him,' Ashworth promised as he patted the sergeant's shoulder. 'I'll get him to see sense.'

'Please do, Jim,' Dutton almost pleaded.

Ashworth gave him a confident wink. 'You just leave him to me.'

* * *

A feeling of trepidation swept over Joyce Regent as she surfaced abruptly from a trouble-filled sleep. Something or someone had activated that enhanced perception which existed throughout her unique bloodline.

Joyce tossed the quilt to one side and scrambled quickly from the bed. Without the tautness of muscle she adopted when in company, her body was flabby; her breasts and stomach having surrendered their firmness to middle age. She pulled on a black bathrobe and stumbled into slippers.

She went on to check all downstairs windows and, finding them intact, was able to relax a little. In the tiny kitchen she prepared coffee and opened a window. Presently the scent of summer flowers mingled with the satisfying aroma of fresh coffee.

The sudden clatter of the letter-box caused Joyce to start, and that feeling of unease returned as she made her way through to the hall. A pile of mail lay on the mat. She scooped it up and flicked through the envelopes, recognizing one from her publisher, another from her agent, several circulars.

But the last one was strange: a plain white envelope, devoid of postmark or handwriting. She opened the letter with hands that shook slightly. As her eyes scanned the writing scrawled across the paper, Joyce's heartbeat quickened; and the letter fell from her grasp as she stifled a scream.

* * *

'That is not your business, Chief Inspector.' There was a cutting edge to Newton's voice, underlining the degree to which Ashworth was trespassing.

'I disagree,' Ashworth said, managing to keep his voice firm and steady.

Newton raised his eyebrows and waited for the 'sir' which did not materialize. They were in the superintendent's office, eyeing each other warily across the desk.

'It's not your place to disagree,' Newton barked.

'It most certainly is,' Ashworth countered, colour creeping into his cheeks. 'If you take the mobiles off the streets, burglaries increase and so does the workload in CID.'

Newton placed his fingertips together and peered over them, stating coldly, 'Ashworth, I have no intention of discussing my policy for the uniformed division with you. Do you understand that?'

Ashworth was clearly put out; in fact he looked as if he had received a physical blow. He recovered quickly, however, and with little civility, said, 'Yes . . . sir.'

'Good. Now, I'd like to discuss matters that are relevant to CID,' Newton continued. 'Drugs — how big a problem are they?'

'Minor. Most of them come in from Bridgenorton. There's little dealing going on locally.'

'Very good,' Newton beamed. 'But be vigilant, Chief Inspector; it won't be long before some youngster realizes he can buy the stuff in bulk from Bridgenorton and sell it at a profit here.'

'Thank you, sir. I must confess, I hadn't thought of that.'

It was evident from Newton's pointed glance that the heavy lacing of sarcasm in that remark had not escaped him.

'Pornography?' he asked.

'There's none in Bridgetown,' Ashworth informed him.

'Not so,' was Newton's curt reply. 'The newsagents are full of it.'

Ashworth frowned. 'I'm not following you, sir.'

'Top shelf material, I believe it's called.'

'Top shelf . . . ?' Then realization hit him. 'Do you mean the girlie magazines?'

'Among other forms of soft pornography, yes, I do.'

'But they come from reputable publishers. They're on sale nationwide.'

Newton gave a tight smile. 'Chief Inspector, you should know the law as well as I do. Some of those publications — all of them, in fact — could corrupt anyone, which makes them illegal.'

'You're joking.'

'I don't joke when I'm on duty,' Newton retorted. 'Children are getting taller — were you aware of that? I want you to get rid of those magazines.'

'I don't believe this,' Ashworth said, laughing loudly.

'You're getting close to insubordination, Chief Inspector,' Newton warned.

Ashworth pinched the bridge of his nose with some urgency as his temper threatened to erupt. 'With all due respect, sir, what you're proposing is ridiculous.'

Newton finally exploded. 'Ashworth,' he yelled, 'you do not tell your commanding officer he's ridiculous.'

'And that I have not done, I'm merely saying that the course of action you are proposing is.'

'Whatever you think of it, my order will be followed to the letter,' Newton thundered, 'because I am your commanding officer.'

Yet again the two men locked eyes, and for a while it looked likely that Ashworth's temper would finally spill over, but he turned away.

'Is that all, sir?'

A chill smile of victory briefly touched Newton's lips. 'No, it's not. The last point I want to raise with you is rather delicate.'

Ashworth waited, preparing to remonstrate.

'Your appearance is a credit to the force,' Newton said, pointing to the chief inspector's smart suit, white shirt, and regimental tie.

Ashworth looked up, surprised.

'Detective Sergeant Bedford is a smartly turned out young lady also. But . . .' The superintendent paused. 'I'm afraid the attire of Detective Constable Abraham does not meet with my approval — far too casual for my liking. Have a word with him about it. I want to see collar, tie, and a suit appropriate for the job.'

'Do you really expect me to tell Josh—'

'Yes, I do, Chief Inspector, I don't talk just to hear the sound of my own voice. Use some diplomacy, of course, but get it done.'

'Is that all, sir? I've a very heavy workload.'

'For the moment, yes,' Newton said, waving a hand in dismissal.

Ashworth had to bite his tongue as he rose from his seat. And he was almost at the door when Newton's voice stopped him in his tracks.

'I'm sure we're going to work very well together, Chief Inspector. Just as soon as you get into my way of doing things, everything will run smoothly. You'll see.'

Ashworth muttered an oath which Newton chose to assume was, 'Yes, sir.'

CHAPTER 4

Tanya followed Katie along the quiet country lane where all was still apart from tall white-flowered weeds waving in the gentle breeze.

'It's started again,' Tanya said, lashing out at the flowers with a long thin twig.

'It has not started again,' Katie scolded, 'and stop behaving like a child.'

'It has, too. I heard her through the wall. I know what "coming" means, you know.'

'Keep your voice down,' Katie spat, looking around the deserted lane. 'We don't want the press snooping about.'

'You said you'd stop it,' Tanya accused.

'I will.'

Katie grabbed the girl's shoulders and shook her lightly. 'Look, she's a creative person, and we both know she needs sex, but I'll stop it.'

Tanya pulled away and stated at the ground. 'I hate her.'

'It'll be all right. After the happening everything will be all right.'

'That frightens me,' Tanya pouted. 'I don't want to think about it.'

'You've got to go through with it. You knew that when we came to the cottage.' Suddenly Katie's voice took on an eerie edge. 'The witch came to me last night. She said, "The happening is nigh. Soon it will be upon you."'

'Don't, Katie, you're scaring me. I know it's going to hurt.'

'It won't. I've told you, the witch'll put you in a trance.'

'Oh, don't, don't,' Tanya shouted, covering her ears. 'I can't bear to think of it.'

'Just remember, after the happening everything will be all right, everything will stop.'

'What about mother? Will that stop?'

'Yes,' Katie said, taking hold of Tanya's, hand, 'that will stop. After the happening we'll start a new life.'

'Promise?'

'I promise.'

'Promise three times.'

'I promise three times,' Katie said impatiently.

* * *

Holly and Josh were investigating the burglaries, and so far had come up with precious little. They both knew that forensic would be tied up for most of the day with not much hope of catching the culprits, and even if the stolen goods were recovered the real owners would probably be reluctant to collect them, preferring to make grossly inflated insurance claims instead.

Holly drove her Micra along the high street. 'Dead loss,' she moaned.

'That about sums it up,' Josh said. 'Are you OK, Holly? You seemed a bit edgy during the interviews.'

'Time of the month, I suppose.'

'Try again,' he said, glancing out of the side window. 'You used that excuse two weeks ago. Try "love life".'

'Why don't I just tell you to mind your own business?' Holly retorted, stopping behind a line of vehicles at the traffic lights.

'Because I'm your mate,' Josh replied easily.

Holly's face fell into a sullen expression. 'It's all over between me and Bruce.'

'Ah.'

'Do you know, I looked at him last night after we'd finished, and I suddenly thought: Why am I doing this?'

Josh seldom displayed any sympathy when Holly's tangled love life went wrong, and now was no exception. He flashed her a smile and said: 'Didn't you know?'

'Yes, of course. I mean, I knew what I was getting out of it. But I sat there watching him push the dinner down, knowing full well that he'd have to eat another when he got home—'

'He has put some weight on over the last few weeks,' Josh cut in.

Holly shot him a withering glance. 'And I just got so mad that I made him eat a pudding as well. And that meant we hardly had any time for bed. I don't know, I just thought: Is it worth becoming a locker-room joke for this?'

She failed to notice that the traffic had started to move, and an irate motorist sounded his horn from behind.

'Balls,' was Holly's automatic response as she let the clutch out.

'How did he take it anyway?'

'He was a little put out,' she said with some satisfaction. 'Perfect set-up for a man, Josh: a bit on the side, not making any demands . . .'

'Never mind,' he laughed, 'you might have broken his heart, but at least his digestion should improve.'

'You're a pig, Abraham. Did you know?'

'What did you think about the Regent woman?'

'Oh, I'd forgotten about her,' Holly said, steering left towards the station. 'Poison-pen letters aren't that serious.'

'The guv'nor will want it looked into.'

'I know,' she sighed, waiting for a gap in the oncoming traffic. 'And I also know who he'll send for a woman-to-woman chat.'

* * *

Ashworth was waiting in CID when they got back. He was pacing the office, glaring with open hatred at the glass wall. They both knew the signs well enough, so steeled themselves for the explosion. But it didn't come. When Ashworth finally spoke, he sounded almost apologetic.

'Josh,' he said, 'I want to talk to you, and I want you to listen.'

'All right, guv.'

Josh settled at his desk, obviously perplexed. Holly perched on the edge, a look of expectancy on her face.

Ashworth cleared his throat. 'Josh, I want you to smarten up — wear a suit with a collar and tie.'

Josh's mouth sagged open. 'Are we supposed to laugh now, guv?'

Ashworth slowly shook his head. 'It's not from me. Newton isn't satisfied with your appearance.'

'He can't do this,' Holly huffed. 'He can't just walk in here without so much as kiss my arse.'

'Holly,' Ashworth warned.

'But, guv, he's got no right.'

Ashworth turned his attention back to Josh. 'Have you got a suit? A tie?'

'I've got a tie and a sports jacket, but I'm not wearing them,' Josh insisted.

Ashworth leant over the desk and looked at his DC. 'Don't go up against Newton, son,' he said quietly. 'You haven't got the clout.'

Both detectives started to protest, but Ashworth cut them dead. 'It won't be for long. Just have some trust.'

Josh subsided. 'All right, guv. I don't have to go home and change today, do I?'

'No,' Ashworth said, pacing the office again. 'If anyone important drops by, we'll hide you in the stationery cupboard.' That quip was delivered with a good deal of animosity.

Josh was gloomy as he left his seat. 'Right, guv, I'll check some things with forensic.'

After he had gone, Ashworth turned to Holly. 'I didn't want to do that,' he said. 'It's hurtful to be told you look a mess, but I don't want Josh flying off the handle and getting himself into trouble.'

He returned to his desk and held up a sheet of paper. 'What's this note about the Regent woman?'

'Central control received a call from her, guv. Seems she's had a poison-pen letter.'

He replaced the note without interest. 'Right, Holly—'

'On my way,' she said, already picking up her shoulder bag. At the door, she stopped. 'Guv?'

'Yes?' he grunted.

'When you said Josh hadn't got the clout to go up against Newton, am I to take it you intend to?'

'Where angels fear to tread, Holly,' he said, with distinct relish. 'Where angels fear to tread.'

'There will go Jim Ashworth,' Holly uttered softly as she closed the door.

* * *

'Don't do it, Mick,' Edith Wright implored her husband.

'Leave it, woman,' he said, putting his pen on the kitchen table as another grating cough brought phlegm into his mouth.

'But they'll catch you,' Edith moaned. 'I know they will.'

Wright turned away so that his wife would not see his need to spit into his handkerchief. 'What can they do?' he rasped. 'The witch's already killing me.'

'You can't believe that, Mick,' Edith said, pulling the thin cardigan around her scrawny body. 'Go to the doctor's.'

'You know I can't be doing with doctors.'

'You'll have to. Don't think I don't know you're coughing up blood. And you're losing weight.'

'For God's sake, let me finish this letter, woman.'

Wright stopped to drink from the cough-medicine bottle and Edith's heart went out to him. But fear made her turn away when he deposited the letter in its envelope.

'You won't drive her out, Mick.'

'If I can't drive her out, I'll do for her. I swear that before God.'

* * *

Jamie Newton's second day at college was no less intimidating. During the lunch-hour he wandered aimlessly along its endless corridors, happy laughter all around. Everywhere students were talking, shouting, running around in senseless horseplay.

He was drawn by bright sunlight from the gardens at the rear. It warmed his skin as he descended the stone steps, picking his way between students sprawled across them.

The garden was perhaps two hundred yards square, finishing where a small rose bed lay behind a low stone wall.

Jamie headed towards it, his trainers flattening the long grass. He felt better away from the others and sat on the wall to contemplate and breathe in the sweet scents of the blooms.

Glancing back at the college building, he wondered what everyone found to talk about, and he envied the ease with which they all seemed to enter into social intercourse. Whenever he was in company, every word he uttered was a forced effort, each encounter sheer torment.

'Hi.'

The voice made him jump.

Sharon crouched beside him. Her tight blue jeans had not been tailored for comfort, and the 'US Dodgers' T-shirt eagerly hugged her young breasts.

A hot rush of blood hit Jamie's cheeks as he mumbled, 'Hello.'

Sharon's pretty young face framed by thick dark hair dimpled into a smile. 'You're in our year, aren't you?'

'Am I? I mean . . . yes, I am.' He felt totally inept, and he really did want her to go away.

'You're good,' Sharon told him brightly. 'The betting is, you'll come out top of the class.'

Jamie knew this to be true; he was an intelligent boy who would succeed at anything he chose to undertake. But the thought of being discussed by others only fuelled his insecurities.

'Do the others talk about me?' he asked haltingly.

'Yeh, all the time. Most of the girls fancy you. Didn't you know?'

This was unexpected, and Jamie surprised even himself by suddenly blurting, 'I didn't want to do computer programming, but my dad made me. I wanted to go to art school.' With the statement uttered, Jamie's gaucherie returned, and he looked away to cover his embarrassment.

'Parents,' Sharon sighed. 'Who needs them? I wanted to go into modelling, but my dad said I've got to get something solid behind me.'

A silence followed, and Jamie racked his brains for something to say.

'Do you go out with girls?' Sharon asked.

'Sometimes,' he said, shrugging in an attempt to appear nonchalant. 'If I fancy them.'

'Want to take me out?'

Jamie turned sharply to see if her expression was mocking. When he saw her sweet, open smile, he became bolder. 'When?'

'Tonight? We could go for a walk over the fields. Have a laugh.'

'OK. Why not?'

Just then the college bell tolled, signalling the resumption of studies.

Jamie spent the afternoon in silent imaginary conversation with Sharon, his every utterance witty and profound while she gazed up at him with undying devotion.

* * *

Holly was relieved to be out of Witch's Cottage.

Sathan, the cat, had spent most of the interview on her lap, every so often rolling over on to his back to reach playfully for her face with a jet-black paw.

That in itself was distracting enough, but each time he turned back he would dig his sharp claws into her legs in an effort to get comfortable. And Joyce Regent did nothing to stop him, just sat there laughing at his antics.

The two youngsters she found distinctly weird. Tanya was fidgety, uneasy, kept flitting in and out of the room. Katie was withdrawn, sullen, and obviously relieved when it was time for Holly to go. She concluded that Joyce was right; they had suffered so much at the hands of the press that they now felt an unhealthy distrust of everyone.

It seemed that Joyce Regent was not overly disturbed by the poison-pen letter itself, which was quite a simple affair: white lined paper, plain white envelope; both cheap brands which could have come from any stationer's.

The message was not particularly chilling, although it did carry a threat.

Leave Bridgetown Witch or history will repeat itself

Holly made a scant study of the bold strokes of the writing before dropping it into a plastic bag for forensic.

Joyce was concerned that the press might be behind the letter. Holly assured her that was unlikely, while thinking how old and haggard the author looked without make-up.

'You don't know what they're capable of,' Joyce told her with acrimony.

'Leave it with us,' Holly called from the garden gate, hoping her lack of enthusiasm did not show in her voice.

Inside the Micra, Holly checked the damage to her tights; the cat had pulled them here and there, but luckily there were no ladders. She brushed the hairs from her skirt as best she could then headed towards the hill behind Witch's Cottage.

Malcolm Headlands was still there, leaning against his Volvo, eating a packet of crisps. He watched with interest as Holly pulled into the lay-by, paying close attention to her legs as she climbed out of the car.

'Lunch,' he explained while she walked towards him. 'Care to join me?' He offered her the crisp bag.

'No, thanks. Have you seen anything?'

'Like what?' he asked, disposing of the empty packet through the open car window.

'Just anything.'

'Hold on, yesterday you were chasing me off, now you want to know if I've seen anything.' He glanced towards the cottage. 'What's going on down there?'

'Nothing,' Holly told him. 'We're just keeping an eye on Mrs Regent.'

Headlands ran long fingers over the contour of his nose, and said, 'Do you see this?'

'That's your nose. Yes, that's definitely your nose.'

'And it can smell a story a mile away.'

'Why do you do this?' Holly asked accusingly. 'Ruin people's lives, I mean.'

He pointed to his expensive car, his quality casual clothes. 'Money.'

'You really are low-life, aren't you?'

Headlands tried to look pained.

'No, sorry, I shouldn't have said that,' Holly jumped in. 'It's disrespectful to low-life.'

Headlands laughed. 'A sense of humour. Now that's unusual in plod.'

'Don't call me "plod". I don't like it.'

'What shall I call you, then?'

She looked at him. 'Holly.'

'Nice name,' he said. 'I'm Malc.' He nodded towards the cottage. 'I don't make her do it, you know. I just report it so the millions who want to read about it can.'

'Ah, but perhaps you invent it sometimes. Make it happen.'

Headlands grinned and shook his head.

'Embroider it a little, then, to make it more interesting.'

'Come on, however hard you try, you can't make me the villain.'

'I followed your story,' Holly said with some scorn. 'Nine times a night?'

'We all like sex—'

'I can take it or leave it,' she cut in, much too quickly.

'But sexy Joyce's in overdrive the whole time.'

'OK.' Holly headed for her car, calling out, 'They'll probably make you a saint when you're dead.'

'How about having a drink with me tonight,' he shouted after her.

'I don't think so.'

'Might be worth your while. I see a lot up here; alcohol could jog my memory, loosen my tongue.'

Holly considered it as she unlocked the car door. She turned back. 'Where?'

'I'm staying at the Colwyn Hotel. In the bar, around nine?'

'I'll be there.'

* * *

Old Ma Shallet turned faded eyes to the door as the shop bell rang out. Straight away, her face cracked into a smile.

'Jim Ashworth,' she said, 'I haven't seen much of you since you packed up smoking. Must be a couple of years now.'

'Something like that, Ma,' he replied warmly, ushering Holly into the shop. 'How are you keeping?'

'Not so bad for an old 'un.' She collected her stick and moved awkwardly from behind the counter. 'What brings you here?'

Ashworth was studying the magazine racks. 'These girlie mags,' he said.

'He always was a devil,' Ma told Holly. 'He used to come in here when he was a lad, and a right cheeky little monkey he was, as well.'

Holly laughed as an embarrassed Ashworth explained, 'I don't want to buy them, Ma. I want you to get them off the premises.'

'Have you taken leave of your senses?' Ma chided. 'He was a right devil for the girls, he was, before that lass, Sarah, took him on.'

Ashworth was now clearly uncomfortable, and Holly watched him fondly as he confronted the tiny woman. 'Ma, you need those magazines out of the shop.'

'Some very respectable people read them,' Ma countered, firmly standing her ground. 'I read *Playgirl* myself till I turned eighty,' she declared, winking at Holly. 'Lost interest, then. It's a terrible thing when the male form stops exciting a woman.'

'You're sending me up, Ma,' Ashworth said with a wry smile.

The old woman looked again at Holly, her eyes gleaming with devilment. 'Jim Ashworth, can you give me a good reason why I should get rid of some of my stock?'

'Yes, I can,' he said, already taking magazines from the rack. 'Because I'm telling you to. Now, just get them out of the shop for a few days.'

'All right, keep your hair on. I'll get my daughter to come over and collect 'em in her car.'

Ashworth placed the pile of magazines on the counter. 'Good.'

'You'll soon have your time taken up with the witch,' Ma said soberly, hobbling back behind the counter.

'And what do you know about that?'

'What me old bones tell me,' she said, closing the counter flap.

'I've no time for riddles, Ma,' Ashworth warned.

'All right, all right. You never did have any patience.' She kept them waiting until all the magazines were hidden behind the counter. Then, straightening up, she said, 'There's them that's very disturbed about the witch coming back.'

Suddenly Ashworth was alert. 'Like who?'

'The aldermen lot, that's who,' Ma replied.

'The aldermen lot?'

'Descendants of the aldermen who put Isobel Perkins to death . . . or what's left of 'em.'

'Who are these people?'

'There's Mick Wright; he delivers the newspapers for the shop. When I told him the news, I thought he was going to have a fit. Then there's Ron Curtis and John Dempsey: them's solicitors or accountants — some such thing, anyway.'

'And this Mick Wright was disturbed?' Ashworth reflected.

'Went white as a sheet, he did.'

'Thank you, Ma, that's very helpful.' He marched to the door. 'You'll be getting a visit from the boys in blue tomorrow, but it's nothing to worry about.'

'I'll get rid of 'em,' she said, looking down at the magazines.

'You do that.' He stopped and turned. 'Don't you think you're getting too old to be running the shop? A lot of criminals are targeting shops nowadays, coming in and emptying the till.'

Ma snorted. 'Who are you calling old, you cheeky beggar. If anybody comes in here after my money, they'll soon go back out.'

Ashworth was about to reply but thought better of it.

Outside, Holly said, 'She's quite a character.'

'Yes, isn't she?'

It was 4 p.m. and the High Street was busy with noisy school children making their way home.

Holly wove her way around a small group of them. 'What now, guv?'

'We visit the newsagents in Cherry Tree and the council estates and warn them off,' he said, heading for the Sierra.

'What about the one in Gladebury Avenue?' Holly asked.

'No need, they don't carry any of the magazines. Let's take our time, shall we? I don't fancy getting back to the nick while it's crawling with councillors.'

'This Joyce Regent thing's bothering me,' Holly said, when they were in the car.

'I know what you mean. Nothing has really happened — just one crank letter. I keep trying to forget it, but I can't. We'll have to look into this Mick Wright.'

‘I’m having a drink with that reporter tonight.’ Holly noticed Ashworth’s raised eyebrows and went on quickly, ‘I’ve a feeling he knows something.’

‘It’s possible. He might have seen who delivered the letter.’

‘I think he could have sent it,’ she remarked, reaching for the seat-belt. ‘The man doesn’t possess many scruples. I’ve no doubt he’d do anything for money.’

‘Where would money come into it?’

‘Joyce Regent is still news. If they can’t dig up any more about her sex life, a twentieth-century witch-hunt could be a scoop.’

Ashworth seemed unimpressed by the theory. ‘Find out what you can,’ he said, starting the engine.

Holly studied his profile. ‘Guv, should we be warning these newsagents about an impending police raid?’

It was a few seconds before he said, ‘No.’

‘I thought not.’

CHAPTER 5

The bar of the Colwyn Hotel was almost empty when Holly arrived at 9 p.m.; and the handful of male patrons openly studied her as she headed towards Malcolm Headlands' table.

He gallantly rose to his feet as she approached.

'Hi, good to see you. What can I get for you?'

'Gin and tonic, please,' Holly said, easing herself into the seat opposite his.

While he was getting the drink, Holly used the time to study his whisky, his cigarettes, but above all, his lighter bearing the inscription, 'Love for ever, Jeanette'.

Soon he was back. 'Is everything in this town olde worlde?' he asked, glancing with distaste at the profusion of beams and horse brasses.

She gave a non-committal shrug.

'That went down well,' he said. 'Let's try something else . . . you're the best-looking woman in the bar.'

'I'm the only woman in the bar.'

'You're killing my patter,' he laughed, nursing his whisky glass.

She sipped her drink. 'What have you got for me, then?'

'Don't you know at your age?'

'Look, cut it out,' Holly warned, 'I'm here on business.'

'What do you want, then?'

She remained silent, and at the sight of her exasperated expression, Headlands retorted, 'Look, something's going down with dirty Joyce and you're not telling me, so why should I tell you anything?'

'You could get done for withholding information.'

'Tell me what you want to know and I'll sing all night,' he said with a wink. 'But you can't do that, can you? Because if you tell me the details, you'll be leading me to the story you're trying to cover up.' He picked up the cigarette packet. 'Mind if I smoke?'

'No.' She watched him light the cigarette. 'Who's Jeanette?'

'We were close,' he said, staring wistfully at the lighter. 'She died in a car crash.'

'Pull the other one, it's got bells on.'

Headlands laughed. 'She had a kid and we split.'

As Holly watched smoke trail towards the ceiling, she said, 'What do you hope to get out of this? You and your colleagues have dug most of the dirt on the Regent woman. If she takes another young lover, it's hardly going to be front page stuff, is it?'

'You're very astute, Holly.' He drew on the cigarette and exhaled slowly. 'If I tell you what I'm after, can we talk a deal?'

'It depends. Try me.'

'As you said, most of the dirty washing's been hung out,' he said, leaning forward eagerly. 'But there's still one big story there. When all this first hit the papers, Joyce was having a fling with a Kevin Thornton. This lad's nineteen, and Joyce was crazy for him.'

Holly finished her drink. 'I don't follow.'

'If you talk to the boys in Joyce's past, you can see a pattern. The woman was totally obsessed with them for about nine months, then she just threw them over and moved on to some new meat. Thornton had been with her for about seven months.'

'Maybe he wanted to go.'

'I don't think so,' Headlands said, sipping his Scotch. 'I reckon he's here in Bridgetown.'

'At the cottage?'

'No, he's probably in a doss-house. Plenty around, even in a town like this. Lots of kids move around the country — he'd blend in.'

'So what are you looking for?'

'I'd just like to keep tabs on him. If I can pick him up when he visits the cottage and find out where he's staying . . .' He spread his hands and shrugged, as if that explained everything.

'I'm still not following you.'

'Well, I reckon Joyce'll get fed up with him soon, and when she does, he'll have a good story to tell. He was with her when the story broke and she knew it was about to hit the papers. He could tell us what she was like then, especially in the sack, and that'll interest the readers. So, when she throws him over, I'll be there waving a nice fat cheque at him.'

'Don't you know what he looks like?'

'No, as far as I know nobody's got a photograph of him. Anyway, these kids are always changing their names to stay on the dodge.' He nodded towards her empty glass. 'Do you want another?'

'No, thanks, I'm driving, but I'll get you one.'

'One of the boys, are you?' he said genially.

Holly smiled as she took his glass. 'I just like to stand my round.'

With the replenished drink in front of him, Holly said, 'When Joyce throws him out, surely he'll realize there's money in it and contact the press himself.'

'Yes, but he won't necessarily contact me.' He held up his glass. 'Cheers.'

Holly inclined her head. 'I wouldn't have thought Joyce's daughters would have allowed the affair to continue. I got the impression they were keeping her on the straight and narrow, especially the eldest.'

'Oh, the little spitfire.' He was silent for a moment while he savoured his Scotch. 'That little lady had a bust-up with some of the lads, broke some cameras and bruised some flesh. Maybe she doesn't know.'

'What's the deal then?'

'I'll be your eyes and ears,' he said eagerly, 'tell you everything that happens around the cottage.'

'And what do you want in return?'

He grinned. 'An exclusive. If anything breaks, I want it before the local press. That way, I can get it to the city a good day before the rest of the pack descends.'

'We won't be looking into any nineteen-year-old kid.'

'No, but you're looking into something, aren't you? There might be a story in it for me, and then I can forget the boy. Let's say I'm just hedging my bets.'

'I can't do a deal like that,' Holly told him flatly.

'You can, of course you can. You'll release the story in any case. All you have to do is tell me first. Oh, come on,' he coaxed. 'Do you want to know what I've seen so far?'

'Try me.'

'Well, not much, actually. Your guv'nor's cramping my style. Thornton can get in and out of that cottage without me knowing.'

'Then you haven't got much to bargain with,' Holly said, as he drained the last of his Scotch.

'There was one thing,' he said after a moment's thought. 'Something that didn't seem quite right. Around midnight a white transit van went past. I noticed because it slowed, as if the driver was looking at the cottage.'

'So?' Holly said, hoping to disguise her interest.

'Well, it was the only vehicle about. It went along the lane and out of sight. About three minutes after that, I heard an engine start from the direction it had taken. I didn't think much about it at the time, but it's possible that the driver parked, walked back to the cottage for some reason, and then legged it back to the van. Is that any help?'

'None at all,' she lied, 'but you've got yourself a deal.'

'Good.' He looked pleased. 'Shall we have a drink on that?'

'Like I said, I'm driving,' Holly told him firmly, picking up her shoulder bag. 'And in any case, I'm off.'

Headlands grinned. 'I don't suppose I could persuade you to come up to my room and view my private etchings, could I?'

Holly pulled a face. 'Down, boy, this is purely business.'

* * *

An eerie silence descended as Jamie helped Sharon over the stile into Bluebell Wood. He rather shyly took her hand, and they wandered along the narrow winding path.

Dense foliage met overhead, blocking out most of the natural light, but rather than creating a sinister air, it had a pleasant, cosy effect. Here, the summer scents seemed more potent, and the rustle of leaves caressed by a soft wind added a magical quality to the silence in the wood.

They had spent the evening in a bar, lingering over two halves of lager. At first, Jamie had worried about his father's reaction to the alcohol on his breath, but very soon, realizing that Sharon seemed actually interested in his thoughts, he forgot his father and talked earnestly about his aspirations for the future.

To her surprise, Sharon was interested; she listened intently, warming to the boy as he explained how art could be put to commercial use in advertising and newspaper design — it didn't have to lead to the wasted life of a struggling artist.

There were times during the evening when she forgot the reason she had befriended this son of a local policeman. Jamie was far more refined, less brash and ill-mannered than most of her peers whose behaviour she emulated in a misguided need to belong within a group.

'Do you smoke?' she asked as they strolled along in an easy silence.

'No, tobacco damages your health.'

'Not fags,' she laughed. 'Grass.'

'Oh,' Jamie said, out of his depth yet again. 'I did try it a couple of times.'

'Do you want some?'

'Yes, why not?' He tried his best to appear casual.

Sharon untangled her hand from Jamie's and extracted a tin from the pocket of her leather jacket. She took out a joint and quickly lit it. Smoke poured from her mouth as she passed the cigarette to Jamie.

He had never smoked before and was filled with panic at the thought of making a fool of himself in front of the girl. Cautiously, he inhaled, willing himself not to cough as the smoke hit his lungs.

Jamie was relieved when it was finished. 'Good stuff,' he remarked, as Sharon dropped the stub and stamped it out.

His head had started to spin, his limbs felt detached, and there were cushions of air beneath his feet as they continued to walk. But he felt great; he felt alive for the first time in his life.

Eventually, they stopped where the wood opened out into fields. 'Let's go back,' Sharon said.

Jamie thought about his father. 'I ought to be getting home.'

'Come on,' she urged. 'Let's have some fun first.' She took his hand and playfully pulled him back along the path.

They stopped by a large oak which had blown over in a gale, and there they kissed. Sharon's arms were around his neck, pulling him closer. Jamie found himself overpowered by her perfume, and her lips were making his whole body tingle and shake.

Sharon pushed against him, forcing him back into the tree, rubbing her stomach against his uncontrollable erection. Jamie gasped for breath when they parted.

Perhaps it was the cannabis, or the thought that he was going against his father; whatever the reason, Jamie felt wonderful, capable of anything. Without thinking, he allowed his hands to slide on to Sharon's breasts. She groaned and undid the fastening of her jacket, granting him access. He fumbled with her T-shirt, finally managing to pull it free from her waistband, as Sharon reached behind to unclip her bra.

And then he was touching soft warm flesh. For the first time, Jamie was experiencing sensations he had hitherto only dreamed of.

Sharon's responses made him more daring, and he helped as she struggled with the fastener of his jeans and searched for the slit in his boxer shorts. His movements were clumsy and hurried, but soon her skirt was pushed clear.

She willingly parted her legs, and Jamie thrilled at the warmth felt through her flimsy pants, and at the unbelievable excitement he experienced when she took him in her hand.

'Please, Sharon, please.'

Without further teasing, she removed her pants, pulled herself up on to the bough of the fallen tree and opened her legs.

His inexperience slowed them somewhat, but after several attempts, Sharon guided him in and on beyond the point of control.

* * *

The door to the transit van slid open, cutting through the eerily still night, and a man jumped awkwardly from the driver's seat, a white envelope clutched in his hand. For a moment he wavered, glancing around nervously. All that could be seen were star-like orange lights dotted along the expressway.

Although the night air was cool, those fingers holding the envelope were sticky with sweat. With a light tread the man made his way along a grass verge leading to the cottage, his whole demeanour suggesting that he expected to be challenged at any moment.

The cottage was in darkness, no chink of light showing through the drawn curtains. With great care he closed the wooden gate and approached the front door. To be so close to the witch disturbed him, and a cold shiver ran along his spine.

Almost too scared to breathe, he pushed open the letter-flap and shoved the envelope through; it hit the rush matting with a faint rustle. The man allowed the flap to fall shut, and scurried back along the path, not breathing freely until he was safely away.

* * *

Jamie was exhausted by the time he arrived home. After leaving Sharon on the Cherry Tree estate, he had run full pelt all the way back to the detached house on the adjoining estate where he lived with his parents.

As his trainers skidded on the gravel drive, he realized with dismay that any slight hope of avoiding a confrontation with his father had died, for the lounge light was still on.

A fine grandfather clock stood at the foot of the stairs in the hallway, and Jamie opened the door in time to hear it chime twelve-thirty. His father was beside it, rigid with rage.

'And where have you been, young man?' Newton demanded, hands clasped tightly behind his ramrod-straight back.

'I've been out with a girl, Dad,' Jamie stammered.

'Until this time of night? Your mother's been worried to death.'

'We just got talking,' Jamie said, inwardly cringing, 'and I forgot the time. I really like her, Dad.'

'Bring her home to meet us, then.' It was spoken as a direct order rather than a pleasant invitation.

Suddenly, Jamie pushed past him into the lounge. 'I don't want to bring her home. It's not cool.'

'Not cool?' Newton barked after him. 'What sort of language is that?'

Jamie ran a hand through his hair and turned to Newton, his large gentle eyes pleading. 'I don't want to argue, Dad.'

'Sit down, boy.'

Jamie made no move; he remained in front of the Regency fire-surround, totally forlorn.

'Sit down,' Newton repeated, pointing to an armchair.

Obediently, Jamie crossed to the strawberry-coloured seat and sat down, staring at the carpet.

'Now, young man, unless I'm very much mistaken, you've been drinking—'

'I had a lager.'

'Don't you dare to interrupt me,' Newton bellowed. 'And by the state of your clothes, I'd say you've been rolling about on the ground rather than talking.'

'Dad . . .'

'Rolling about with some cheap little trollop.' Newton pointed a warning finger. 'I will not tolerate that sort of behaviour while you're living in my house.'

'Sharon's not a trollop,' Jamie shouted, jumping from the chair.

'Do not answer me back,' Newton thundered. 'Girls who go drinking and allow boys to paw them about are trollops.'

'But, Dad, I'm not a boy, I'm a man.'

'You're as far away from being a man as it's possible to get,' Newton sneered, with open contempt. 'In future, you'll get home by ten o'clock and I want to meet any friends you make before you take them out. Is that understood, boy?'

All of that new-found confidence and self-respect so eagerly derived from Sharon now threatened to evaporate before the low self-image inflicted upon him by his father, but Jamie resolved to fight.

'Why do you have to ruin everything for me?' he yelled. 'Why can't you ever listen to what I want?'

'Don't raise your voice to me,' Newton said, visibly shaken.

'Why? What are you going to do — hit me? Is that what you're going to do?'

'Don't think you're too old for that, my boy.'

'You can't keep on putting me down all the time. You make my life a misery, just like you make Mum's.'

'You ungrateful brat.' Newton's hand came from nowhere, taking Jamie off guard as it caught his face, knocking him sideways. 'Now get to bed.'

'No, I won't,' Jamie said, beating his fists upon his father's chest. There was little force behind the blows, but the suddenness of the attack left Newton reeling.

'Why can't you ever listen?' Jamie screamed. 'Just shut your fucking know-all mouth and listen for once.'

'Jamie, stop it,' Newton commanded, grabbing his son's arms.

Jamie broke away and ran from the room. The front door slammed as Newton, stunned and shocked, lurched towards the hall.

'Get back here. Do you hear me? Jamie!'

CHAPTER 6

Peanuts noticed it first, and she followed Ashworth around, looking up at him with large, quizzical eyes.

Sarah was next to spot it. She made no comment, but after her husband had left for work, she felt rather perplexed. And while sorting through the fridge, making a shopping list, she absently muttered, 'Batteries.'

Martin Dutton, a long-standing acquaintance of Ashworth's, noticed immediately and all through their morning chat he stared at the chief inspector in mild disbelief.

To Ashworth's chagrin, Newton overlooked it. But then, he was preoccupied: his son had failed to return home, and the spate of car thefts and burglaries had not abated. Even so, throughout the morning's briefing, the main problem on his mind was how to get rid of Ashworth as quickly as possible.

Josh's mind was most definitely not in the CID office, so he too failed to notice. He was certain the collar and tie would eventually asphyxiate him; and the herringbone sports jacket which had replaced his suede blouson made him feel stiff and formal.

Worse still, news of the order for him to smarten up had spread like wildfire throughout the station and now everywhere he went uniformed officers would wolf whistle as he walked past. Even his automatically muttered, 'Balls,' did little to soothe his irritation.

It took Holly sometime to become aware of it. Ashworth breezed into the office, listened while she explained that Joyce Regent had received another poison-pen letter, and then rifled through the burglary and car-theft reports, ordering that uniformed would have to deal with them.

After leaving Josh with instructions to accompany the officers on the pornography raid and report directly to him, he strode out of the office, telling Holly to follow.

It was when they were both seated in the Sierra that she noticed. Apart from Sarah, Holly probably understood him better than anyone else, and she immediately knew the reasoning behind it.

'This Regent thing's getting to be a pain,' he announced between muttered curses, as he reversed the vehicle in the congested car park.

Holly dug into her shoulder bag for her notebook. 'I found out the address for Mick Wright,' she said.

'Good girl. How did it go with that reporter chap last night?'

'Ah.' She stared straight ahead. 'I've done a deal with him. He'll be our eyes and ears at the cottage . . .'

'Oh, do come on,' Ashworth said crossly, as he waited for an opening in the traffic.

'. . . and in return we give him any story before it breaks.'

Ashworth turned sharply towards her. 'You've done what?'

'Keep your eyes on the road, guv.'

'Holly, you can't do deals with the press. It contravenes regulations.'

'Does it?' she said, surprised. 'You mean like warning newsagents about porn?'

Ashworth chuckled. 'I don't know why I let you get away with so much.'

They were crossing the River Thane when Ashworth said, 'Didn't you suspect this reporter of sending the letters?'

'Yes,' she admitted. 'If we eliminate Mick Wright, Malc will become my prime suspect.'

'Malc, is it?' Ashworth teased.

Holly ignored him. 'And while it might not be a serious offence for a half-crazed man to write to a witch he thinks has cursed him, a journalist going out of his way to make a story is a different matter altogether.'

* * *

Malcolm Headlands spotted Ashworth's car as it pulled up outside Witch's Cottage. With practised ease, he focused the long-distance lens and within seconds the blurred picture filling the viewfinder became a clear-cut image.

He watched Ashworth climb from the car and then swung the camera to the passenger side. Holly was just emerging, swinging her legs from the vehicle, her skirt riding quite a way above her knees.

'Give us a flash, girl,' Headlands whispered, training the camera on her legs.

As if in answer to his request, Holly leant back inside the car for her shoulder bag long enough for him to catch the briefest glimpse of her white pants.

'Yes,' he smiled, focusing the camera on her face.

Holly winked in his direction and gave a cheeky grin.

'You're going to be a lot of fun, Holly,' Headlands chortled. 'A lot of fun.'

* * *

When Joyce Regent opened the front door, it was obvious that she had not dressed for the occasion. Her baggy black trousers were creased; so too was the loud check man's shirt she was wearing, and her tied-back hair was greasy.

'Well, you two took your time getting here.'

The detectives were taken aback.

'We came as soon as we could,' Ashworth said, as they were ushered into the hall.

The cat was sitting on the bottom stair; it spat and snarled the moment Ashworth walked in.

'Shoo, shoo,' Joyce called. 'Sorry, he can't stand men. He's all right with women but as soon as a man walks in he goes wild.'

'Well, he'll have to put up with me,' Ashworth muttered, still put out by their initial reception.

With one final loathsome glare, the cat bounded up the stairs.

'In the lounge,' Joyce said, leading the way.

The chaos of his last visit had been sorted out: three-piece suite in place, walls lined with bookcases, and centre of the room now home to a large glass-topped coffee table. Joyce pointed to it.

'The letter's on there,' she said. 'I've handled it as little as possible.'

Ashworth crossed to the table and stared down at the letter.

Leave now witch or you'll burn.

It was identical to the first: paper, envelope, handwriting.

'And it arrived this morning?' he asked.

'It was on the mat when I came down this morning.'

'Right.' Ashworth signalled to Holly, who stepped forward to seal the letter in a polythene bag.

'Joyce, I wouldn't worry too much about this,' she said, with a smile of reassurance. 'I can see it's getting to you.'

'Oh God, I'm sorry,' Joyce said, slumping on the settee. 'Please do forgive me.' She gave Ashworth a humble look. 'It's my artistic temperament coming to the fore. Believe me, I'm hell to live with.'

'We'll clear this up,' Ashworth assured her. 'If you get any more letters, I'll put an officer outside full time.'

'It's not the letters that worry me so much,' she said, getting up to stare out of the window. 'It's that reporter watching the house all the time.'

'There's not a lot we can do about him. He's not breaking any law.'

Joyce turned to him. 'You see, I'm going to town to stay with my agent for a few days. It's Katie's idea,' she said. 'And I'm worried about leaving the girls here alone, with him up there.'

'Let's hope he follows you,' Holly said.

'That's what Katie's hoping for. If he sees there's nothing going on, perhaps he'll back off.'

'Joyce, can I go up and see your bedroom?' Holly asked suddenly.

'My bedroom? Whatever for?'

'I just want to see what sort of view that reporter has of the window.'

Joyce shrugged: 'Oh, all right, I'll take you up.'

Holly shot an imploring glance at Ashworth. He responded immediately.

'Miss Regent,' he said, 'could you give me details of how long you'll be away, and where we can contact you if necessary?'

'Yes, of course.' She glanced at Holly. 'Can you find your own way up? It's the large bedroom at the front.'

Holly raced up the stairs but came to a dead halt at the top. On the landing she was overwhelmed by a strange sensation. It was hard to identify at first, but then, with a shudder, she realized it was like icy fingers feeling along her shoulder blades.

'Get a grip of yourself,' she muttered, opening the door to Joyce's bedroom.

It was an ultra-modern room with mirror-fronted sliding wardrobes and matching dressing table. The bed was king-sized and covered with a black quilt.

Holly pulled it back and peered at the sheet. Satisfied, she patted the cover into place and made her way downstairs.

Joyce was waiting in the hall. 'The chief inspector's already outside,' she said. 'A call came through on the radio, or something.'

'Thanks,' Holly smiled, unlatching the front door, 'and have a nice time in London.'

'I'll try. I'm not really looking forward to the trip. And sorry I was so bad tempered.'

Ashworth was waiting in the car, a smug, satisfied smile on his face. 'Josh's been on the radio. They've covered Ma's, the Cherry Tree and council estate newsagents and they're all clear. So now it's just Gladebury Avenue.' He started the engine. 'Why did you want to get upstairs?'

As the car pulled away, Holly said, 'Malc, the reporter, has a theory that the last of Joyce's young lovers is in Bridgetown. Anyway, somebody's definitely giving it to her; I found semen stains all over the sheet.'

'It's got nothing to do with us,' Ashworth reminded her. 'They're consenting adults.'

'I know, guv, but there's something weird about that cottage. I just feel something terrible's going to happen there.'

Ashworth was disturbed by Holly's remark. He too had experienced the same disquieting premonition, but for the moment he decided to say nothing.

* * *

Craig Summers viciously gripped Sharon by the chin, his thumb and forefinger digging into her skin.

'Don't hand me this bullshit about him not being a bad guy,' he snarled.

The others crowded around.

'Back off, Craig,' Sharon warned, attempting to slap his hand away.

'I want that weirdo in trouble. His old man's chief pig.'

They were in the garden at the back of the college. It was midmorning break, and their behaviour was attracting the attention of a tutor. A small man in cord trousers and sports jacket with leather-patched elbows, he flitted around the periphery for a while, uncertain as to whether he should interfere.

Finally, he decided to approach. 'Are you all right, Sharon?' he called. 'Craig, let her go.'

Craig released his grip, and Sharon shot the man a wide smile. 'I'm fine, Mr Dunkley . . . really.'

The tutor retreated a little, but kept a suspicious eye on the group.

'I'm just saying that the guy's not bad,' Sharon said. 'He really hates his old man. And he's fun to be with when you get to know him.'

Rod Calway and Carl Chown waited for Craig's lead, while Laurie picked at her fingernails with the measured indifference she usually adopted when not at the centre of attention.

'I'm saying he'll come in with us,' Sharon said. 'He's really fed up with his old man, honest.'

'So we wouldn't be breaking up the happy home,' Craig pondered. 'Where is he today? Why isn't he in college?'

'She let him have it,' Carl leered, 'and he's such a wimp, he's knackered.'

'I don't know,' Sharon said, giving Carl a withering glare.

'Look, there he is,' Laurie said, pointing across the garden.

All heads swivelled round.

Jamie was on the steps, his eyes searching the garden. His hair was uncombed, and his clothing creased.

Craig gave Sharon a shove. 'Go and see what he's doing.'

The moment he spotted the girl, Jamie broke into a run, a huge smile lighting up his young face.

'Hi,' she said.

'Hello.' He took her hand. 'I had a row with my dad last night. I walked out.'

'Where did you sleep?'

'In the park. Look, I'm not coming back to college. I just wanted to know if I can see you tonight.'

'But where are you going to stay?'

'I don't know,' he said, worry suddenly wiping away his smile.

Sharon thought for a few moments. 'Hold on, Craig's got a pad. He'll put you up for a couple of nights. He's just moved down from London, and he's OK.'

Jamie brightened as Sharon gestured to Craig. The youth swaggered over with arrogant self-confidence.

Sharon said, 'Craig, you know Jamie.'

'Yeh,' he replied, viewing his supposed enemy cautiously.

'Listen, he's had a row with his old man, and split. Can you put him up?'

Craig's eyes widened with surprise; perhaps he'd misjudged after all. 'Yeh, why not?' he said. 'Do you know Hazeldene Road?'

Jamie nodded.

'It's the flat at the top. Number seven.'

Sharon turned back to Jamie. 'Are you staying this afternoon?'

'No, I'm going to split,' he said, enjoying his new vocabulary.

'I'll be in about six,' Craig told him.

Jamie looked expectantly at Sharon.

'I'll see you at Craig's tonight,' she said.

* * *

Josh came through on the radio as the Sierra pulled up outside Mick Wright's cottage.

'OK, Josh, go ahead,' Holly said.

'We've done the newsagents in Gladebury Avenue. We found girlie magazines, soft porn — quite a lot, in fact.'

'Describe some of it to me,' Holly giggled. 'In great detail.'

She caught Ashworth's reproachful stare and mouthed, 'Sorry,' as Josh continued. 'The guy in the shop only works there. The owner's being contacted, and the material's on its way to the nick.'

'Message received, Josh, now straighten your tie and comb your hair.' Holly laughed, quickly replacing the handset before he could reply. 'Well, guv, it looks as though you were wrong — they do carry porn.'

'So it would seem. They must have had a change of policy.'

'And Newton's got his tickle despite our efforts.'

'The best laid plans of mice and men, Holly,' Ashworth reflected.

They knocked on the door of number forty-three. It was opened by Edith Wright. 'Yes?'

'Chief Inspector Ashworth, madam, Bridgetown CID, and this is DS Bedford.'

'What do you want?' she mumbled, ignoring their warrant cards.

'We'd like a word with Mr Mick Wright, if that's possible,' Ashworth said gently.

'You can't. He's not in.'

'Who is it, woman?' Wright called from the end of the passage.

Ashworth looked in to see a gaunt figure peering towards them.

'Oh, Mick, it's the police.'

Wright hurried to the doorway. 'What do you want?' he asked brusquely.

'We're looking into a complaint about poison-pen letters, sir,' Holly politely informed him.

Edith squealed, 'I told you, Mick. I told you.'

'Shut up, woman,' Wright shouted, before surrendering to another bout of coughing.

'Can we come in, sir,' Ashworth enquired.

'No, you can't,' Wright wheezed. 'I'll not speak to you till my lawyer's present. Ring him, woman.'

The front door slammed shut.

Ashworth was quite amazed. 'I think we've found the sender of the letters,' he said.

* * *

Whenever Sergeant Dutton was annoyed, the colour of his bald head acted as an accurate indicator to the height of his annoyance. The colours were wide-ranging, from slightly pink for mild irritation to crimson for seething anger.

Today, his dome was glowing like a red 'stop' sign. The reason for this was the pile upon pile of erotic magazines from the newsagents in Gladebury Avenue. Now classed as evidence, they had been deposited in interview room number one, and were acting as a magnet for nearly all personnel in the building. Dutton had lost count of the number of times he was forced to abandon reception in order to clear the room of uniformed officers of both sexes.

On the last occasion, WPC Jenny Perry was assuring her female colleagues that the man in the photograph was wearing a false penis; either that, or she had attracted a lot of bad luck in her own sex life. A harassed Dutton had once again cleared the room amidst several shouted offers to show Jenny something far larger.

Now he was forced to stand guard outside the room which, to his mind, was just another example of Superintendent Newton making his job more difficult.

* * *

It was some twenty minutes before Ashworth and Holly were allowed entry into the Wrights' residence.

While Ashworth hurred and purred inside the Sierra, Ronald Curtis' Bentley glided smoothly to a halt a few yards away. Shortly afterwards the latest Rover model arrived, carrying John Dempsey.

Ten minutes later the smartly dressed Curtis emerged from the cottage and approached the Sierra. Ashworth wound down the window.

'Sorry to keep you waiting, Chief Inspector,' he said pleasantly. 'I'm Ronald Curtis, Mr Wright's solicitor.'

'We can come in now, can we?' Ashworth asked tersely.

'Yes, please do,' Curtis said, leading the way.

Sounds of Mick Wright's coughing could be heard as soon as they stepped into the hall. Curtis ushered them into the tiny front room, empty but for a dark brown two-seater settee, one armchair, and an old sideboard, and yet there was still barely room enough left for the six of them.

Wright was on the settee, a handkerchief in his hand. Edith, beside him, became visibly agitated when the detectives entered the room. John Dempsey was staring out of the front window, seemingly trying to distance himself from the situation.

Curtis, now sounding more like a solicitor, said, 'What's all this about, Chief Inspector?'

'We're making inquiries into poison-pen letters that have been turning up at Witch's Cottage,' Ashworth replied impatiently.

'And are you accusing Mr Wright of sending those letters?'

'No,' Ashworth said, 'but I do know a white transit van, similar to the one driven by Mr Wright, has been seen in the vicinity of the cottage of late.'

'Of course it has,' Wright stammered. 'I have to drive along there for me work—'

'No, Mick,' Curtis snapped, shaking a finger. Then to Ashworth, 'Have you any evidence to connect my client with these letters?'

'None,' Ashworth admitted.

'Then I think you'd better leave.'

Ashworth's quota of patience was fast diminishing; he fixed the solicitor with a baleful stare and said, 'Within this room is the whole of the aldermen group, I take it?'

Curtis faltered at the question, but quickly recovered. 'Does that have any bearing on what we've been discussing?'

'You tell me. I know all about the curse and the prophecy, so I'd say those with most to fear from Joyce Regent moving into the cottage are all in this room.'

'The witch has done for me,' Wright lamented wildly.

'Mick, don't,' Curtis said, alarmed at the outburst.

Ashworth went on in a level tone, 'All I have left to say is that two letters have been sent. Now, if no more turn up, I won't be moving heaven and earth to find out who sent them. Am I making myself understood?'

He carefully studied the group while the meaning of his words became clear. 'I'm just trying to save time — my time. All right?'

Edith's face showed relief, while her husband stared dully at the floor.

'Then I'll leave you in peace,' Ashworth said, glancing at Holly and nodding towards the door.

'I'll see you out,' Curtis called, following them through into the passage.

As soon as they left the room, Wright's coughing began in earnest.

'He should get that cough seen to,' Holly remarked.

'He's going to the doctor's tomorrow,' Curtis said, standing aside at the door for them to pass.

Ashworth stopped on the threshold. 'You know he sent those letters,' he stated bluntly.

'It's not impossible,' Curtis replied, with a lawyer's caution.

'Dissuade him from writing anymore.' He was about to go when he said, 'Tell me, Mr Curtis, surely in this day and age no one really believes this witch's curse stuff, do they?'

Curtis leant forward, his expression serious. 'Chief Inspector, I regard myself as an intelligent, educated man, and it still frightens me,' he said. 'When it goes back in your family for generations, you see it from a different viewpoint, I can tell you.' He sighed. 'It's foolish, I know, but my wife is pregnant, and I'm worried to death that there's going to be something wrong with the baby.'

'But not scared enough to be sending letters,' Ashworth ventured.

'No,' he conceded, 'but then Mick's not well educated. I am trying to do something, though.'

Ashworth was surprised. 'And what might that be?'

'I'm trying to challenge that Regent woman's right to the cottage. She's so many times removed from the bloodline, you see, and the cottage is only supposed to be occupied by direct descendants of the witch. I think the property should revert back to the state. There, does that convince you about how worried I am?'

During the drive back to the station, Ashworth was silent. Now that he had met the aldermen group, now that he had seen the effect past events had had on their lives, that deep feeling of foreboding intensified within him.

Perhaps something awful *was* about to happen.

CHAPTER 7

'But Katie, I need it,' Joyce sobbed, 'you know that. I need it all the time. I can't work unless I'm relaxed.'

'I do know,' Katie said firmly, 'but it has to be away from the house. You're upsetting Tanya.'

They were in the author's bedroom. Katie was sitting on the window-seat while Joyce dressed.

'I don't know why I asked you to come here,' she pouted.

'Don't you?' Katie asked coldly, watching Joyce's bra conceal those large sagging breasts.

'Well, yes, I suppose I do.'

'I don't want Tanya upset, not with that reporter hanging about. He could wreck everything.'

Katie looked out of the window, straining to see where Headlands was standing in the lay-by, still watching the cottage.

'All right,' Joyce said meekly, 'not in the house.'

Katie rose to leave. 'It's for your own good.'

'I know,' Joyce sighed.

'Look, perhaps I could get Tanya out of the cottage this afternoon.'

'Oh, dear Katie,' Joyce enthused. 'I don't want her upset, but you do know my needs.'

'We'll work it out. Once this whole thing has died down, it'll all get back to normal. Tanya thinks the cottage is haunted, you know.'

'Is that what's wrong with her? She seems to be forever moping about and eating.'

'She'll get over it. I'll have a word with her this weekend.'

'Don't dabble in anything you don't understand,' Joyce warned. 'Now, when can you get rid of Tanya? Take as much money from my bag as you need.'

Katie smiled. 'Is that a bribe?'

'Yes,' she said, her eagerness pathetic.

'In about an hour,' Katie said, viewing her with disgust.

* * *

Ashworth had to fight back a smile at the sight of the usually placid Martin Dutton, pacing up and down outside the interview room.

'You look happy, Martin,' he said cheerfully.

'Don't start, Jim, I'm just not in the mood. I thought you were going to knock this porn thing on the head.'

'It takes time,' Ashworth laughed. 'Lighten up, man. See the funny side of things.'

'Lighten up?' Dutton retorted. 'I feel like throwing up. Have a guess what Newton's doing now — he's pushing Neighbourhood Watch and anti-car-theft schemes in the worst-hit areas, instead of just letting my boys get on with the job.'

Ashworth sobered. 'I know what he's trying to do,' he said. 'And he's going the wrong way about it.'

'Well, I'm glad somebody knows what he's up to,' Dutton moaned.

'Oh, yes, I'm beginning to read the man. A smaller, slimline force on a lower budget means a happy band of councillors.'

'I don't know what you mean, Jim.'

'You will, in the fullness of time.' Ashworth looked towards the stairs. 'But now I think it's time to put a warning shot across his bows.'

‘Couldn’t you aim it at his head?’ Dutton muttered to his retreating figure.

‘Come in,’ Newton called in answer to Ashworth’s brisk knock. ‘Ah, Ashworth, sit down. I believe you had some success with the pornography raids.’

‘A little,’ Ashworth said, easing into his seat. ‘Three of the newsagents were clear, but Samson’s in Gladebury Avenue was carrying quite a lot of the stuff.’

‘Funny that the others were clear,’ Newton pondered, eyeing Ashworth with suspicion. ‘It looks almost as if they were tipped off.’

‘Should we be looking for a mole within our midst?’ Ashworth asked, barely keeping his face straight.

‘No, I don’t think so. After all, he’s not a very good mole — he missed Samson’s.’ Newton’s eyes twinkled. ‘I just hope that in future people will realize that I miss very little.’

‘I’m sure they will, sir.’

‘You think this whole pornography thing is a waste of time, don’t you, Chief Inspector?’

‘Since you ask me, sir, yes.’

Newton leant forward. ‘I’m not the fool you take me for.’

Ashworth raised his eyebrows as if to question that remark.

‘Dumb insolence — that would have been the term used to describe your attitude in my army days.’

Newton stood up, placed his hands on the desk, maintaining eye contact with the chief inspector. ‘I’ll be honest with you, Ashworth, I think that we are heading for a clash of wills.’

‘I do hope not, sir,’ Ashworth replied amicably.

‘I don’t expect a conviction on the pornography, but if the newsagents know they’re going to be raided from time to time, and have the threat of prosecution forever hanging over their heads . . .’ He spread his hands. ‘Well, it’s such a small part of their trade, they’ll soon stop carrying it.’

‘Very clever, sir,’ Ashworth said.

'Yes, it's that sort of thing that helps keep the council happy. And a happy council means a happy chief constable, and that means a happy superintendent, which in turn means a happy chief inspector.'

'I see,' Ashworth said, 'Well, that all sounds very . . . happy. But there's one thing puzzling me, sir. I'm sure a lot of the councillors will be happy with this, but I doubt whether Archie Samson, the newsagent, will be.'

'That's of little interest to me,' Newton snapped.

There was a long pause. 'Councillor Archie Samson, that is.' An innocent smile settled on Ashworth's face. 'A very important man, is Archie.'

Newton's mouth dropped open. 'Do you mean to say, you let me raid the shop of a—'

'I didn't let you do anything, sir.'

As far as Newton was concerned, the battle-lines were now drawn and Ashworth could only agree. Unless one of them pulled back, a serious confrontation, sometime in the future, was inevitable.

Newton managed to regain his self-control. He pulled himself erect and glared down at Ashworth. 'This interview is now over, Chief Inspector.'

'Thank you, sir,' Ashworth said as he sauntered towards the door.

* * *

That afternoon, Jamie Newton visited his mother to assure her that he was all right. He loved his mother; she always listened to him. She listened now and promised not to interfere in his life. He collected some clothes, pocketed his bank books and kissed her at the door.

She was tearful. 'Keep in touch, won't you?'

'I'll ring you every day, Mum,' he promised.

'Your dad will come round. I'll work on him.'

'It's no good, Mum, he'll never let me go to art school.'

His mother kissed him again, hugging him to herself, loath to let him go.

'I hate him, Mum,' Jamie declared vehemently. 'I'd do anything to get back at him.'

Then it was time to leave. And pushing all second thoughts away, Jamie raced off without looking back.

He had some difficulty in finding Craig's place. Hazeldene Road was located in the Victorian part of Bridgetown, and was lined with huge houses, most of which had been converted into student flats. He trudged along, hands in the pockets of his jeans.

Finally, he approached number twenty-five, manoeuvring past black rubbish sacks stacked at the side of its tarnished door. They gave off a disgustingly pungent odour which lingered even in the hall. He had to climb three flights of stairs, past doors painted gaudy reds, oranges and lime greens. At the very top, he knocked on the door to flat number seven.

'It's open,' Craig called.

Jamie entered and found himself in a large room. Beanbags were spread all over the dirty blue carpet and tattered curtains were already pulled across the filthy windows.

Craig was in the kitchen doorway, eating baked beans from a chipped white plate. 'Hi, Jamie,' he said.

'Hello,' Jamie replied from a spot just inside the door.

'This is it,' Craig said, waving his fork. 'Dump your stuff down anywhere. There's no rules here, you can do what you like. Sometimes I vanish for a while, 'cause I'm giving it to somebody. She pays really well, so I'm thinking about dropping out of college.'

Jamie struggled out of his backpack, placing it neatly in a corner. As he gazed around at the filth, he felt a keen revulsion and was engulfed by a feeling of acute loneliness. Those alien surroundings made him feel very small, very small indeed.

* * *

Holly was surprised to feel a tingle of excitement when she pulled into the lay-by. Headlands smiled broadly as she hurried towards him.

She gave a tiny salute. 'Reporting to base, sir.'

'What have you got?'

'Nothing really. Just thought I'd let you know that Joyce is going to London. She'll be staying with her agent for a few days.'

'Is she, now?' In the gathering gloom he shot Holly a hopeful look. 'I don't suppose you'll tell me why you were at the cottage today.'

She shook her head and smiled teasingly. 'Nope.'

'Thought not.'

'Seen anything?' she asked, looking back at the cottage.

'The bedroom curtains were drawn for about an hour and a half this afternoon.'

'Exciting,' she said.

Headlands grinned. 'It could have been . . . if you were on the other side of the curtains.'

'Malc, I was looking at Joyce today and . . .' She hesitated. 'Well, she's not exactly the best-looking woman in the world, is she? How does she get all those young boys?'

'Money.'

'What do you mean — she buys it?'

'Not exactly. I mean, she doesn't actually say, here's a hundred pounds, give me an hour of fun. But she's a rich lady. The boys live well off her.'

Holly stood fiddling with her car keys, reluctant to leave. She said, 'So what will you do this weekend? Follow Joyce, I suppose.'

'Yes, I suppose.' His tone suggested he was not relishing the prospect.

'Why don't you leave her alone? Let her have a bit of dick in peace.'

'She's getting plenty of that, don't worry.'

'Then you'd be better off here,' she reasoned. 'Who knows, this boyfriend might just show himself.'

'It's a pretty dead place to spend the weekend.'

'I could liven it up for you.'

Headlands studied her with sudden interest. 'And how would you do that?'

'I could invite you to my place,' she said. 'I do a pretty mean spaghetti Bolognese. We could have a bottle of wine.'

'And?' he prompted.

'And watch some telly.'

He laughed. 'You've got a date.'

Holly gave him the address, offered only a cheek to his pouting lips, then returned to her car.

Once inside she gave herself a good ticking off, an occurrence which was becoming something of a habit these days. But why shouldn't she see him? After all, wasn't she trying to find out if he was sending the letters? It was good police work, that's all: subtle; imaginative.

Checking the road behind, Holly caught a glimpse of her image in the rear-view mirror, and gave herself a wink — besides, that's a bloody interesting bulge in his trousers.

* * *

The squalor of the large room which Craig called a flat was getting to Jamie but, determined not to return home, he fought to make the best of it.

The others arrived at about 8 p.m. They sat around on the beanbags, smoking cannabis and drinking lager. Craig was friendly enough, so were the two girls; but Carl was still hostile, and Rod was simply withdrawn.

'Do all ponces paint and draw?' Carl asked on one of the few occasions when the lager can was not at his lips.

Jamie started to stammer a reply when Sharon cut in. 'What do you draw, Jamie?'

'Anything,' he said, looking around. 'I'll draw Craig, if you like.'

Jamie got to his feet and reeled; his head was light and his legs felt flaccid. He staggered to his rucksack, collected his pad and pencils, and squatted down to study Craig. Eventually he began to draw.

For ten minutes his face was a study of concentration. And then, with a flourish, he produced the drawing. 'There.'

They passed it around.

'Hey, that's great,' Laurie exclaimed. 'It looks just like him.'

Jamie took a gulp of lager to cover his embarrassment. 'It was just a quickie,' he said shyly. 'I didn't have time to do it properly.'

They all agreed that it was a good likeness.

'Do me next,' Laurie said, reclining on the beanbag.

'Make it interesting,' Craig suggested. 'Take your clothes off.'

'Yeh, come on,' Carl and Rod chorused. 'Get 'em off. Get 'em off.'

Laurie jumped up and slowly began to bump and grind around the room, humming 'The Stripper' tune as she removed her clothing.

By the time she was down to her underwear, the boys were silent and an air of expectancy filled the room.

Laurie unclipped her bra but held it in place with cupped hands. Slowly, she lowered it to expose her unbelievably firm white breasts. Tossing the garment to one side, she hooked her thumbs into the elastic of her pants.

'All close your eyes,' she called, laughing.

'No way,' they shouted back.

With great deliberation, Laurie pushed them down and kicked them off. She stood before them, her head thrown back haughtily.

Jamie's breath caught in his throat as he viewed the triangle of hair, the slim waist. The others cheered and jibed while Jamie sat there fascinated.

Laurie positioned herself against a wall, her legs held lewdly apart. Jamie's hand was shaking as he tried to draw; and considering he had only ever seen a naked female in books or on screen, a good likeness began to emerge very quickly.

He forced himself to concentrate, looking from her body to the drawing-pad as if he had seen it all before.

And the detached part of him, the artist, did a fine job; even Carl admitted that the picture was good.

After a whispered conversation with Laurie, Craig signalled Jamie to join him in the kitchen. They stood against the heavily stained white sink which smelt appallingly of the drains.

'Look, man,' Craig said, 'do you want us to split while you have Laurie?'

'But I was with Sharon last night,' Jamie stuttered. 'I thought we had a thing going.'

'Where are you coming from, man? The girls pass it around. It's no big deal.'

'Oh, well, I mean, I know that, man,' Jamie said, trying to appear confident. 'That's how it is, right?'

'Right. And Laurie's got the hots for you.'

'It's just that some girls can be funny,' Jamie said, hooking his thumbs into the waistband of his jeans. 'They can think they own a guy.'

'We'll go to the off-licence. Be about an hour.'

'Here, let me give you some bread,' Jamie offered, digging into his back pocket. 'Call it my shout.'

'We don't buy it,' Craig laughed. 'We nick the stuff. It adds some fun to life.'

* * *

Far into the night, Jamie drifted on the edge of sleep. Thoughts of his experience with Laurie were still with him, appearing through veils of memory as he lay on the floor, covered by two dirty blankets.

He had smoked too much, drunk too much, and the room would not stay still; it was forever moving, revolving, bringing with it a taste of nausea, made more intense by the smells of tobacco, dust, and human bodies which rose from the carpet. He tossed and turned, his young mind troubled. In the last few days his whole world had turned around, leaving him to thrash about in the unknown, to make his own decisions, rightly or wrongly.

Away from the influence of his totalitarian father, the suffocating love of his mother, Jamie had gained knowledge of so many new and exciting things. Most of these were wrong, but they were pleasurable, and brought with them that which Jamie sought above all else: acceptance, a sense of belonging.

It tasted sweet, and even after such short acquaintance, Jamie found he was addicted.

CHAPTER 8

Next morning, Ashworth's appearance was giving cause for concern.

Sarah broached the subject at breakfast and listened, open-mouthed, to his explanation. Later, at the station, Martin Dutton and Bobby Adams stared in amazement while Ashworth took them into his confidence.

'Do you think he's gone mad, Sarge?' Bobby asked, when Ashworth was safely out of earshot.

Dutton scratched his bald head. 'Newton's sending us all mad.'

'What shall I do about the porn, Sarge?'

'Follow orders, Bobby. We spent all yesterday getting it into the station, and today we're to take it back. We're to apologise to the newsagent and explain that it was a mistake. There wasn't a complaint from a member of the public after all.' He sighed. 'Why aren't I the laughing policeman?'

Bobby gave him a curious glance. 'I'll get on with it then,' he said, disappearing through a door at the rear of reception.

'Bobby,' Dutton called. 'Spread the news of what Jim Ashworth's doing as you go round the station.' He allowed himself a smile, gleefully rubbing his hands. 'This is shaping up into a real battle royal, and I know who my money's on.'

'My car's been stolen.'

The voice startled Dutton. He turned to face a disgruntled man, dressed in a smart business suit.

'When I got up this morning, it was gone.'

'Oh, right, sir,' Dutton said, bringing his attention back to the job. 'I'd better take some details.'

* * *

Superintendent Newton's eyes were glued to Ashworth's face.

'You're what?' he spluttered, from behind his desk.

'I'm growing a beard,' Ashworth told him calmly. 'There's nothing in regulations to forbid it.'

'There's quite a lot in regulations about the appearance of police officers—'

'To be interpreted by the commanding officer and applied as he sees fit,' Ashworth countered.

'Exactly.' Newton's fist struck the desk top, providing an outlet for his impotent rage, and immediately he straightened the blotter which had become misaligned. 'This is in direct retaliation for me wanting Abraham to smarten up. I'm right, aren't I?'

'Yes, you are.'

The superintendent left his seat slowly and leant across the desk. 'Ashworth,' he said, 'I am usually a man of great restraint—'

'Don't restrain yourself on my account,' Ashworth cut in.

'—but you are going too far. Why are you interfering? Abraham can speak for himself.'

'Yes, but if he lost his temper, you'd haul him up in front of Ken Savage.'

'I could haul you up in front of Ken Savage,' Newton barked.

'You could,' Ashworth said, 'and I'd be willing to go.'

'I will not have you undermining my position,' Newton insisted. 'The running of this station is my responsibility.'

'But you can't run it along such rigid lines. This is the 1990s. People are no longer willing to be servile.'

Newton's control was beginning to erode. He said, 'Chief Inspector, I will not tolerate any more of this. I know you went behind my back over the newsagents business.'

'That I did,' Ashworth readily admitted. 'I wasn't prepared to see innocent citizens persecuted just because you'd got a bee in your bonnet.'

'A bee in my bonnet?' Newton spat. 'Ashworth, your behaviour was totally improper.'

Ashworth nodded. 'Yes, it was, because yours was unreasonable.'

'I do not believe this,' Newton said, his laugh almost maniacal. 'You have just admitted your behaviour was improper.'

'I've never denied it,' Ashworth replied, attempting to keep a lid on his temper. 'But no more improper than classing something as pornography until it happens to be in the hands of a councillor.'

Newton returned to his seat, his colour rising. 'Ashworth, I think the problem here is that no one has ever stood up to you, but I intend to, and I promise you one thing, I will break you.'

'Will that be all?' Ashworth asked, pinching the bridge of his nose.

'One of us has to change our attitude,' Newton said as Ashworth reached the door. 'Or it's going to be impossible to continue working together.'

'I couldn't agree more,' Ashworth said, slamming the door loudly.

* * *

'Why would the guv'nor do that?' Josh wanted to know as he swivelled around in his chair, the computer bleeping behind him.

Holly perched on the edge of her desk. 'I think he was a bit pissed off about having to order you to smarten up.'

'But to grow a beard . . .'

'I know. I think the great man feels he has to do something.'

'I suppose so.'

Josh returned his attention to the computer screen, and Holly smiled at his back.

'Do you know, Josh, now that you're wearing all that gear and you're washing every day . . .' She slid to her feet and curled her arms around his neck. 'Ooh, you sit there all pink and scrubbed, and I could eat you, I really could.'

'Get off,' he said, pushing her away good-naturedly. 'Holly, I know he's doing it for me, but don't you think it's all a bit, well, childish?'

'Yes,' she said, giggling uncontrollably. 'Yes, I do, but I think he's lovely.'

* * *

Bridgetown settled into the weekend.

Ashworth did what he enjoyed most during a weekend at home with Sarah: he pottered about the garden or walked the dog by day; and by night, he watched television or listened to music. He was a man of habit, firmly entrenched in his ways.

Mick and Edith Wright spent the two days in a torment of worry. Their GP had sent Mick to the hospital on Friday for a series of X-rays, the results of which would be known on Monday.

Edith could only sit and witness the sight of her man weeping like a child, all the while swearing vengeance on the witch.

Joyce Regent probably enjoyed herself more than most, back in London with no press in attendance. Her agent, a kindly man, ever mindful of his ten per cent, made sure that a succession of well-rewarded young boys kept his client happy in the privacy of his mews flat.

Holly entertained Headlands, cooked him a meal, became slightly drunk yet managed to repel his advances;

but unfortunately, she enjoyed his company so much that the poison-pen letters completely slipped her mind.

John Newton also spent the weekend at home, more worried about his son than he cared to admit. Although he was an intransigent, unpopular man, Newton was far from evil. It was just that in any given situation he believed that he alone knew best. The fact that he had risen to the rank of superintendent at such an early age only served to reinforce that view.

In his job, Newton was willing to forgo popularity in his drive for an efficient police force. Even the love he felt towards his wife and son took second place to his desire to do the best for them. One day, when the results of his sound judgement and common sense became apparent, he felt sure they would thank him.

* * *

On Monday morning, Joyce Regent received a telephone call from Katie. She took it in her agent's bedroom. A naked boy of sixteen reclined on the bed, uninterested.

'What do you mean, I can come home now?' she spat into the receiver. 'First you send me away, and then you order me back. You're taking over my life, Katie, and I don't like it.'

She listened intently to the reply and glanced across at the boy as she said resignedly. 'All right, yes, I'll come home.'

Joyce replaced the receiver and stood for a while staring down at it. 'I must have my freedom,' she muttered. 'I must.'

* * *

'There's no easy way to break this news,' the consultant said, peering over the top of his spectacles. 'It's lung cancer, I'm afraid. Too advanced to operate, but there is chemotherapy.'

Edith squeezed her husband's hand as she tried to take in the words, and without warning tears sprang into her eyes.

Mick Wright was pale but surprisingly calm. 'How long have I got?' he asked quietly.

The consultant considered the question. 'Months, I would say, rather than years. Of course, we can ease the cough and the suffering.'

He turned to Edith, who was now crying openly. 'I'm sorry to be so brutal, Mrs Wright, but when a patient asks, I feel I have to be honest.'

Mick Wright got to his feet, a perplexed look stealing across his face. 'So that's it,' he said. 'You've just told me I'm done for.' He turned abruptly and hurried out of the room.

'Forgive my husband,' Edith said, turning to follow.

'It's all right,' the consultant soothed. 'In the circumstances I would expect it.'

* * *

Later that day Ashworth was at his desk, scratching at the stubble on his chin. His facial hair had never grown rapidly, so it would be another six or eight weeks before the beard reached fruition. And he knew full well that it would irritate almost as much as the stubble. By now, Ashworth was regretting his ploy, seeing it as no more than a futile petty gesture; but he was a stubborn man, and once embarked on a course of action he found it virtually impossible to discontinue.

Holly burst into the office, muttering a string of mild expletives. After throwing her bag on to her desk, she turned to Ashworth.

'I'm bushed, totally knackered. I've had it up to here,' she said, tapping her forehead. 'And what's more, I'm pissed off.'

She waited for some sort of rebuke from Ashworth, but he simply smiled.

'I've had enough, guv,' she moaned, kicking out at the leg of her desk in frustration.

'How's it going?' Ashworth asked.

'We're clearing up some of the burglaries . . .'

The number of break-ins had increased so dramatically that all personnel — plain-clothed and uniformed — were now having to work on them.

'But now Newton's come up with something else.'

Ashworth's eyebrows arched.

'Now he wants anybody found carrying even a small amount of drugs hauled in.'

'And what's the general reaction to that?' Ashworth asked, as he rubbed at his embryo moustache.

'Most of them are totally demoralized, guv. If Newton would just let them carry on normal patrols, a lot of the burglaries wouldn't be happening.' She hitched herself up on to the desk and shook her head. 'But no, now they're having to chase everybody with enough cannabis to roll a joint.'

'The magistrates' courts are full to overflowing,' Ashworth said with a grim smile. 'And it looks like Newton's clearing up a crime wave when, in fact, he's causing it.'

Holly looked at him. 'Do you think that's why he's doing it?'

'It's not his ultimate aim, but it's part of it.' He changed the subject. 'No more letters have turned up at Witch's Cottage. I rang this morning. The eldest girl answered. She was none too pleasant, but that runs in the family.' He fell silent and stared into space.

'Is there something wrong, guv?'

'Do you think I'm anything like Newton?' he blurted out.

'Come again?'

'Do you think I'm anything like Newton? Come on, you can be honest.'

'Ah, I'm beginning to see what's bothering you.'

'You're hedging,' he warned.

Holly took a deep breath. 'There are similarities,' she said, 'but you do have a lot of redeeming qualities.'

'That's blunt. You're getting to be like me.'

'I know.' Holly smiled across at him. 'At times,' she said, 'you alienate me and Josh—'

'And everyone I've ever worked with,' Ashworth interjected morosely.

'Yes, but you have the sensitivity to realize it. You don't ride roughshod over people — that's the difference between you and Newton.'

She stopped suddenly, a little embarrassed by the way the discussion was developing. She had worked with Ashworth for twelve months, and this was the first time she had seen him with his guard down.

'Surely Sarah convinces you you're not an ogre.'

Ashworth sighed. 'Don't misinterpret this — I think the world of Sarah, but she has her life, and I have mine. We meet up at various times in the day, but sometimes I feel we don't pay as much attention to each other as we should.' He shrugged. 'Perhaps couples get too used to each other after a time.'

'Now, come on,' Holly scolded as she jumped down from the desk, 'this is no way for my big, bad guv'nor to behave. Self-pity doesn't suit you. Get up.'

Ashworth meekly obeyed, and Holly guided him to the coat-rack. 'I think it's time you went home,' she said, reaching for his old waxed-cotton jacket.

'I'm sorry. Maybe I shouldn't sit around thinking.'

'You shouldn't,' Holly said, helping him on with his coat. 'There're burglars, drug addicts, and people reading dirty magazines out there. You should be chasing them.'

* * *

A ginger-and-white cat strolled along the drive, all manner of noises sounding in his ears: the distant drone of traffic; movements from within the house; the hum of a television set; a scratching sound as a dog made its bed comfortable. Most of those noises would have gone undetected by the human ear, but away from his cosy home with endless supplies of canned food, Fluffy became the wild animal he truly was, always on the alert, always courting danger.

He stretched up a paw to dislodge the lid of a dustbin. The plastic top made little sound as it landed on the concrete but he waited, listened, golden eyes glowing in the night. When no human shouts came, the cat gracefully jumped up on to the rim of the dustbin, balanced himself and set about shredding the enclosed rubbish sack with sharp claws.

All kinds of smells assailed his nostrils as the bag came apart: used tea bags, days-old cooked vegetables, but also something nice — the enticing scent of a chicken carcass. His paw probed the bag, touched bone, and he drew it back, tossing the carcass into the drive. He was on it almost before it had landed. Very quickly, with the breastbone clamped between his teeth, the cat made off across the road.

He stalked into a nearby field, stopped, and deposited his find on the ground. After circling it twice, he leapt upon it, biting and clawing to simulate the kill. Then he settled down to eat his prize.

The cat was totally engrossed, completely unaware that he, the hunter, had now become the hunted.

A strong hand gripped the loose fur of his neck. Startled, the cat kicked out and howled, his back rigid as cruel fingers worked their way under his collar, making it impossible for him to break away.

CHAPTER 9

Jamie felt his heart rise into his mouth as the laconic assistant in the off-licence looked up at him.

'Yes?' the girl asked.

'Twenty John Players Special,' Jamie said.

He was the decoy. His job was to keep the assistant busy while the others sidled up one aisle, down another, grabbing as many bottles of wine and lager packs as they could carry.

The assistant reached behind just as the gang started.

'Hey, what you doing?' she shouted.

Carl Chown gave her a V-sign as he pocketed a litre of wine.

The girl was incensed and ran around the counter, starting towards them. Carl reached for another bottle, but his fingers failed to grip and the bottle fell to the floor, red wine flowing everywhere.

As the assistant stared in horror at the mess, Carl stepped back and punched her face. She fell awkwardly into a display of mixer drinks. Bottles smashed and tonic fizzed as blood poured from the girl's nose.

'Run,' Carl yelled. 'Get the fuck out of here.'

In the confusion that followed, they made their escape.

But not Jamie. He stood rooted to the spot, looking down at the assistant. She was still sprawled on the floor, a hand to her nose, whimpering. Blood seeped between her fingers and dripped on to her overall.

'Call the police,' she begged.

Jamie edged towards her, his whole being wanting to offer help and comfort. But then he stopped.

The door was open. He could get away.

The girl was still pleading, but Jamie ignored her. Instead, hating himself, he ran from the shop and disappeared into the night.

* * *

Joyce arrived home late evening to find Tanya in bed with a mysterious bug, and her declared intention to call the doctor was met with panic. The girl was obviously distraught and would not be pacified until Joyce agreed to wait and see how she was in the morning.

Katie was as bossy and — she had to admit — as obnoxious as ever, and Joyce definitely felt a parting of the ways approaching. Not relishing the prospect of another row, she locked herself in the bedroom with a half-bottle of brandy which was soon emptied.

She awoke shortly after dawn, hung over and demoralized. On any given morning, Joyce needed a pot of strong coffee and three cigarettes to give her a kick-start, but today it would take a little longer for her to re-join the world. Presently, she dragged herself from the bed and padded down to the kitchen, lighting a cigarette on the way.

It was while she was preparing the coffee that Joyce noticed two farm labourers staring at the cottage from the lane. At first she thought little of it, but then worry gripped her. Could they have brought another letter? She rushed into the hall and laughed with relief; there were no letters on the mat.

As she circled the lounge, drinking her second cup of coffee, Joyce happened to glance out of the window. A car was slowing down, and she could see the driver staring towards the cottage. Puzzled, she continued to watch. Seconds later, another car came along; it slowed, the driver gaped at the dwelling, then drove off.

'What the hell's happening now?' she muttered, making sure her bathrobe was fastened.

She was about to go to the front door when the postman appeared at the gate. His mouth sagged open as he stared with revulsion at the front door, seemingly unwilling to approach.

Now she was really worried. Placing the coffee cup on the table, Joyce marched into the hall and flung open the door. And as her eyes followed the postman's pointing finger, she let out a hideous shriek.

* * *

Cancer was the first thought to enter Mick Wright's mind when he came awake. He lay staring at the ceiling; and although it was a chill September morning, his body was hot and sweating beneath the sheets.

As he lay there, he fancied he could feel the growth expanding in his lungs, pushing out the soft tissue until it pressed against his rib-cage. That new medicine prescribed by the doctor had eased the cough almost immediately, which was a relief. And although he was under a sentence of death, Wright felt a fresh surge of spirit. He would get well, he told himself.

Edith entered the bedroom, clutching a steaming mug of tea. She set it down on the bedside table and glanced at her husband with eyes that were red from crying.

Taking his hand, she sat on the bed. 'You'll get better, Mick. I know you will. Once they start that chemotherapy thing.'

'I won't be starting it, woman,' Wright said obstinately. 'There's only one way to deal with this, and that's to get the witch to lift the curse.'

'Oh, no, Mick, please,' Edith implored. 'Don't be messing with that woman anymore.'

* * *

Headlands spotted the commotion, which sparked off an adrenalin rush, prompting him into action. He hurriedly checked that the camera contained enough film to cover any eventuality, then continued to watch the postman.

The man was obviously distressed; he kept flagging down passing cars, but none of the drivers seemed willing to become involved. They all looked towards the cottage with horror, then accelerated away.

Headlands let the Volvo coast down the hill, bringing it to a halt at the side of the cottage. He had no intention of alerting anyone inside to his presence until he had got his photographs. Leaving the engine running, he casually strolled to where the postman was leaning against the fence.

'Have you seen that, mate?' the man asked with alarm.

Headlands's journalistic make-up thrilled at the sight of the ginger-and-white cat impaled on the door. When on a job there was no place within him for revulsion, horror, or even distaste; he simply focused the camera and got his pictures.

Then the image in the viewfinder altered as Joyce opened the door. She was livid, and she lurched down the path, her bathrobe parting to expose ample breasts.

'Nice,' Headlands said as the shutter clicked. 'Nice.'

'You parasitic bastard,' she shrieked.

The journalist, unconcerned, continued taking photographs while the amazed postman looked on.

Katie came running from the cottage, shouting, 'Leave him to me.'

Headlands took a couple more shots, all the while backing away. But as soon as Katie's enraged face filled the viewfinder, he turned and fled. He skidded to a halt at the Volvo, looked back to where Katie was bearing down on him with a distinctly unladylike gait, then jumped into the car and drove off down the hill.

Katie aimed a kick at his rear bumper but missed, mouthing 'Bastard' as Headlands gave a cheery wave.

* * *

'Jesus Christ, guv, I feel sick,' Holly exclaimed.

'I'm not surprised,' he said. 'What kind of lunatic would do a thing like this?'

Despite his own feeling of nausea, Ashworth strained forward and studied the cat. The knife pinning it to the door had been driven through the heart. Pink flesh showed through its white fur, and a thin trickle of blood had run down the door to mingle with the words written in white chalk:

A dead cat witch
next it's
you

Ashworth looked at Holly and sighed.

'Do you think it's Mick Wright?' she queried.

'Doesn't add up,' he said, unable to take his eyes off the cat. 'Yesterday we warned the man off. He wouldn't do a thing like this straight afterwards.'

'Unless he was deranged,' Holly said.

Ashworth's grunted reply suggested he was not overly impressed with the idea. 'Forensic?' he murmured.

'On their way.'

'Let's go and see Mrs Regent, then.' Pushing the door open, he took one more look at the animal. 'Poor little beggar.'

Joyce was in the lounge, still clad in her bathrobe. She paced the floor, her bare feet sounding on the boards.

'Well?' she demanded, before lighting the cigarette which dangled from her mouth.

Ashworth was fast tiring of her ungracious manner. '"Well" doesn't come into it,' he said, without ceremony. 'Did you or your daughters hear anything last night?'

'Oh yes, of course we did,' Joyce said, throwing her arms around dramatically. 'I thought, what's that? It sounds like a cat being nailed to the door.' She glared at Ashworth. 'What a bloody silly question.'

Holly, fearing her superior might erupt, jumped in quickly. 'Be fair, Joyce. How can we establish who did this without asking questions?'

The author's temper subsided, but only slightly. 'No, we didn't hear anything,' she said, still pacing, incapable of remaining still. 'It was a windy night and the house makes a lot of noise.'

'I'll have to ask your daughters the same question,' he told her.

'There's no need for that.'

Ashworth grew impatient as he watched her stubbing out the half-smoked cigarette. 'I'll still have to ask them,' he insisted.

Joyce rounded on him. 'Tanya's ill in bed. I won't have her upset. Do you realize the effect something like this could have on a child?'

'All right,' Ashworth conceded. 'Your eldest daughter then.'

Joyce closed her eyes briefly, then walked to the door. 'Katie,' she called.

After a couple of minutes Katie slouched into the room, scruffily dressed in loose-fitting black jogging bottoms almost concealed by a baggy black T-shirt which reached to the knees. 'Yes?'

Joyce lit another cigarette. 'The chief inspector wants to know if you heard anything last night.'

'No,' Katie said with a definite shake of the head.

'Satisfied?' Joyce asked. Then, crossing to the window, 'It's that bastard up there. That's who's responsible. He was down here taking photographs.' She turned to glare at Ashworth. 'Have you questioned him yet?'

'No, we haven't,' Ashworth said mildly, although his temper was rising, 'because we're interviewing you, Mrs Regent.'

'It's Ms Regent, not Mrs,' Joyce informed him tartly.

'I don't care what it is,' Ashworth retorted. 'We're police officers and I'd like you to keep a civil tongue in your head while you're dealing with us.'

'Get out,' Joyce screamed. 'Go and catch the people who are making my life a misery.'

Holly coughed diplomatically. 'Maybe we should go, guv.' She inclined her head towards the door.

'Right.' Ashworth left the room without another word.

Sathan, the cat, was perched on the stairs, ready to pounce.

'Don't you start,' Ashworth warned. He waited for Holly in the Sierra.

'That bloody woman's getting on my nerves,' he huffed as she climbed into the passenger seat. 'The daughter uses words as if they're rationed, and the mother paces about, raving her head off.'

'She's a nervous wreck,' Holly said. 'I'm surprised she stays still long enough to get laid.' She bit a fingernail, lost in thought. 'Perhaps that's why they have to be young . . . so they've got the energy to bounce around the room after her.'

Ashworth laughed. 'I let you get away with too much, you know. I really should take you in hand.'

'Promises, promises,' she murmured under her breath.

'Where's forensic?' he wanted to know. 'How long are they going to be?'

'No idea, guv.' She turned to look at him questioningly. 'Shall we calm down?'

'I'm quite calm,' he said irritably, glancing out of the side window. 'What do you think to this idea that it could be the reporter?'

'No way,' she said, shaking her head. 'I don't think he'd go as far as knifing a cat.'

After a pause, Ashworth said, 'Are you . . . involved with him in any way?'

'No,' she replied staunchly. 'I've let my heart rule my head a bit too much lately. I know I've done some—'

'Hold on,' he cut in. 'I'm Jim Ashworth, not Marje Proops. I just wanted to know whether your opinion was biased in any way. I'm not after sorting your life out.'

'Rest assured, guv, he hasn't so much as sucked my big toe.'

Ashworth looked at her feet, and asked innocently, 'What would he want to suck your toe for?'

'Forget it,' Holly grinned. 'But, no, my opinion is in no way clouded by any involvement.'

'Good.' He looked at his wristwatch.

'Guv?'

Ashworth grunted.

'When we get to Malc, can I ask the questions?'

'Why?'

'Well, how can I put this diplomatically? You're in your obstreperous mood, and I think you'd rub him up the wrong way.'

'That's diplomatic?'

* * *

'Katie, get down here this minute,' Joyce bellowed from the foot of the stairs. 'You do not walk out on me when I'm talking.'

Katie, sullen-faced, descended the stairs and flounced into the lounge, saying, 'I asked a straight question — did you go with anybody while you were in London?'

'Yes, yes, yes, I did,' Joyce yelled, cradling her head in her hands. 'I'm sick of you running my life. I had a good time, OK?'

Katie took a cigarette from the packet on the coffee table and lit it. 'And what if the press had picked it up?'

'But they didn't, did they?' Joyce flared. 'I'm serving you notice, Katie. I want you out of here.'

'You can't just throw me out.'

'Can't I? Can't I?' she taunted.

'Stop it,' Katie shrieked. 'Just stop it.'

'I'm sick of you ruining my fun. Sick of it. Just get out.'

'I need time to find a place. You can't just throw me out.'

'You have two days. And keep out of my way, because I've got somebody coming round tonight.'

'Yes, I bet you have,' Katie reflected as Joyce strode from the room.

* * *

The tyres of the Sierra threw up gravel chippings as it came to a halt in the lay-by. Headlands watched expectantly as they climbed out. He gave Holly a smile.

'Turn-up for the book, eh?'

Ashworth scrutinized the journalist. 'I don't suppose you saw anything?'

Headlands shook his head. 'Not who put the cat there, no.'

'You've got your story now,' Holly said. 'I suppose this'll be all over the papers tomorrow.'

'Depends.'

'On what?' Ashworth asked, worrying the stubble on his chin.

Headlands dug his hands into the pockets of his expensive trousers and rested his back against the car. 'Look at it from my point of view — not much of a story as it stands, is it?'

'Worth some money, I'd have thought,' Holly replied. 'The Regent woman's still news . . .'

'Look, I'll level with you. The last thing I want is the whole press pack down here at the moment, because I think there's a far bigger story to come. Now, if you could keep the lid on this locally, I'd be willing to keep it under wraps.'

Ashworth considered this. 'All right, I can see to that.'

He started back to the Sierra while Holly fingered.

'Do you want to come for a meal tonight?' she asked.

'Just a meal?'

'Just a meal.'

'OK, about eight.'

CHAPTER 10

Josh rapped on the Wrights' front door for a second time, but still there was no response.

'Looks like they're out, lover,' Holly remarked.

'Open up — police,' Josh called, knocking louder.

'You've been watching too many episodes of *The Bill*,' Holly teased. 'Hang on . . .' She delved quickly into her shoulder bag. 'Oh, damn it, I've left my axe back at the nick.'

'Very funny,' Josh said. 'But there's somebody in. I saw the upstairs curtains move as we pulled up.'

Holly backed away from the door and stared up at the bedroom window. For a split second she caught sight of Edith's pinched, pale features behind the glass, then the woman vanished.

'You're right,' she said. 'I've just seen the wife.'

Josh banged on the door with more force. 'Open up — police. And we're not going away until you've answered the door.'

Then came sounds of a lock turning and the door opened to reveal Edith Wright. She looked at Holly.

'What do you want?'

'Is your husband in?' Josh asked.

'No, he's not.'

Although the woman's attitude was hostile, tears were brimming in her eyes.

'Are you all right?' Holly asked gently.

'Oh yes, I'm all right,' Edith told her, even as her shoulders hunched and fresh tears flowed down her cheeks. 'They told my Mick he's got cancer, so it doesn't matter how much you lot bother us now.'

'Can we come inside?' Holly said.

'Do what you want.' Edith turned from them and made her way along the passage.

'What do we do now?' Josh whispered.

Holly gave him a helpless look. 'I don't know. We'll have to ask the questions, I suppose.'

They followed the woman through to the kitchen. She was filling the kettle. 'You'll have to forgive me,' she said with dignity, while taking mugs and the teapot from a cabinet, 'but I'm under a bit of a strain.'

Holly made a move towards her. 'Here, let me make the tea.'

Edith shook her head rapidly. 'No, no, it's all right, I'm better when I'm busy. You two sit down.'

They sat at the kitchen table, feeling decidedly awkward, while Edith waited for the kettle to boil.

Josh cleared his throat. 'Where's Mr Wright?'

'I told you, he's out,' Edith said, keeping her back towards him. The electric kettle clicked off, and Edith said no more until the tea was made. Finally she turned to them. 'Is this about them letters?'

'I'm afraid it's a little more than that,' Holly said.

She went on to tell her about the cat impaled on the door.

Edith bristled. 'And you think my Mick did that?' she said, staring at Holly in disbelief. 'He wouldn't hurt a dumb animal.'

Holly went on, 'I'm sorry to have to ask you these questions, Mrs Wright, but was your husband in all last night?'

'Yes,' Edith declared, her lower lip trembling. 'We sat where you two are sitting now. We were putting our affairs in order, what bit of money we've got, insurance . . .' She took a tissue from the pocket of her pinafore dress and blew her nose. 'Mick's worried there won't be enough for a decent funeral . . .' Her control finally slipped and the tears came fast and furious. 'And what's going to happen to me after he's gone?'

Holly, too, felt tears spring into her eyes. She had been where Edith Wright was now; and as those locked-away memories of her own husband's illness began to surface, she pushed them away, and said firmly, 'We have to do this, Mrs Wright. Your husband has almost admitted sending those letters.'

'No, he hasn't,' a sobbing Edith countered. 'I know what you're trying to do — you're trying to get me to say something against Mick, but it ain't going to work.'

'Please don't upset yourself,' Holly said, getting to her feet.

'I'd like you to leave now, if that's all you've come about.' There was open animosity in the words.

'Yes, of course,' Josh said. 'We'll see ourselves out.'

'I really am sorry,' Holly called from the doorway.

'Just go, please,' Edith implored.

Holly closed the door quietly.

'I don't need this, Josh,' she muttered once they were inside the Micra. 'You do realize, don't you, that every time something happens to that bloody Regent woman, we'll have to haul Mick Wright in.'

'We'll still need to speak to him about this though.'

'I know.' Holly hit out at the steering-wheel. 'Why did the poor sod have to send those letters? Mind you,' she huffed, 'that woman and her bloody daughters are so vile, I could start sending letters myself.'

'Holly?'

'What?'

He nodded towards the Wrights' cottage. 'Personal involvement?'

'Aren't you getting involved?' she bridled. 'Don't you feel anything?'

* * *

Ashworth felt not the faintest trace of trepidation as he approached Superintendent Newton's office. Yesterday, there was something he had felt compelled to say, so he had said it. And today there was another matter which needed to be aired.

He had no doubt that a gigantic row was brewing between them, but he had no desire to stay out of the firing-line in the hope that it might go away. Ashworth was not a man to run or hide. He marched along the white-walled corridors of Bridgetown station, mounted the stairs briskly, and knocked on the superintendent's door.

'Come in,' Newton called.

Ashworth pulled himself erect and entered the office.

'Ah, Ashworth, further thoughts on our meeting of yesterday, I hope.'

'No, sir, this is to do with another matter.'

'Speak,' Newton ordered.

Ashworth felt his hackles rise. He had not been asked to sit and therefore stood before the desk, arms at his sides, and in an acutely stiff manner relayed to Newton details of the poison-pen letters and the dead cat on the cottage door.

Newton listened with exaggerated patience until he had finished. 'So?' he said.

'So, I'd like a twenty-four-hour watch put on Joyce Regent. I feel she's in some danger.'

'A twenty-four-hour . . . ? Are you out of your mind, man?'

'I feel the woman is in danger,' Ashworth reiterated.

'You feel? You feel? Police officers are not paid to feel, they deal in facts. Bring this Wright character in and if there's enough evidence, charge him.'

'There is no evidence,' Ashworth replied stiffly. 'Forensic have come up with nothing on the letters.'

'Then put the fear of God into him. From what I've heard the man doesn't sound too bright.' He waved his hand dismissively, muttering, 'Do not waste my time with this, this, trivia.'

Ashworth held his breath and counted to ten, but it made no difference, his anger was still boiling and he glared at Newton, saying, 'Look, if you insist on my calling you "sir", I must ask that you address me by my proper rank — chief inspector.'

Newton rose from his chair, his face flushed. 'You are getting to be a thorn in my side,' he barked.

'Am I? Then pretty soon I'm going to fester unless I'm treated with a little more courtesy.'

'Do you want a row . . . Chief Inspector?'

'I'd very much like one, sir,' Ashworth retorted. 'Where shall we start? There are a number of matters I'd like to discuss.'

Any further hostilities were curtailed by a tentative knock on the door.

'Come in,' Newton called with menace, keeping his eyes on Ashworth's face.

Holly could sense the atmosphere as she gingerly entered the room. She mouthed an apology to Newton and turned to Ashworth. 'Sorry to bother you, guv, but Mick Wright's just been brought in. It's been alleged that he attacked Joyce Regent. Apparently he tried to strangle her.'

* * *

Mick Wright was slumped over the interview table, with Josh seated opposite and a uniformed officer in attendance beside the door. After morosely fiddling with a packet of cigarettes on the table, Wright lit one, immediately bringing on immediately that painful hacking cough.

'I should have done for the witch,' he spluttered. 'Done for her there and then.'

'Mick,' Josh said, 'you're not doing your case any good.'

Wright tried to clear his throat, then rasped, 'My case? What does any of that matter now?' He leant towards Josh and said earnestly, 'That woman was telling a load of lies. It didn't happen like she said.'

'Save it for the chief inspector,' Josh cautioned. 'And when he gets here just be careful what you say.'

The words had scarcely left his mouth when Ashworth entered the room, his face like thunder. Holly was following close behind.

He came to an abrupt halt and gazed down at Wright with exasperation. 'What have you been doing, old son?'

'I was only trying to save my life.'

As Wright turned to him, Ashworth noticed a swelling on the side of his head, just below the left eye. Josh vacated his seat and wandered over to Holly. Ashworth sat to face the man.

'Joyce Regent claims you tried to strangle her. What have you got to say for yourself?'

'I went there to plead with her to lift the curse, that's all. She stood there screaming at me, her language was really bad. And then she attacked me.' He fingered the bump on the side of his face and winced. 'She was hitting me with her fists, she was.'

Ashworth glanced towards Holly. 'That's not the way she tells it. She told my detective sergeant here that you turned up at the cottage and started hurling abuse at her. Then you got your hands around her throat. She's got the marks on her neck to prove it. She also said you threatened the life of her eldest daughter when she tried to intervene.'

Wright's eyes were haunted as he took in the three detectives, and he looked across at the uniformed officer before saying simply, 'I've got cancer. I've only got a few months to live.'

'My DS also told me that, and I'm very sorry, Mick.'

'Sorry? You're sorry?' The distraught man cradled his head in his hands. 'You don't know what it's like to have somebody tell you you're going to die.' He turned desperate eyes on all three of them, declaring, 'I didn't kill no cat like she said. And the witch attacked me. I was just trying to defend myself.'

'All right, Mick, calm down,' Ashworth said, patting the man's arm. 'Did you send the letters?'

'Yes,' he admitted, his shoulders slumping in defeat. 'I sent the letters, but I haven't done anything else.'

There was a knock on the door and Holly slipped across quietly to open it. Bobby Adams stood ill at ease in the doorway. They held a whispered conversation, after which Holly followed him into the corridor and closed the door.

Ashworth returned his attention to Mick Wright. 'You can see my dilemma here, can't you? You've admitted sending the letters.'

He nodded. 'Yes, I can,' he said. Then, becoming agitated, 'But I was desperate.'

'Calm down, Mick,' Ashworth soothed. 'What about the cat pinned to the door?'

'I didn't do that, I swear to God.' He fell forward then, coughing, gripping the table as pain shot through his scrawny chest.

Ashworth allowed him time to collect himself, then said, 'And yet all the signs point to you attacking the Regent woman.'

The bout of coughing had taken away what little fight he had left. 'Think what you want,' he said resignedly. 'Do what you want. What difference does it make now?'

Holly popped her head around the door. 'Guv, could I see you for a minute?'

'Excuse me, Mick,' Ashworth said. At the door he stopped. 'Is there anything we can get for you? Tea? Coffee?'

Wright gave a shake of his head, keeping his eyes on the tabletop.

The corridor was busy, being as it was the main link between reception and the canteen. Ashworth leant against the wall and waited for Holly to speak.

'I've just had Malc Headlands on the phone,' she told him. 'He bears out what Mick's been saying—'

She was interrupted by a particularly noisy group of uniformed officers making their way along the corridor. Ashworth's stern glare brought about immediate quiet, and the officers passed by with an almost reverential restraint.

Holly went on, 'He says Mick turned up and accosted Joyce Regent. He was shouting, but there was no violence. Then Joyce went absolutely berserk, according to Malc. She attacked Mick before he got his hands around her neck. Then Katie tried to pull him off, and Mick threatened to kill both of them.'

Ashworth said nothing, stood deep in thought for a few minutes.

'Guv?' Holly prompted.

'Sorry, it just seems to me that by admitting he sent those letters, Wright's put himself in a bad position. From now on every time something happens to Joyce Regent, he'll be blamed. So, if someone did mean to harm her, they'd be in a perfect position to implicate him.'

'I know, but they'd better hurry up, guv. I don't think the man's going to be here very much longer.'

'Yes,' Ashworth sighed. 'What do I do now?'

'We can't hold him,' Holly said.

'No, we can't. Will you take his statement?'

She nodded.

'Then caution him,' Ashworth continued. 'Really put the fear of God into him. I don't want him anywhere near that Regent clan. Oh, and can you take Headlands's statement?'

'Will do, guv.'

Ashworth still seemed preoccupied. 'Who in the name of God would kill a cat and impale it on the front door? Who would have anything to gain from doing that?'

'In his present state of mind, Mick Wright would,' Holly suggested.

'That's what I mean. Make it a strong caution, Holly.'

* * *

Around the town centre uniformed officers were out in some force, sauntering along in pairs, seemingly without purpose. In the High Street they would pause to gaze into shop windows, would self-consciously chat to passers-by.

At the same time Jamie and the rest of the gang were roaming the streets, equally bored. Craig called a halt outside the fish and chip shop.

'Let's nick a car,' the belligerent Carl suggested.

Craig dismissed the idea. 'No,' he said. 'All the fuzz're round the centre. No point in nicking a car if they don't chase you.'

'There's still three mobiles,' Jamie sneered. 'They could latch on to us.'

He had been with the group for just a few days but already his metamorphosis was complete: his faltering step replaced by a swagger, his good manners overturned by pig ignorance; and his language now that of a lout.

'The fuzz ain't that clever,' Rod Calway broke in.

'We could nick one in town, right under their noses,' Jamie ventured. 'They'd have to chase us, then.'

As they spoke a large Peugeot estate pulled up outside the chippy and the driver alighted, leaving the engine running.

'That would take bottle,' Craig said, as they stared at the car with its exhaust vibrating, a haze of vapour escaping from it.

'I've got the bottle,' Jamie announced with a grin.

'You ain't got no bottle,' Carl scoffed.

'Shut your mouth,' Craig said. He looked towards Jamie. 'Prove it, man.'

Jamie glanced over his shoulder. The man was shaking salt and vinegar over his fish and chips.

'Beggars Meadow, in an hour, OK?' He sprinted towards the car. 'You coming, Laurie?'

The girl squealed with delight as she followed, her high heels clicking on the pavement.

Jamie threw open the car door and bundled her across the driver's seat, then he jumped in and slammed the door shut.

The car owner looked on astounded. He dropped his fish and chips and scrambled out of the shop, shouting, 'Hey!'

While Jamie struggled to put the car into gear, he glanced back. The man was hurtling towards them, a murderous expression on his face. 'I'll kill you, you little bastard,' he snarled.

As he passed the gang, Craig stuck out a foot and the man went sprawling on to the hard pavement with a cry of frustration.

There came a scream of tyres and the smell of burning rubber as the car sped away.

'Run,' Craig ordered.

They made it to an alley at the side of the fish and chip shop just as every uniformed officer in Bridgetown — or so it seemed — arrived on the scene. After establishing what had taken place, one of them moved away from the crowd and radioed central control.

'Yes, Sarge, car stolen from outside Morgan's chippy. Young lad and a girl. The owner left the keys in and the engine running.'

He went on to give the car registration number, and lowered his voice to agree with his sergeant that the man was indeed a prat of the first order. 'Car's heading over the river bridge,' he said. 'And, Sarge, this boy's really motoring.'

Jamie slowed the car after they had crossed the bridge. Laurie sat with her hand in his lap, fondling him.

'Open it up, Jamie,' she urged. 'Let's really go.'

'Not yet.' He knew that any prestige and admiration would come from his actions after the police began their pursuit.

And he did not have to wait long. Within minutes, sounds of a siren came from behind, and a flashing blue light filled his rear-view mirror.

Jamie's heart was thumping, and his mouth felt dry as he stared into the mirror to identify the pursuing vehicle. It was a single-manned Ford Escort.

'Hang on,' he warned, as his foot pressed down on the accelerator.

The Peugeot shot forward, its powerful engine throbbing beneath the bonnet. Jamie pushed away Laurie's distracting hand and watched the speedometer rise to sixty, seventy. Still the police car stuck to their tail.

A winding lane stretched before him in the arc of the headlights as the speedometer touched eighty.

'Go. Make the fucking thing go,' Laurie called out, her face alive with excitement. 'Hit the ton, Jamie'.

The lane was perilously narrow with no room for manoeuvre should a car approach from the opposite direction. Throwing caution to the wind, Jamie drove into an oncoming bend without slowing. The Peugeot lurched to one side, tilting on two wheels, and skidded around the corner. Jamie steered into the skid and the car righted itself, crashing down on all four wheels with such force that the glass in the headlights shattered.

A long straight stretch of road opened out ahead. Jamie pushed the accelerator to the floor and laughed as the speedometer climbed towards the hundred-miles-an-hour mark.

It was then that the patrol car gave up the chase.

CHAPTER 11

'You break a word of this story, and I'll break your arm,' Holly warned.

Headlands put on his hurt look. 'When will you learn to trust me?'

They were sprawled on the carpet in the front room of Holly's house. Earlier, over tuna salad, she had told him everything that had happened to Joyce Regent. He had listened avidly, saying very little. They were now sipping drinks, enjoying each other's company.

Holly rested her head against the armchair and stretched out. 'You're quiet,' she said.

As Headlands glanced across at her, she realized that his eyes were having an effect. One half of her wanted to go to bed with him. But the half containing her brain told her not to appear too easy; and as that half was controlled by intellect as opposed to instinct it was the part she chose to heed.

'I was just thinking about Joyce,' he said. 'She managed to get a boy into the cottage this afternoon.'

He reached into his jacket and took out a series of photographs, passing a couple to Holly.

'Well, as the back of a head goes, they're very nice,' she remarked with a smile.

Headlands laughed and sipped his drink.

She looked again at the rear view of a boy dressed in blue jeans and colourful T-shirt. 'Do you think this is Kevin Thornton?'

Headlands shrugged. 'I don't know. It could be, he's the most likely candidate.'

'Shouldn't you be watching from the lay-by, hoping to get a cheap thrill?'

He studied her with a measured gaze, a smile reaching his lips. 'I decided to come here instead, for a real thrill.'

'Tuna salad and a drink? My, you are easily excited.'

'You can't resist me for much longer, you know. You're denying yourself the experience of a lifetime.'

Holly's green eyes teased him as she laughed. 'You city boys think you know everything, don't you? But I could show you a thing or two.'

'Oh yes?' he said, gazing directly at her crotch.

Realizing that the banter was leading in the wrong direction, she checked herself and swiftly changed the subject. 'You don't seem very interested in young Kevin all of a sudden.'

Headlands sipped his Scotch and shifted his position. 'I'm not, at the moment,' he admitted. 'Like I said, I think there's a far bigger story brewing.'

'Do you want another?' Holly asked, struggling to her feet.

He nodded.

'So what do you think this story is?' she said, pouring fresh drinks.

'I'd say someone means to harm Joyce Regent.'

The tonic fizzed angrily in her gin as Holly turned and looked at him. 'What makes you say that?'

He shrugged and patted the carpet for her to join him in front of the settee. 'I don't know, really, but it seems to me that this Mick Wright bloke's being set up.'

'Now that's interesting,' Holly said, returning with the drinks. 'Ashworth thinks much the same.' She passed Headlands his Scotch and stretched out beside him. 'So much so that he wanted a twenty-four-hour police watch kept on the woman.'

He placed his drink on the carpet and lit a cigarette. Exhaling slowly, he said, 'And my bet is, it's our Kevin boy.'

'No, I wouldn't think so. The first thing we look for is motive and the boy hasn't got one.'

'Or one that's obvious,' Headlands suggested.

'Like what? He's hardly the spurned lover, is he? And if the goose that laid the golden eggs decided she'd had enough of him, so what? OK, there'd be no more easy pickings, but if money bothered him that much he could always sell his story to the press. You told me yourself they'd jump at his story.'

'Yes,' he said doubtfully.

Holly turned to him, tried to read his expression. 'Do you know something we don't?' She sounded suspicious.

'When will you learn to trust me?' he said, wearing that same hurt expression until his face broke into a smile.

'Never,' she told him. 'Come on, tell me what you know.'

Headlands seemed to be considering this, and his look was taunting as he said, 'What's it worth?'

'How about if I guarantee you can walk out of here without any broken limbs?'

The gin had started its magic and, deliciously relaxed now, Holly was enjoying their verbal foreplay.

'OK, that seems like a fair exchange,' Headlands said, with an easy smile. 'Anyway, I haven't got much. Last night I rang a guy I've worked with on and off. He's still trying to track Kevin down, and he's found an address where the boy lived a few months before moving in with Joyce.'

'And?'

'He hasn't managed to get his hands on any photographs yet, or any new leads, but it does seem that young Kevin was a nasty piece of work. He was doing heroin and dealing to finance his habit . . .'

He stopped and raised his eyebrows in amazement as Holly, sitting cross-legged against the settee, knocked back the full glass of gin and tonic in one go.

'Drink up,' she ordered. 'I need to relax.'

'Let me get them this time,' he said, reaching out for Holly's glass.

'He moved in with a sixteen-year-old girl,' Headlands continued, as he refilled the glasses. 'And he was having the girl's sister behind her back.'

'So?' Holly said, watching him pour a very liberal measure of gin into her glass.

'The sister was thirteen. It seems he has a taste for young flesh — preferably virgins he can corrupt.'

'Ah.' She accepted the drink and sampled it. 'My God,' she said, grimacing, 'are you trying to get me drunk?'

'Yes,' he grinned. 'Thought it might improve my chances.'

She gave him a challenging look, then suddenly crouched before him, saying eagerly, 'This has given me an idea. Say Kevin did the same thing at Joyce's. Mother and two daughters,' she added meaningfully.

'Hold on, the eldest girl's got to be eighteen at least.'

'Yes, I know that, but she's hardly a sex symbol, is she? Pretty face, but not much of a body. It's not beyond the realms of possibility that she was still a virgin when he moved in.'

'But—'

'No, hear me out,' she insisted. 'If he was having the daughters and Joyce found out, she could well have killed Kevin, and that's why you can't find him.'

'So who killed the cat then?'

'I'm coming to that. Say some friends of Kevin's found out about this and decided to kill Joyce for revenge.'

Headlands started to speak, but Holly waved him down. 'Or here's another little scenario — say Kevin's alive and was kicked out by Joyce because he was bunking-up her daughters. Say the girls are so incensed by this, so infatuated with him, that they're planning to kill their mother.'

'Are you serious?'

'No, three parts pissed,' she giggled, collapsing on the floor.

Headlands grinned. 'You had me going there. I thought I was with a maniac.'

'Policewomen do have a sense of humour,' she told him.

'And what else have they got?' he asked, placing his glass a safe distance away and slipping an arm around her shoulders.

Holly pushed the arm away. 'Much the same as any other female,' she said.

'Then I'd like it.' The arm crept slowly around her waist.

'But you're not going to get it,' Holly assured him.

'Come on, Holly, what's wrong with you? I've never had a woman say no before.'

She was giggling uncontrollably, attempting to wriggle from his grip. 'Ah, you see, since they started charging for eye tests, there're a lot of short-sighted women about.'

Headlands was gently sliding his hand up and down the side of her body, causing throbs of pleasure in parts not remotely connected with her side. Her head was spinning pleasantly from the gin, and she was aware of his male scent even through his aftershave.

She tried to protest, her movements half-hearted. 'No, Malc.'

'Don't say no, Holly.' He smiled, confident that he was close to shattering her resistance.

When he kissed her lips, Holly's arms went automatically around his neck, pulling him down on top of her. And as his hand gently cupped her breast, she made no attempt to push it away. The kiss was gentle, lingering, and when it ended, Holly's breath came in ragged gasps.

She was aware of urgent fingers fighting with the buttons of her blouse, undoing sufficient to allow access for his hand. Shifting her position a little, Holly lifted her back from the floor, enabling him to push aside her bra. A long moan broke in her throat as he caressed her breast, its nipple hardening and tingling.

A tremulous quiver travelled the length of her body, and her pleasure increased with every touch of his hands and lips.

The feelings threatened to become overwhelming, when suddenly she pushed him away and somehow managed to sit erect. 'No, Malc, no,' she said.

That petulant look was back on Headlands's face, but this time it was real. 'What's the matter?'

'I'm sorry, I want to go to the toilet.'

'Just my luck,' he said, running an impatient hand through his hair. 'The girl wants to go to the toilet.'

Holly was on her feet, fastening the buttons of her blouse. 'No, I don't,' she said, 'it was the first thing that came into my head.' She gave him an apologetic smile. 'I am sorry, Malc, I just don't want to do it.'

'Jesus, Holly, what are you trying to do to me? You come on like that, then you switch off.'

'It's not that I don't like you. I do. I really fancy you, but I want to try being a good girl for a change. Let me phone you a taxi, yes?'

A subdued Headlands looked up at her and said, 'Do you mind if I just sit here for a while? Trying to stand up could be a bit embarrassing for the next ten minutes or so.'

* * *

Soft rain spattered against the bedroom window of Witch's Cottage, its sound barely loud enough to drown out Joyce's voice drifting in from the adjoining bedroom. Her speech was slurred by brandy, and she was acting out her depraved desires which found their outlet in bizarre fantasies involving her favoured young boys.

Katie listened, with annoyance bubbling inside, to the chiding sounds of 'Auntie Joyce' chastising the young boy caught in an indecent solitary act. Katie had heard it all before. The pretend threats to tell the boy's mother. His ridiculous rehearsed promises not to do it again. Then — as Joyce's excitement grew — her assurance that his secret would be safe so long as she could join in the fun.

Their lovemaking continued with a noisy urgency; the boy moaning with pleasure as 'Auntie Joyce' soothed and praised. And with every erotic sound, Katie's anger deepened.

Two days before, Tanya had moved out of the bedroom because she could no longer bear to listen. And now, Katie, exhaling sharply, also left the room to sleep elsewhere.

* * *

Ken Savage liked his new office in Bridgenorton Police Station. Its leather-covered desk top and executive chair were more in keeping with his status of chief constable for the county than his old furniture at Bridgetown.

The habitual cigarette was in his mouth, the familiar headache and queasy hung-over stomach still with him. His telephone rang, irritating him as most things did first thing in the morning.

He picked up the receiver and growled, 'Hello.'

'Good morning, Chief Constable, it's Superintendent Newton here.'

'Ah, Newton, I was going to make contact with you today,' Savage said, sorting through some papers on his desk. 'I'm more than somewhat alarmed by the rising crime figures for Bridgetown.'

'I can set your mind at rest about that, sir,' Newton's voice purred. 'They're falling fast now. The main problem was the rather outdated and lackadaisical approach of all personnel, but I'm getting on top of it.'

As Savage had maintained sole charge at Bridgetown Station prior to the arrival of Superintendent Newton, he did not take kindly to the assertion that his officers had been allowed to produce less than their best. He decided to put Newton in his place.

'That's not what the figures show on paper, Superintendent. The number of burglaries, especially, has risen substantially in the past weeks. Now, the figures might be dropping, as you say, but only back to the level they were at before your appointment.'

Savage almost smiled as he listened to the panicky stutterings flowing from the earpiece.

He drew on his cigarette and waited. 'Well? What can I do for you?'

'It is rather delicate, sir.'

'Come on, man, I'm busy,' Savage snapped. 'Spit it out.'

'I'm . . . well, I'm having a little trouble with Chief Inspector Ashworth, sir.'

'Really?' Savage tried his level best to sound surprised. 'What sort of trouble?'

'It's his attitude, sir. Let me give you an example — I had to issue an order to the effect that I wanted DC Abraham to smarten up. In retaliation for this, Ashworth is growing a beard.'

Savage clamped his hand over the mouthpiece and laughed aloud.

'The man looks like a tramp,' Newton told him.

Savage smothered his mirth, and said, 'A lot of police officers have beards nowadays.'

'That's true, sir, but it's the man's attitude which rankles. He refuses to accept that I'm the senior officer.'

'Have you anything more specific? Is he carrying out his duties to your satisfaction?'

'I've no real complaints as yet, sir.'

'Then I can't see what I can do. Ashworth's been there a long time. It'll take him a while to adjust to a new man at the helm.'

'I wonder if you could have a word with him, sir,' Newton said hopefully. 'Let him know his behaviour is not going unnoticed at the very top.'

'I'm loath to do that, Superintendent, unless you're ready to make a formal complaint about his behaviour. And from what you've said, I don't think that's warranted.'

'No, sir.' Newton sounded dejected.

'Sort it out yourself, Superintendent,' Savage ordered curtly. 'You're the senior officer — keep the man in his place.'

Newton said quickly, 'Oh, don't worry about that, sir, I will. I just thought a word from you wouldn't come amiss, but I'll read the riot act to the man as and when it becomes necessary.'

'Well done.' He allowed the receiver to drop into its cradle. 'And the best of bloody luck.'

Savage chuckled as he opened a drawer of his desk, taking out a half-bottle of whisky.

'Growing a beard, eh?' he chortled, topping up his morning tea with a good measure of the liquor. 'That's going over the top, Jim, even by your standards.'

* * *

Joyce Regent rose early the following day. After showering, she drank two cups of coffee and smoked her customary three cigarettes, while the rising sun fast dissolved away that soft grey so peculiar to an autumn dawn.

By the time she had woken the boy and they were ready to leave, her mood was good. Last night her sexual gratification had reached new heights, leaving within her a mellow contentment. And her spirits were raised still further by an early morning reconnoitre which revealed that Malcolm Headlands was nowhere in the area.

She waited in the hall, and presently the boy made his way down the stairs. He had fine blond hair, a slender build and an almost pretty face, and looked years younger than his actual age.

Joyce smiled affectionately. 'When we get to the car, duck down so no one can see you.'

The boy nodded.

'It won't be for long, I promise. Just as soon as I can get rid of that reporter, you can stay at the cottage.' She collected her handbag from the hall table and took out a small wad of bank notes. The boy's eyes widened.

Joyce kissed him tenderly, briefly caressed his crotch. 'I could do with you this morning,' she said, staring into the boy's sleepy face, 'but I can't take the risk.' She pushed the money into his hand. 'There. Now, don't forget, I'll pick you up late afternoon.'

The boy pocketed the money without counting it and stood obediently at the door.

'Come on,' Joyce said, 'before the bloodhound arrives.'

* * *

At about the same time, inside the Wrights' cottage, Edith came awake slowly, blinking her eyes against the strong sunlight which streamed through the open curtains.

Force of habit led her to reach across for her husband. His side of the bed was still warm, but empty. Muttering softly to herself, Edith threw back the covers and climbed out of bed.

She found him sitting at the kitchen table, a steaming mug of tea before him, a cigarette between his fingers. His skin was now permanently grey, and the deathly hollows beneath his eyes had deepened.

'Mick?' she said tentatively.

'Everything's all right, girl. Don't worry yourself.'

The tender edge which now lightened his voice had been absent for sometime. Edith pulled up a chair and sat down, her eyes questioning him.

'I've been sitting here thinking,' he said.

'Don't torment yourself—'

'I'm dying, Edith.'

'Don't, Mick.'

Wright took her hand, encircled it with his own, their fingers interlaced. 'I'm dying, girl,' he said softly. 'As we sit here, I'm dying. I always wondered what it would be like. It's something both of us have got to come to terms with. Once we've done that, everything'll be easier.'

Edith found she could not speak; mere words seemed so inadequate. She watched her husband stub out the cigarette.

His face took on a distant look, and he said, 'I watched the sun come up this morning. I always saw them things, you know, the beauty of them: the sun, the trees, flowers. But, I don't know, perhaps it's because I didn't have a good education or nothing that I couldn't express myself. I always thought people would ask what right had I got to talk about beauty and everything — an ignorant little sod like me?' He smiled at his wife and sighed. 'So I used to act tough, unfeeling, like all that stuff was for women and nancy boys. But I saw it all, everything that was round me.'

Tears were flowing freely down Edith's face as years of repressed emotion forced their way to the surface.

'Edith, I always . . . I always . . .' He peered down at the table as he struggled to find the right words. Then suddenly his eyes were bright, kind, as he gazed at her. 'I always wanted to tell you how much I loved you. How glad, no, how privileged I was to have you, but the words wouldn't come. I was frightened you'd laugh.'

Edith squeezed her husband's hand as a tender smile transformed her tired, worn features. She rose slowly from the chair and wrapped her arms around his neck, her tears tumbling on to his cheeks.

'And I love you, Mick. I love you,' she murmured. 'Don't die. Please, don't die.'

CHAPTER 12

Ashworth was indeed beginning to resemble a tramp. At first sight all one noticed was that black stubble, shot through with silver, which erupted from the lower half of his face. The smart suit, the brilliant white shirt and sharply knotted tie went unnoticed. He strolled to the reception desk for a quick word with Martin Dutton.

'Coming along well, Jim,' the sergeant commented, running a hand around his own chin.

'Yes,' Ashworth said doubtfully. 'How are things with you, Martin?'

'Improving, Jim, improving. Things are slowing down a bit. We've got five Neighbourhood Watch schemes off the ground, so the burglaries are slowing down. And the recent spate of car thefts have made drivers more security conscious.' He leant an elbow on the desk. 'Do you think Newton's methods could be paying off?'

'No, I don't,' Ashworth said stubbornly.

'Ah, say no more.' He viewed Ashworth's contemptuous expression and went on in a conspiratorial voice, 'The grapevine has it that Newton's son's left home.'

'I'm not at all surprised.'

'One of the cleaners heard him talking to his wife on the phone. It seems the boy walked out after a row with him.'

'Martin, is this leading anywhere?'

Dutton peered cautiously around, first left and then right. He lowered his voice. 'There's a gang of youngsters we're looking for. Four lads and two girls. And what I've heard is that Newton's boy is one of them.'

'Really? And what has this gang done?'

'Nothing we can pin on them or we'd have them in. But they've been stealing from shops, taking cars, that sort of mischief. I don't mind telling you, the whole nick's waiting for that lad to get caught so his old man can catch it in the neck.'

'Martin, whatever's happened to you?' Ashworth inquired with a frown. 'I've never known you to be vindictive.'

'Know thyself, Jim, as they say. That man's brought something out in me. I don't think there's an officer in this nick that wouldn't like to see him come a cropper.'

'Amen to that,' Ashworth said.

'I'll tell you something else he's done . . .' Although the reception area was empty, Dutton lowered his voice to a whisper. 'He went to Ken Savage about your attitude.'

Ashworth now showed interest. 'Did he really?'

Bobby Adams came through the door behind the desk, and, not possessing the confidence to join in a conversation with his superiors, he chose to stand stiffly to attention just out of earshot.

'But Savage didn't want to know,' Dutton went on. 'The betting is he doesn't want to lock horns with you unless he has to.'

Ashworth's look was incredulous. 'Martin, where do you get all this gossip from?'

'The grapevine, Jim,' he said, tapping the side of his nose. 'The grapevine.'

Holly came bustling into reception. She had on a black skirt and jacket, both of which hugged her recently acquired curves. A touch of white showed at her throat where a cameo brooch was fastened.

Dutton pursed his lips in appreciation. 'My God, Jim, that lass is getting bonny. And she's coming out of herself. When she first came here you could hardly get a word out of her.'

'Yes, and now she can be quite a handful at times,' Ashworth said fondly.

Dutton laughed. 'I wouldn't mind a handful of her.'

Ashworth stared at the man with a pretence of shock. 'It wouldn't do you any good at your age,' he mocked.

'My missus wouldn't let me, anyway,' Dutton told him with a rueful smile.

Ashworth wandered across to Holly who was fumbling in her shoulder bag at the foot of the stairs.

'You all right, guv?' she asked. 'You look a bit puzzled.'

'I'm not sure.' He glanced back at Dutton. 'Some of the things Martin's coming out with of late . . . I'm seeing another side of him.'

'Perhaps he's getting it regularly,' she suggested with an impish grin, as they started up the stairs.

'Holly,' Ashworth warned sternly.

'And he's not the only one we're seeing another side of,' she said, quickening her step to keep up with him. 'I mean, I wouldn't have dared say anything like that to you a few months ago.'

'And you shouldn't now, young lady.' He stopped to muse. 'Perhaps it's seeing what a pompous, overbearing person like Newton can do to morale which is making us all lighten up a little.'

'I don't know, guv. That's too deep for me, especially first thing in the morning.'

Ashworth started off up the stairs again. 'Anything new on the Regent case?'

She told him of her meal with Headlands, and everything — well, almost everything — that had been said.

'Nothing there,' he grunted, as they reached the door to CID.

Instead of opening the door, Holly stood staring up at him.

'What's the matter?' he asked, rather disconcerted.

'I was just thinking, your beard looks really . . . now, what's the word I'm looking for?' She clicked her fingers and her face lit up. 'Nice? No, that's not it.'

Ashworth opened the door. 'Get in,' he ordered amicably.

* * *

Joyce parked her car on the grass verge and carefully locked it. There was a fence to her right which bordered Beeches Wood, a vast expanse of timber and bramble on the north side of town.

She climbed the fence and picked her way through thick undergrowth to reach a path. This was a nice spot, it was always quiet; and Joyce strolled along, her hands dug deep into the pockets of her lightweight waterproof jacket, enjoying the peace.

In common with many creative people, she was a strange mixture. The darker side of her nature, over which she exercised little control, pulled her towards excesses, prompted her to fulfil that strong sexual appetite by any means available. As one partner began to bore, she would swiftly move on to another, always seeking the ultimate thrill.

By contrast she could be quiet, well-bred, sensitive to the feelings of others. Even when her nature was at its most volatile, she could still appreciate beauty where others might fail to see it. She was able to choose an arrangement of words which were as easy on the eye as a symphony orchestra was on the ear. Sometimes, as now, she felt great peace in isolation, cut off from the world and all of its prying eyes.

She stopped by a wide stream and laughed with joy as water-rats paddled furiously through the water, scrambling to safety on the opposite bank. After a while, Joyce continued her walk through the wood until the dense undergrowth finally blocked her passage. There she sat on a ravaged tree trunk, felled long ago, and smoked a cigarette, taking little notice of the rustling sounds which seemed to be all around as a haunting breeze stirred the trees.

Dark clouds stole towards the sun, blocking its rays inch by inch; and a shadow crept over the wood as the sun disappeared, advancing until it bathed the area in a premature twilight.

Joyce stamped out the cigarette, flicked the butt into the stream and watched for a few seconds as it swirled away on the current. It was time to head back towards the car. As she walked the wind increased, until overhead the trees became one great mass of rustling, swaying foliage.

Joyce quickened her step as the temperature suddenly fell and rain started. She could hear the drops hitting the leaves, where most of them clung, way above her head. All around, the trees seemed to moan, buffeted by the increasingly sharp wind.

She made her way back along the path, or so she thought. A dead end lay ahead, the track blocked by fallen trees, brambles, and ankle-deep mud. Up above, the leaves, overloaded with rainwater, finally gave up their burden, and showered it upon her.

Panic welled up in her throat as Joyce realized she had taken a wrong turning. She retraced her steps at a run, searching fruitlessly for the path. By the time she had taken two more wrong turns, Joyce was convinced she was in the heart of the wood, heading further and further away from the car.

No sooner had the rain started than it cleared, and the sun managed to break free of the clouds. At the same time, Joyce came to a clearing, seeing in the distance the fence and beyond it her car. She laughed with relief.

The first blow caught her in the face, smashing her nose. Her attacker had leapt without warning from the rear of a large oak tree to her left. Blood poured from her face, drenching her jacket, and through it Joyce recognized her assailant, was about to call his name.

But the sound died in her throat when the wooden club smashed into her skull, rendering her unconscious, unable now to feel the blows raining down upon her.

* * *

Holly was surreptitiously watching Ashworth as he sat behind his desk, tapping his forefingers on its top, and she wondered whether he'd ever had a secret desire to be a drummer. Josh was positioned in front of the computer, staring at the screen but doing little else. It was one of those dreary mornings in CID when nothing seemed to be happening.

Holly's mind, when idle, was prone to wandering. She considered Ashworth. He was incredibly fit and well preserved for a man in middle age, but — she continually reminded herself — married, and settled. Even so, she found herself wondering whether, somewhere inside him, there might be a tiny part which was still a boy, an irresponsible teenager who, if tempted, would find it impossible not to succumb.

You've been seeing too much of Joyce Regent, she silently chided herself; young boys, indeed. Momentarily forgetting where she was, Holly laughed out loud, attracting puzzled glances from the others. She was relieved when her telephone buzzed, eradicating the need for an explanation.

She lifted the receiver. 'DS Bedford.'

The humour soon faded from her face as she listened, coming quickly to her feet, all the while scribbling details on a piece of paper.

'On our way,' she said. 'Joyce Regent, guv, she's been found badly battered in Beeches Wood. Forensic are on their way. Uniformed are already there to make sure the paramedics don't disturb anything.'

'Right,' Ashworth said, donning his waxed-cotton coat. 'Let's go.'

'I want to ring Malc.'

'Just make it snappy,' he called from the corridor.

* * *

The wood was now bathed in warm, comforting sunlight, its rays slanting elegantly through the still branches to dance on the brook.

As Ashworth pulled the Sierra on to the grass verge, he spotted Headlands waiting by the fence. He was checking his light meter, the camera around his neck, forever at the ready to record the stress and suffering of its victims.

The reporter acknowledged him with a tight smile and a wave of his hand. But his face brightened considerably when Holly's Micra pulled up behind the Sierra. Ashworth waited for Holly to join him, then made his way stolidly to the wood. Headlands moved towards them, but Ashworth ignored him and clambered over the fence.

Holly was about to follow when the reporter grabbed her arm. 'A quick word, Holly.'

'Not now, Malc,' she whispered. 'Ring me tonight.'

She climbed the fence with energetic ease and fell in beside the chief inspector.

Ashworth scowled. 'I know he's got his story at last, but does he have to look so damned cheerful about it?'

Holly decided to keep a tactful silence.

Near to the spot where Joyce Regent had been attacked, they were joined by the new pathologist, Doctor Alex Ferguson. He was a young man, barely thirty, wearing green waterproofs.

'Chief Inspector.' His tone was formal, his hand outstretched.

'Doctor Ferguson,' Ashworth said, shaking the man's hand. 'What have you got?'

'A woman in her forties—'

'We know who she is,' Ashworth interjected, determined that they should not waste time. 'What about her injuries?'

They walked past uniformed officers working industriously to seal off the site. To their left the forensic team had begun combing the wood.

'Oh yes, she's a local celebrity, isn't she?' Ferguson said. 'She's been badly beaten about the head. I'd say it was an iron bar or something similar.'

'Chances of survival?' Ashworth asked.

'Nil.'

Ferguson took off his bifocals and buffed them up with a handkerchief. He was holding them up to the light when he said, 'Whoever attacked the woman left her for dead. She's on her way to hospital now, but I'd give her an hour at the most.'

'Holly, get to the hospital,' Ashworth ordered.

'Will do, guv.'

As Holly ran back to the road, Ashworth stood surveying the scene. 'Excuse me, Doctor,' he said. 'I'd better check with forensic.'

'I've already done that. I thought it might save time.'

'Good man,' Ashworth said.

'There's very little to go on as yet. That's where the attack took place.' He pointed to some undergrowth, a short distance away. 'They believe her attacker may have hidden among that lot. All they've found so far is a single shoe-print, but the rain dripping from the trees has all but obliterated the pattern of the sole. What they can be sure of, though, is that it's somewhere around a size seven.'

'A bit small for a man, wouldn't you say?' Ashworth mused, peering down at his own size twelves.

'It could be nothing to do with the attack, of course. Lots of people use the wood,' Ferguson said. 'She was found by a woman out walking her dog. She's in one of the police vehicles, I believe, badly shaken up.'

'Small wonder,' Ashworth said.

He thanked the doctor and wandered off towards the nearest uniformed officer to ask the location of the witness.

He found her trembling in a patrol car parked on the road. She was in the front passenger seat, drinking tea from a thermos-flask cup. A golden retriever sat whining in the back. When Ashworth opened the door to climb in, the dog let out a series of vicious barks.

'Be quiet, Rocky.' The woman gave Ashworth a weak smile. 'He won't hurt you. He's a big softy really.'

She leant across the seat and ordered the dog to sit. It did and carried on with its piteous whining.

Ashworth sat in the driver's seat and produced his warrant card. 'Chief Inspector Ashworth,' he said. 'I believe you discovered the injured woman.'

'Yes, that's right. I don't think I'll ever get over this.'

She was a tiny woman, probably in her forties, but she resembled a bewildered child as she sat there in a deep-purple track suit.

'It was Rocky who found her, really. I'd just let him off the lead and I heard him barking like mad. When I went to see what was going on, I found him standing over that poor woman. There was a large pool of blood and she was, well, just lying in the middle of it.' The woman shuddered as she relived the horror. 'I just panicked and ran to call the police.'

'Did you walk to the wood?' Ashworth asked.

The woman nodded as she placed the plastic cup on the dashboard. 'From Pinewood estate.'

'And did you see anybody on your way here?'

'Oh yes, lots of people. It's very busy until you reach the roundabout.'

'But did you see anybody in the lane leading up to here?'

The woman looked confused. 'I honestly can't remember. I think there was a boy, a teenaged boy, walking along.'

'But you're not sure?'

The retriever took to barking again.

'Oh, do be quiet, Rocky,' the woman said, glaring back at the dog. 'Now let me think — there was a lad in the lane. He was wearing a grey sweatshirt, and I think it had a hood. He had blond hair, and I remember thinking how pretty he looked, sort of sensitive.' She blushed.

'Anything else?' Ashworth asked.

She bit on her lower lip, her brow creased in thought. 'Yes, his jeans were skin-tight, really close-fitting.'

'Was he carrying anything?'

'I don't remember.'

'Thank you very much,' he said. 'Somebody will call on you to take a formal statement.'

Ashworth climbed out of the car to the accompaniment of the barking retriever and walked smartly towards Malcolm Headlands.

'I'd have thought you'd be off by now,' he said, far from affable. 'You've got what you came for.'

Headlands pulled himself up on to the fence and smiled down at the chief inspector. 'You don't like me very much, do you?'

'No, I don't,' Ashworth admitted.

'And I haven't got what I came for, not until you give me the full story.'

'That's something I'm not prepared to do. You made your arrangement with Holly so you'll have to speak to her.'

Headlands sighed. 'Look, I can accept that you don't like me, but do you have to be quite so hostile?'

Ashworth huffed. 'Has it escaped your notice that if you and others like you hadn't hounded Joyce Regent, she wouldn't have come here and this wouldn't have happened?'

'Bullshit,' Headlands exclaimed. 'Most of those kids she was messing about with would knife you for the price of a fix.'

'So you think one of her lovers attacked her?'

'That's my bet.' He considered Ashworth for a moment. 'I don't know if Holly told you, but I saw a boy going into the cottage yesterday.'

'Yes, she did.' Ashworth hesitated. 'I believe you got a shot of the back of his head. Tell me, what colour hair had he got?'

Headlands's eyes narrowed. 'Blond. Long.'

Ashworth reflected upon this information in the light of what the eyewitness had told him. 'You think Kevin Thornton has something to do with this, don't you?'

The journalist's nod was emphatic.

Ashworth was far from convinced. He said, 'What motive would he have had?'

Headlands shrugged. 'Just because the motive doesn't come out and hit you in the face, doesn't mean there isn't one. Any number of things could have gone wrong between him and Joyce, giving him a good reason in his mind to try and kill her.'

'And he very nearly succeeded,' Ashworth mused.

'Witches' curses? Mick Wright terrified to the point of murder? It's not very likely, is it?'

'I hope not,' Ashworth said softly. 'I really do.' He turned on the reporter. 'Anyway, you'll have to get in touch with Holly, you're getting nothing out of me.'

'I've already got quite a lot,' Headlands said, with a disarming smile.

'Oh?'

'I now know Joyce isn't dead, but pretty close to it. I also know you're quite interested in a young boy, and by the look on your face when I told you, long blond hair comes into it somewhere.' He winked. 'You're not the only one capable of a little detection.'

Ashworth was driving back to the station before he allowed himself a smile at the fact that Headlands had gone a long way towards outwitting him.

* * *

The hospital smelt as hospitals always do. And although the smell itself was not unpleasant, its association with death and disease made Holly uncomfortable.

Her heels sounded on the tiled flooring as she hurried along the corridor. At the far end were swing doors over which hung a sign stating, 'accident and emergency'. The flexible rubber doors bent before her fingers as she pushed them open. Inside, porters shouted, patients complained about being kept waiting, and there was a general air of tension about the staff, a feeling that they were forever working against the clock.

She strode towards the reception desk and showed her warrant card to the harassed woman labouring behind it.

'DS Bedford, Bridgetown CID. I'm looking for Joyce Regent.'

'Through those doors,' the receptionist said, pointing. 'Ask one of the nurses which cubicle she's in.'

She gave Holly a brief smile then turned her attention to a middle-aged man in overalls with a large bandage across his right eye.

There was an urgency in Holly's step. She now sensed that time was of the essence.

Once through the doors she approached an extremely weary young doctor as he stepped out of a cubicle. 'I'm looking for Joyce Regent,' she told him, holding out her warrant card.

'I've just cleaned her up and seen to her injuries,' he said, digging his hands into the deep pockets of his white coat. 'She has a severely fractured skull, a broken nose, and God knows what else.'

'Any chance of her living?' Holly asked.

'None whatsoever. It's a wonder she's still alive. She keeps muttering something—'

'Can I see her?'

The doctor pulled aside the curtain of a cubicle and Holly pushed past him to reach the side of Joyce's bed.

She looked clean, peaceful, and although barely conscious, she started tossing her head to and fro on the pillow as if aware that someone was standing there.

Her lips moved. Holly was unable to hear any sound so she leant forward. But all that came from Joyce was laboured breathing, the air rasping in and out of her lungs.

'I think you'd better leave,' the doctor whispered. 'She's going.'

A low rattling noise began in her throat. And with what seemed like a supreme effort, she mumbled, 'He . . . he . . .'

Holly's heart was racing. 'Give me a minute,' she begged the doctor.

'Kill . . .'

The word was carried out on a long breath. And it was so long before she inhaled again that Holly feared she might be dead.

Holly bent down towards her. 'What, Joyce, what?'

The doctor was disturbed. He touched Holly's arm and signalled for her to leave, but she gave him a pleading look and turned back to the bed.

The woman was trying so hard to speak, to impart her final message. Her body tensed visibly beneath the sheets as she managed to whisper, 'Katie.'

The rattle came back into her throat and her body began to shake. Holly turned frightened eyes towards the doctor who was already moving to the bedside.

But it was too late. Joyce's eyes and mouth gaped open, and then she was still.

Holly was trembling as the doctor pulled the white sheet up over her face. He said, 'I wouldn't read too much into that, if I were you. Immediately prior to death, people say all kinds of weird and wonderful things.'

Holly looked down at the bed with dismay. 'I think she's just told me that her daughter's been killed as well.'

As she rushed from the cubicle, the doctor called, 'I'll make the arrangements for the pathologist.'

By the time she had reached the car park, Holly had recovered sufficiently to radio control. She asked them to pass on the news to the chief inspector.

CHAPTER 13

Ashworth was not looking forward to reaching Witch's Cottage. Joyce Regent's murder was horrific enough, but the thought of finding her daughter in a similar state brought a tight knot of worry to his chest. Despite his reluctance, he drove at speed and was soon parking the Sierra.

He walked with Josh along the garden path to the cottage and exhaled deeply before knocking on the door. Net curtains at the lounge window twitched, and then they heard the padding of stockinged feet on the bare boards of the hall and the hissing of the cat.

It was Katie who opened the door, dressed as ever in an oversized top — this one bearing the logo of an American football team — and jeans which were equally baggy.

'Yes?' The voice was sullen.

Ashworth was greatly relieved, and for once decided to ignore the antagonism in the greeting. 'May we come inside, Miss Regent?'

Katie viewed the two detectives with alarm. 'What do you want?'

'I think this would be better dealt with inside,' Ashworth said gently.

'Joyce's not at home. Perhaps you should come back when she is.'

'It's about your mother,' Ashworth said. 'Something's happened, I'm afraid.'

'You'd better come in, then.' With reluctance, Katie stood aside for them to enter. 'In the lounge.'

They walked into the room and found Tanya sitting on the window-seat. She looked fragile, less robust than in the past, and her cheeks were colourless. Her customary unsightly clothes, those which matched Katie's, were now gone and instead she wore a pretty floral dress.

'What's the matter, Katie?' she asked in her childish voice.

Josh remained at the door while Ashworth stood in front of the fireplace. He cleared his throat. 'There's no easy way to tell you this . . . your mother has been attacked and badly beaten. I'm afraid she died shortly after being admitted to hospital.'

He watched them closely for their reactions. Katie stood stock still, that attractive face showing no emotion.

Tanya simply held her breath for a long moment. A shaking hand was raised to her mouth. 'Katie, oh Katie,' she said. 'What are we going to do?'

Katie crossed to her quickly and gripped her shoulders. 'Go to your room, Tanya. I'll deal with this. We'll talk when the police have gone. Go on.'

Tanya stared at Ashworth, seemed about to speak but Katie pushed her towards the door, and she ran from the room.

'Where was she attacked?' Katie asked, after she had gone.

'In a place called Beeches Wood. Look, I know this might sound insensitive, but we do have questions which need to be answered.'

'Ask away,' Katie said, settling on the window-seat.

'When did you last see your mother?' Ashworth quizzed.

'Yesterday. Last night. She was coming out of the bathroom to go to bed. It was about ten o'clock.'

'Thank you, that's very helpful. So you didn't see her today at any time?'

Ashworth looked towards Josh who was taking everything down in his notepad.

'No, I didn't. I heard her. She left the house somewhere around eight o'clock.'

'Was she alone?'

Katie hesitated for a second. 'I don't know. As I said, I didn't see her. I just heard the front door close and the car start.'

Ashworth began pacing. 'I've got a feeling there's something you're not telling us, so I'm going to ask you if Kevin Thornton was ever in this cottage.'

'What's Kevin got to do with any of this?'

'I'm simply asking a question.'

'You think Kevin did that to her?' Katie said hotly. 'You must be out of your mind. Mick Wright did it. Remember him? He wrote hate mail, stuck that cat on the door, and then he attacked us. Shouldn't you be talking to him?'

'Calm down, young lady,' Ashworth cautioned.

'No, I won't. I don't want that all over the papers again. She's dead, for Christ's sake. Does her sex life have to come out again?'

'We'll do all we can to keep it under wraps,' Ashworth said. 'But we do have to know if Thornton was ever here.'

Katie stared into space, a little of the anger spent. 'Yes, Kevin was here.'

'Did he live here?'

'No, he didn't. I wouldn't allow it. Joyce kept bringing him here, which worried me to death after that reporter turned up.'

'Was he here last night? And be truthful, because we know someone was.'

'I don't think so. Kevin had been gone for days before she went to London. This was someone new.'

'But you've no idea who it was?' Ashworth probed. 'This lad was in the house but you didn't see or hear him?'

'Look, I saw her at ten. She was coming out of the bathroom, fully dressed and ready to play one of her pathetic little sex games. And, yes, I heard them in the bedroom, but I'm certain it wasn't Kevin.'

'How do you know it wasn't?' Ashworth asked with a meaningful stare.

'Because Joyce told me she'd got someone new coming round. Kevin had gone home.'

'And where's home?'

'I don't know. I don't know,' Katie said, smashing a fist repeatedly on the window-seat.

Ashworth decided it was time to push his advantage. He said, 'Was your mother the only one having a relationship with Kevin?'

'What sort of question's that?'

'A direct one. Did you have any sort of friendship with Kevin Thornton?'

Katie gave an empty laugh. 'If only you knew how funny that is.'

'What about Tanya?'

'Tanya's just a child. Just a child, for God's sake.'

'She might be, but Kevin Thornton was into children, from what I can gather.' Ashworth squatted on his haunches in front of the window-seat. 'Look, you must understand that Thornton is vitally important to my investigation. Do you know where I can find him?'

Katie turned away from him. 'No, I don't.'

'Did he leave anything here?' Ashworth pressed. 'Any clothes?'

'Not to my knowledge, no.'

'Can we take a look upstairs?'

They were led slowly to the top floor.

On the landing, Ashworth baulked. Something had unnerved him. A feeling so nearly imperceptible, so transient, as to be almost imagined. It was as if a piece of lace, cold lace, had been pulled across his face. He felt it on his skin for no more than a second, and then it was gone, leaving behind it a chill, a dread. Ashworth touched his cheek, shook his head to free himself of the sensation, then followed the others into the main bedroom.

Katie was standing in front of the sliding doors to the wardrobe. 'Look where you like.'

Josh opened the doors, which glided effortlessly on expensive runners, and checked inside. He then went on to riffle through the chest of drawers. Finally, he straightened up.

'No, guv, all female clothing.'

'I'm afraid someone will have to identify the body,' Ashworth said gently.

'I'll do that. You might as well know, I didn't get on with her, but I didn't want her to die. She wanted me to leave. No, to be more precise, she was throwing me out. I was cramping her style. And now she's dead . . .'

As Katie faltered, clearly close to tears, Ashworth almost felt pity, but he brushed it aside.

'I think that'll be all for the moment,' he said. 'I'm sorry about what's happened.'

Katie sneered as Josh opened the front door. 'Are you sorry? You don't seem to be. It's so obvious who did it, but you want to rake all the muck up again, don't you? You want it all over the papers again.'

Ashworth stepped out into the sunlight, saying, 'I'm sorry you see it that way, I really am.'

The moment Josh followed him out, the door was slammed in their faces.

Josh hurried after the striding Ashworth, fiddling with his collar and tie. 'You were a bit hard on her, guv.'

'She doesn't inspire sympathy, does she? Her sister was obviously in shock, and yet she ordered her out.'

'She is only a kid.'

Josh waited for Ashworth to get into the Sierra and open the passenger door, then climbed into his seat, saying, 'I think Katie just wanted to protect her.'

'Or maybe she was frightened of what Tanya might tell us,' Ashworth suggested, as he scratched at the lengthening stubble on his chin.

'Don't follow, guv.'

'Just a hunch — a young boy was seen in the lane around the time of the assault. It could have been Kevin Thornton.'

'Guv, I'm dreading this as much as you are,' Josh said, securing his seat-belt, 'but we'll still have to bring Mick Wright in, won't we?'

Ashworth started the engine. 'I know that. I asked Holly to check with the hospital as to how advanced the man's condition is.' He steered into the road and sighed. 'This is one I'm not looking forward to, Josh.'

* * *

Holly was pleased that her interpretation of Joyce Regent's last words was wrong. With an easier mind, she watched Ashworth remove his coat, and said:

'Newton's been in here every ten minutes looking for you.'

'Good,' he replied, his voice heavy with sarcasm. He settled behind his desk. 'What have you got?'

'Mick Wright's in a bad way. He's only got a matter of months to live.' She hesitated briefly, then said, 'We really ought to bring him in, guv. If he hasn't got a cast-iron alibi, we've got enough to hold him.'

'Yes, I know,' Ashworth mused.

The door was flung open, startling them all, and Superintendent Newton strode into the office.

'I've been looking everywhere for you, Ashworth,' he accused, standing rigidly to attention.

'Well, now you've found me,' Ashworth replied, with a touch of impertinence.

'Why hasn't Mick Wright been brought in for interview?'

'I'm just checking things with my team, and then I'll be deciding my next move.'

'No need for that, just bring the man in. That's an order.' Newton turned abruptly and marched from the office.

'Guv?' Holly said hesitantly, 'I know Katie's still alive, but—'

'All right, Holly,' Ashworth snapped, 'I have worked it out.' He crossed to the glass wall and looked out over Bridgetown. With his back still towards her, he said, 'What Joyce Regent was trying to tell you on her deathbed was that Wright would try to kill Katie, just as he'd threatened.'

He turned abruptly and gave a deep sigh. 'I hear the station book is quoting ten-to-one odds that somebody will thump Newton, but only evens that it'll be me. Well, the odds on that have just shortened.'

* * *

The deathly grey in Mick Wright's face deepened.

'Somebody's done for the witch?'

'Yes, Mick,' Ashworth said, 'and that means we'll have to ask you some questions.'

'You don't think it was Mick who done it?' Edith said, dashing in front of her husband as if to protect him.

'Don't fret yourself, girl,' Mick said quietly. 'They've got to ask their questions. I must be the number one suspect. You go and make us some tea.'

Edith surveyed Ashworth and then Holly with a worried expression before departing to the kitchen.

'Sit down,' Wright invited.

Ashworth settled his bulk on the settee, while Holly perched herself on the edge of the armchair.

Mick Wright remained standing, quite at ease. 'Somebody's done for her, then. I can't say I'm sorry.'

'Where were you this morning?' Holly asked.

'I went out for a walk,' he told her. 'Believe me, girl, when you've been told your days are numbered, it takes time to come to terms with.'

'But *where* did you go?' She smiled. 'We'd love to eliminate you from our inquiries.'

'I had a chat with Edith first thing, and after that I went out, walked through the town—'

'Did anybody see you?'

'Hold on, girl,' Wright said, holding up a hand, 'I know what you're after. I left here at ten. I went into town, called in at Ma's paper shop, and we had a bit of a chat. Then I went to where I work, had a cup of tea with the lads to get my breath back. I left there and walked around, taking it nice and slow, like. There was a heavy shower, so I sheltered in a bus stop and then came back here.'

Ashworth exchanged a look with Holly. He said, 'Did you go anywhere near Beeches Wood?'

'No,' Wright said rather quickly. 'Why should I?'

'That's where Joyce Regent was attacked.'

'I wasn't there,' he insisted. 'I got back here at twelve o'clock.'

Ashworth searched the man's face, tried to read his expression. 'If you were there, we'll find out.'

'But I wasn't there,' Wright reiterated strongly. 'God, you're determined to pin this on me, ain't you.'

Ashworth averted his gaze. 'All right, Mick, I'll be honest with you. What's on record — the letters, your attack on Joyce Regent — makes you a suspect. But until I get the pathologist and forensic reports, I won't do anything. Will you cooperate with us?'

'How?' the man asked guardedly.

'Will you let us have the clothes and shoes you were wearing this morning?'

'Yes, 'course, mind you they're wet just now. Edith washed them as soon as I got back.'

Ashworth closed his eyes and rubbed his new beard with annoyance. Presently, he looked up at Wright. 'Why did she do that?'

'Because they were wet. I got soaked before I reached the bus shelter.'

Ashworth sighed. 'And I suppose she cleaned your shoes . . .'

'Well, yes, they were muddy.'

'They were muddy,' Ashworth repeated, exhaling sharply. 'What size shoes do you take, Mick?'

Wright glanced down at his feet. 'Tens.'

'At least that's something,' Ashworth murmured.

* * *

The remainder of the day was given up to the laborious task of sifting through countless forensic reports. Although the police were still combing the wood, they had so far turned up nothing which could be of any help.

There were no fingerprints on the knife used to impale the cat. And the shoe-print was proving to be of little use.

The owner of the shoe had placed his or her foot on a particularly muddy piece of ground, leaving what would have been a precise indentation. However, rainwater from the trees had washed away all distinguishing features, leaving the police with no more to go on than the fact that it was a size seven.

Mick Wright's freshly washed and still wet trousers had predictably produced nothing. More importantly, neither had his unwashed sports jacket. No traces of blood, mud, or any other such substance which might tie him to Beeches Wood and Joyce Regent's death.

Ashworth felt like throwing the reports into the air, such was the depth of his frustration.

Holly returned from interviewing Mrs Bagshaw, the woman whose dog had found the body, the woman who claimed to have seen a young boy in the adjacent lane. Although distressed earlier by the day's events, Holly strolled into the office, seemingly recovered, and sat at her desk with eyes twinkling while Ashworth read the statement. Indeed, as she sat there smiling to herself, he viewed her with some curiosity as his eyes scanned the paper.

It was 4 p.m. when Doctor Ferguson rang with the post-mortem results. Joyce's death had been brought about by repeated blows to the head, resulting in extensive bleeding inside the brain. And due to the presence of minute splinters of wood in the wounds, he concluded that the murder weapon was a blunt wooden instrument. Scratch marks on her hands and legs — probably caused by brambles — were still bleeding freely on his arrival at the scene of the attack, which led him to believe that the crime was committed immediately prior to the discovery of her body. There were no signs of sexual assault.

Ashworth passed this information on to his two detectives, neither of whom made any comment.

'There's nothing there to put Wright in the frame,' he remarked.

Holly said, 'He's already in it, guv. There's nothing in there that takes him out.'

Ashworth sat weighing the facts.

'There's enough circumstantial evidence to bring him in,' Holly ventured.

'Not yet,' Ashworth said, his manner abrupt. 'Leave it until tomorrow.' He gathered up the papers and left the office without saying more.

'What's he delaying for?' Josh asked. 'Newton's going to do his nut.'

'He doesn't think Wright did it,' Holly said.

'Well, he's giving Newton a stick to beat him with. Mick could be destroying evidence left, right, and centre.'

'Josh, you know as well as I do, if we bring Wright in he'll be remanded to a prison hospital where, in a couple of months' time, he'll die, long before this ever gets to court. And to us that'll mean case closed.'

'That's what's going to happen in any case,' Josh countered. 'So like I said, why the delay?'

Holly started to giggle as she studied her notebook.

'Can you find anything funny in this?'

'Just thoughts,' she said, turning the page, 'just thoughts.'

Her telephone buzzed, and she was still smiling when she lifted the receiver. But as she listened, her giggly mood faded swiftly.

'Oh dear,' she said, replacing the receiver. 'That's another nail in your coffin, Mick.' No sooner had the utterance left her mouth than she regretted her choice of words.

CHAPTER 14

Ashworth passed a restless night. Not for him an escape into fleeting fantasies that slipped from memory once eyes were opened and mind focused.

At one point, on the brink of oblivion, he was visited by Isobel Perkins, her long red hair flowing in the wind as she mocked him.

He watched himself imploring her to name the killer, only to hear her laugh. And the harsh wind carried the words, 'They will all die for what they did to me. And if you stand in my way, so shall you.'

The buzz of the alarm clock brought him awake. Sarah was still sleeping, so he crept out of bed, thankful that it was morning, and went downstairs to make tea and exercise the dog.

Later, Bridgetown Police Station was bustling with activity. The full story of Joyce's murder had finally broken in the national press, giving Headlands his exclusive. And now reporters from the tabloids, hungry for details, had converged on Bridgetown.

Holly, true to her word, had held back the story from the local press, leaving it until they had time only to announce it in their 'Stop Press' columns, so local journalists also formed part of the scramble for information. Television crews were all about, unloading their cameras. Technicians ran off cable, checked sound levels, while make-up girls fussed around the presenters.

Ashworth shouldered his way through the crowds and into front reception.

'Ashworth.' Newton's voice stopped him in his tracks. The superintendent came striding across reception. 'Why haven't you brought Wright in?'

Ashworth sighed. 'I questioned him yesterday, and I can't find any concrete evidence against him.'

'Nonsense,' Newton snapped. 'The man's admitted sending threatening letters. It's on record that he attacked the dead woman on an earlier occasion. What more do you want?'

'The man is very ill,' Ashworth said.

'I'm well aware, but that doesn't alter anything.'

'All right, then can I suggest that if Wright is charged, we agree to bail so long as he books into hospital where we can keep him under a twenty-four-hour guard?'

'What's all this twenty-four-hour guard you keep on about?' Newton huffed. 'I haven't got the manpower for that.'

'If you'd complied with my first request for a guard on Joyce Regent we wouldn't be standing here now,' Ashworth retorted. 'If you'd listened then, the woman might still be alive.'

'What sort of snide remark is that?'

'I don't make snide remarks,' Ashworth replied calmly. 'I'm merely stating the facts.'

'Bring Wright in and charge him,' Newton said, with great deliberation. 'I don't care if the man's barely alive, this thing must be cleared up today.' He looked towards the road, preening himself. 'I've got television interviews to think about.'

Ashworth flexed his right hand several times before walking away. Newton watched until his solid bulk had vanished up the stairs.

He was worried. The man had a valid point about his refusal to offer the Regent woman protection. A thing like that could bounce back on him unless he took steps to ensure it did not.

The reception doors swung open, interrupting his thoughts. A young man, carrying a clipboard, approached.

'Robert Howard, BBC,' he announced.

'Ah, Mr Howard,' Newton said, stepping forward eagerly to offer the man his hand. 'I'm Superintendent Newton. We spoke on the telephone. Can I offer you some refreshments?'

* * *

Ashworth was still bristling when he got back to CID. His furious expression warned Holly and Josh that there would be no friendly pleasantries this particular morning.

He straight away walked to the glass wall and stared down into the street. 'Haven't the press or TV got anything better to do?' he scowled.

'Guv?' Holly said tentatively. 'Something came in about Mick Wright last night.'

There was hope in Ashworth's face when he turned to her. 'Oh yes?'

'It's not good news, guv.'

He sat heavily in his chair, his mouth returning to its sullen line. 'What is it, then?'

'He was spotted near Beeches Wood at the time of the murder.' She picked up a statement from her desk. 'A man who used to work with Mick — Tom Spencer — saw him, and because the whole town's buzzing with the murder, he reported it. I took his statement last night.' She passed it to Ashworth.

He scanned the page, then threw the statement on to his desk and sat back in the chair. 'That removes any slight choice I might have had.'

'Looks like it to me.'

'But it's still all circumstantial,' Ashworth argued.

'Yes,' Holly agreed, 'but if we don't take that man off the street, and then something happens to either of the Regent girls, we'll be crucified.'

'I know,' Ashworth mused.

* * *

Holly took Josh along to bring Mick Wright in.

The man was quite passive, seemingly resigned to his fate. Edith, however, was totally uncooperative. As they were about to leave the kitchen, she became hysterical, throwing chairs and saucepans in their path, screaming for them to leave her husband alone.

Josh tried his best to reason with the woman, but she attacked him, kicking out and flaying him with her fingernails. The sight of that diminutive middle-aged woman getting the better of a young police officer would have looked comical in different circumstances. As it was, Edith's outburst, and the vigour with which she fought for her man, touched Holly's heart. Even so, she felt forced to intervene, but even her extensive martial arts expertise was not sufficient to subdue the woman.

Throughout the harrowing spectacle, Mick Wright stayed slumped against the wall, his face showing disbelief. Just as Holly decided that real force would be needed to control the situation, Wright stepped in. He advanced towards his wife and, in a surprisingly strong voice, ordered her to stop.

Edith yielded immediately and stood before the detectives, breathing heavily, arms slack at her sides, but still trembling with fear and rage.

'Give us a minute together, will you?' Wright asked. 'There's things I need to say.'

They waited beyond the kitchen door. Five minutes later, Wright emerged, his eyes moist. 'She's all right now,' he told them softly.

Holly put a hand on his arm. 'Mick, would you like me to get somebody to come and sit with her?'

'No, you needn't bother, I've phoned her sister. She'll be better with family around her.' He knocked her hand away and pointed a finger. 'Just you make sure you let her know what's happening to me. I read the papers, you know, and the way you lot treat the kin of accused people—'

'She'll be kept fully informed,' Holly assured him promptly. 'Don't worry about that.'

Outside, it appeared that the whole of the lane had turned out to witness his departure. For a few seconds, Wright considered his neighbours standing on their doorsteps like carrion crows awaiting a death. He seemed about to call to them, but shook his head instead and ducked into the back seat of the Micra. Josh climbed in beside him as Holly started the engine.

When they neared the station, Josh removed his jacket and instructed Wright to cover his head with it. Three minutes later, they were pulling into the station car park.

All at once the press pack converged, swarming around the car like busy ants. The photographers jostled one another, pushed and shoved, cameras held aloft in the hope of getting a better shot.

Amid the clicking of shutters, the flashing of bulbs, Holly caught sight of Headlands and stuck out her tongue. He grinned and took her photograph.

Inside the station, they placed Wright in interview room number one. Before the man had settled in his seat, Ashworth appeared in the doorway, his bulk almost filling it.

'Hello, Mick,' he said genially. 'Can I get you anything?'

'A cup of tea, and I wouldn't mind a packet of fags.'

'See to it,' Ashworth barked at the uniformed officer by the door, who immediately left the room.

Mick Wright was sitting with hands in lap, staring straight ahead. Ashworth moved into his line of vision.

'You know why you're here . . .'

'Not for a cup of tea and a packet of fags, that's for sure.' He looked up then. 'Are you going to charge me?'

Ashworth sat down to face him. 'Do you want your solicitor present?'

Wright shook his head. 'No, Ron Curtis has left Bridgetown. And in any case, he wouldn't want to be involved in this.'

The uniformed officer returned with a tray holding a mug of tea, the cigarettes and a box of matches. He placed it in front of Wright and once again positioned himself beside the door.

Ashworth heard Holly activate the tape recorder, giving the time and the names of those present.

'It's your right to have a solicitor here,' Ashworth said.

The man shrugged as he tore at the Cellophane on the cigarette packet. 'Don't make much difference, does it? You're going to charge me.' He put a cigarette to his mouth and lit it. 'I didn't do it, you know.'

Ashworth coughed as a cloud of smoke wafted towards him.

Wright said, 'I made a statement yesterday and I've nothing more to add.'

'Someone saw you near Beeches Wood at the time of the murder,' Ashworth told him gently.

What little fight the man had left quickly evaporated. He slumped forward, his face distorted in a fit of sobbing.

'I knew if you found out I was there, that would do it . . .'

'I've got to charge you,' Ashworth cut in.

Wright sniffed. 'You'd better get on with it, then.'

While the caution was being read to him, he realized for the first time his desperate predicament. Strain showed in his face, his shoulders sagged, and he drew heavily on the cigarette.

'What happens now?' he asked Ashworth.

'You're to be held in a prison hospital until your appearance before the magistrates. When you do come up in court, your lawyer can request bail.'

'What are my chances of getting it?' he said, as he extinguished the cigarette.

'Slight.'

'Even in my condition?'

Ashworth, reluctant to look the man in the face, said, 'We're talking premeditated murder here, Mick. The prosecution are going to claim that you killed Joyce Regent because you believed she was a witch and that she had put a curse on you. They'll reason strongly that if you're allowed out on bail, you might—'

'I might do the same to her spawn . . . the two little witches that'll take her place,' Wright finished with a bitter tone.

Ashworth stood up. 'That's about it,' he said.

Wright picked up the tea and sipped it. 'I wish I had done for her, now,' he muttered.

'Do yourself a favour,' Ashworth advised. 'Don't say anything else until you've talked to a solicitor.' He started towards the door.

'Mr Ashworth,' Wright called. 'Thanks for being honest with me. You seem like a fair bloke. Will you see that Edith's all right?'

'I'll do what I can, Mick.'

His voice was gruff and Holly was not altogether sure that the slight watering of his eyes was caused by the smoky atmosphere of the room.

* * *

Superintendent Newton frequently glanced from left to right as he drove along the High Street. Ever since his television appearance, during which he had announced the arrest of a man for the murder of Joyce Regent, he was convinced that he would be recognized by all.

His Audi purred across the bridge over the River Thane and headed for Witch's Cottage. He was on his way to see the bereaved under the guise of informing them in person that a man had been apprehended; but in all truth, the real purpose of his visit was to cover himself against any charges that Ashworth might bring.

The cottage and surrounding areas were quiet when he pulled up. He locked the car and hurried along the garden path, eager to get this done.

As Newton knocked on the door, he noticed with disgust the traces of cat's blood still remaining there. The door was opened by Katie, who waited for the police officer to speak.

'Superintendent Newton,' he announced with a click of his heels. 'And you are?'

'I'm Katie.'

'Ah. May I come in?'

With little grace, Katie stood to one side and waved him into the hall. The cat, crouched on the bottom stair, spat and growled with back arched before bounding up the stairs and out of sight.

'In there,' Katie said, indicating the lounge.

Tanya was resting on the settee. She seemed to flinch at the sight of the superintendent. Instantly, Katie rushed forward.

'Don't worry, Tanya, it's just a policeman come to see us.' Then, turning to Newton. 'She's a nervous wreck since, you know . . . what happened.'

'Quite understandable,' Newton said stiffly as he removed his peaked cap. 'May I offer you both my condolences. And although I know it won't bring your mother back, I hope it will be a small crumb of comfort to know that a man has been charged in connection with the crime.'

They exchanged relieved looks.

'Well, now, I can see you're pleased with that.' He gave an embarrassed cough. 'Do you think I might sit down?'

'Oh yes, sorry,' Katie said, moving a pile of books from a chair. 'Is it that Mick Wright?'

Newton lowered himself into the seat. 'The very same,' he said.

'And is that the end of the investigation? No more questions or upsets?'

'Well, of course we won't be looking for anyone else to assist us,' Newton replied, 'because for the moment our inquiries are complete.'

'What do you mean, for the moment?'

Newton was beginning to feel uncomfortable beneath Katie's suspicious gaze. 'I mean if Wright's case goes to court and he's acquitted, we'll have to look at it again.' He swallowed, and added quickly, 'But I can assure you that is highly unlikely.'

Katie sat beside Tanya on the settee and gently took her hand. 'So it's finally over.'

'Yes, you can rest assured that it is.'

Newton sat undecided for a matter of seconds and then, although loath to do so, he broached the subject which was the real reason for his visit.

'There is one other thing,' he said, faltering slightly. 'A few days before your mother's unfortunate death, I received a request from Chief Inspector Ashworth that she should have a police guard. Naturally, in the circumstances — the business with the dead cat and what have you — I considered this. And I . . . I rang your mother to see if she wanted protection. I don't suppose either of you remembers that?'

'No,' Katie said flatly.

'What a pity,' Newton mused. 'I should have gone through proper channels, you see, had it all down in writing, in report form. But your mother refused my offer, so I left it there. Now, the chief inspector doesn't think that Wright is guilty, and I fear he may try to use this against me.'

'Would that hold anything up?'

'It would complicate matters, yes.'

'If I said that I remembered your phone call, would it help?'

'Oh yes, it would help enormously.'

'All right, I'll do it.'

Newton sighed inwardly and strove to keep the relief from showing on his face. 'I'm only thinking about you girls. This must be a difficult period for you both, and I intend to do all I can to relieve any pressure.'

After Newton's departure, they sat together in a comfortable silence. Presently, Tanya said, 'Do you remember that man ringing mother?'

'No, of course not. He's made a cock-up and he's just trying to cover himself.'

'Oh, I see.' Her brow wrinkled. 'I don't like that Mr Ashworth. He's too nosy.'

'Don't worry about him,' Katie soothed, slipping a protective arm around Tanya's shoulder. 'Do you want to be happy?'

Tanya's eyes sparkled. 'You mean?'

Katie smiled warmly and withdrew a small white packet from behind a cushion on the settee.

'Yes, yes, yes,' Tanya enthused. 'Oh, Katie, I *am* happy. For the first time in my life I'm really happy, and I don't want anything to spoil it.'

'What could?'

The girl's mood changed abruptly. She pouted petulantly, and said, 'If that man Ashworth found out and—'

'Shush,' Katie said, placing a finger across Tanya's lips, 'now don't start that again. Nobody's going to find out. Anyway, we've got our own friend in the police now. My betting is that Newton refused Ashworth's request for a guard, and if he hadn't, dear Mama would still be here.'

'Dear Mama,' Tanya said, shrieking with laughter. 'Oh, Katie, you're so funny.'

* * *

Malcolm Headlands was in high spirits when he called on Holly that evening. She poured drinks for them in the front room and they touched glasses.

'Cheers,' Headlands said. 'And thanks, that was a great story you gave me. The lads are mad that I got it a day before anybody else.'

Holly stretched out on the floor in front of the armchair and sipped her drink. 'Have they left Bridgetown, the rest of the reporters?'

Headlands settled in his spot by the settee and nodded. 'There's nothing to keep them here now everything's wrapped up. The next big one's after the trial, when we try to persuade the Regent girls to tell their story.' He mimed flicking through a wad of money.

Holly's notepad was on the settee. Headlands reached across for it and thumbed through its pages. He squinted, holding the book at arm's length. 'I thought my handwriting was bad,' he said. 'What's this? Cock, cock, cock. Is that what you think about all day?'

Getting to her feet, Holly rushed at him, her face bright with devilment. 'Give,' she said, her hand outstretched.

Headlands held the book behind his back, engaging Holly in a mock fight. Eventually, she wrestled it out of his grip and fell, laughing, in front of her chair.

'I wrote that when I was taking the statement of the woman who found Joyce battered in the wood. Just before she came across the body she saw a boy in the lane. She said his jeans were very tight.' Holly's cheeks dimpled as she giggled. 'Well, it was obvious there was only one part of him she looked at properly. She wasn't really sure about hair colour, height, but, my God, talk about bored housewife — I bet she could have described his equipment in minute detail if I'd let her.' Her smile slipped. 'Anyway, it cheered me up, and I needed that after watching Joyce die.'

Headlands's eyebrows rose suggestively. 'Do you study outlines?'

'Are you leaving Bridgetown, too?' Holly asked, skilfully changing the subject.

He stretched and stifled a yawn. 'I might stay on a couple of days, just to unwind.'

'What about Kevin Thornton?' she said hopefully. 'Aren't you still interested in him?'

'He's on the back burner. I couldn't write anything about him, it would prejudice the trial.'

Holly stared into her glass. 'There won't be a trial,' she said solemnly. 'Poor old Mick Wright'll be dead before then.'

'Holly, have you got a problem with this?'

'Yes,' she admitted quietly. 'I don't think he did it.'

'Well, I've typed the story up, and with all the facts it's impossible not to think he did it.'

'I know, that's what's so odd about it. It's all too cut and dried.'

Headlands pursed his lips. 'The man's out of his head, one way or another. You can't apply logic to his behaviour.'

Holly laughed. 'Just what I need tonight — a smart arse.'

'You know what I think? Wright's dying and you're letting that cloud your judgement.'

Holly seemed not to hear him. She said, 'What would a bestselling author be worth? Millions? Say the girls, disgusted with their mother's behaviour, killed her.'

Headlands gave her his long-suffering look.

'Or,' Holly went on, 'the older girl, frightened she might be cut out of the will, killed her. We all know she was being thrown out because Joyce thought she was cramping her style.' She saw Headlands's mocking expression and laughed. 'Well, it is possible.'

'Yes,' he said, putting his empty glass on the carpet. 'Or Saddam Hussein might have got wind that Joyce was about to visit Iraq and, fearing that most of his young male population were in grave danger of enjoying themselves, panicked and had her assassinated. Possible, but not very probable.'

'Yes, all right,' Holly said, giggling, 'but Ashworth's not convinced it was Mick.'

'Too bad, he'll just have to let it go now, won't he?'

'You don't know Jim Ashworth. If he doesn't want to let go, he just hangs on.'

'Wait a minute,' Headlands said, waving a finger, 'do I detect a note of the DS fancying her boss?'

Holly's laugh was too loud, and even to her ears it sounded strained, false. 'Don't be silly,' she said. 'He's old enough to be my dad.'

Headlands shot her a knowing look, and in order to avert the conversation she said, 'Couldn't you help?'

'Me? How?'

'Couldn't you stay a few weeks? Dig around a bit?'

'Are you kidding?'

'Oh, come on, Malc,' she said, edging towards him. 'I helped you with your story. It wouldn't have been an exclusive if it hadn't been for me. You owe me one.'

'No, no, no,' he insisted firmly. 'Unpaid police work's not in my line, and in any case I can't stand Ashworth.'

'Please,' she wheedled, crouching by his side so that her skirt rode up to reveal her stocking tops and suspenders. 'Please?'

His resolve began to weaken as he stared at her thighs. 'All right,' he said, 'but just for a couple of weeks. And only because I owe you one.'

Holly leant forward and kissed him briefly. 'You're great, do you know that?'

'I've been conned,' Headlands complained with a laugh.

He got to his feet. 'I couldn't take a shower, could I?'

'Yes, you know where the bathroom is.'

'Cheers.'

'There're clean towels in the airing cupboard,' she called as he vanished into the hall.

'Roger and out,' he shouted back.

She smiled as she collected the glasses.

Headlands's voice reached her from the landing. 'Holly, I don't know where the airing cupboard is.'

'It's . . . Oh, hold on.' She left the glasses by the spirit bottles and ran up the stairs. 'It's in the bedroom.'

He was waiting for her on the landing, his shirt removed, his hair ruffled. Holly tried not to stare at his physique, that deep hairless chest, the flat hard stomach, but found it hard to resist. His bare feet made no sound on the carpet as he followed her into the bedroom.

She passed him two thick bath towels and he grinned. 'Thanks.'

She watched him walk to the door, noticed that the small knot of muscles behind his shoulders rippled, and was aware of his aftershave all around her.

The bathroom door clicked shut, but Holly noticed that he left it unlocked. She stood in the doorway of the bedroom and listened to his belt buckle clanging against the door as he hung up his trousers.

'I bet he wears boxer shorts,' she murmured. 'Yes, definitely boxer shorts.'

Her eyes were drawn to the bathroom door, which was all that stood between them, and she saw his nakedness in her imagination. She heard him pull the curtain across the bath and turn on the shower. With a resigned sigh, Holly wandered back into the bedroom and sat in front of the dressing table.

'Oh dear,' she said to her reflection, as she started to unbutton her blouse.

CHAPTER 15

During the whole of his adult life, Mick Wright had cried only twice. The first time was when he learned of the terminal cancer devastating his lungs. That night he had buried his head in the pillow and cried like an infant, great heaving sobs which racked his body.

He appeared to have come to terms with his sentence of death, but inside his mind was unable to grasp that even in a few short months he might no longer be alive. And he could not so much as begin to contemplate what lay beyond this life.

But on that night, when cancer put up a barrier between himself and the future, Edith had been there to comfort him. Emotionally stultified as they both were, the experience had been moving, a time of spiritual growth. And during that long night he learned that the greatest gift a man could possess was the love of someone who cared enough to be devastated by the thought of his death.

But now Edith wasn't there. He was locked in a ward filled with prisoners. There were guards on the door.

'Oh God, let me bugger off out of it tonight,' he whispered into a pillow damp with tears.

* * *

Pauline Talbot was almost frantic. Titch, her small brown and white terrier, had got free of the lead and bolted into Bluebell Wood.

She stood by the stile, shouting, 'Titch. Titch, good boy. Come here.'

But the dog would not obey. Pauline considered what her husband would say if she went home with nothing but the lead and the news that she had lost the little animal which they both worshipped.

'Titch!' she called again in desperation.

When the dog failed to return, she overcame her fear and climbed the stile. Although Joyce Regent's attack had happened in a wood on the other side of Bridgetown, the thought of her death did little to calm Pauline's nerves as she made her way haltingly through the darkening copse.

She had to swallow a scream when, without warning, an owl took off from the branch of an oak tree, its large beating wings black against the late evening sky. She breathed shallowly and could feel her heart pounding against her rib-cage as she stood still, listening for any sound that might betray the dog.

And it was then that she heard something — the low whimpering sound of her pet.

'Titch?' she called, hurrying towards the noise. 'Titch, what's wrong?'

She found him within a large circle of bushes. Branches lashed at her face as she fought her way through the trees to get to him.

The dog was digging furiously, earth flying out from under his paws. He was panting strangely, his tiny body trembling.

Relief flowed through Pauline. 'You naughty boy,' she scolded tenderly, as she clipped the lead to his collar. But the dog was reluctant to leave the spot. He continued to paw at the ground.

'Walk,' Pauline commanded. 'Walk, Titch.'

All attempts to drag the dog away proved futile, and in the end she was forced to scoop the writhing body up in her arms. He struggled within her grasp, and let out piercing yelps, but Pauline held him tightly and carried him back towards the stile.

* * *

Martin Dutton had taken the call and was now hesitating before passing it on to central control for fear of the barracking it would receive.

'I can't just leave the woman standing in the wood,' he muttered irritably to himself.

He picked up the telephone in front reception and punched out the digits.

'Central control.' It was PC Russell Green, the station wag. Dutton's heart sank.

'Russ, it's Martin. I've just had a funny one.'

'Really, Sarge? And you need to talk to somebody about it, is that it?'

'Very funny, Russ. No, I've just had a woman on the phone complaining that her dog keeps digging holes in Bluebell Wood.'

PC Green tut-tutted. 'Whatever next?' he said. 'What does she want us to do, arrest it or just give it a caution?'

'When you're ready to stop acting like a prat, Russ, I'll carry on.'

'Sorry, Sarge, but I don't see the problem.'

'The woman's certain there's something buried there.'

'A bone?' Green suggested with a snigger. But when he heard Dutton's testy sigh, he went on quickly, 'I'll get a mobile out there if I can find one. Is the woman still on the scene?'

'Yes. It's a Mrs Talbot.'

* * *

Holly whistled loudly as she walked along the corridor. Her mood was light and her eyes sparkled.

She opened the door to CID to find Josh sitting at the VDU, but Ashworth was not at his desk.

'Hello, lover,' she said brightly, running her fingers across Josh's neck as she passed. 'That hair's getting a bit long. Smarten it up.'

'Malc's got there, then,' he said, without taking his eyes off the computer screen.

'I don't know what you mean.' She began sorting through papers on her desk and then stopped and looked at him. 'Have I ever told you how much you irritate me, Abraham?'

'Frequently.'

She sat down and was suddenly serious. 'Josh, you won't mention this to the guv'nor, will you?'

'What, about Malc, you mean? Why should I?' Then he turned to her, frowning in disbelief. 'You're not making a play for Ashworth, as well? Oh, Holly, you wouldn't dare.'

She blushed. 'Don't be ridiculous. No, I just don't want him to know, that's all. He'll think I have sex with every man I come into contact with.'

'You do,' Josh said, turning back to the screen so she wouldn't see his mischievous grin.

'I'll have you know, there're a lot of conditions a man has to meet before he gets into my bed.'

'He has to be alive for a start,' Josh quipped.

'Or at least still warm.' Holly laughed, rapping both hands on the desk top.

When Josh turned again to look at her, his face was straight, all humour gone. 'I do worry about you.'

She got up and walked to him. 'Yes, I know,' she said warmly, 'and I love you to death for it. But this is my life, right?'

'I know, but—'

'But nothing. Listen, I've been there, Josh, everlasting love and all that. When Jason died, I didn't think I'd ever come through it, but I have. And now I don't want any emotional involvement with anybody, because if it happened again, I don't know what I'd do.'

Josh inhaled deeply and made a face. 'Sorry, I can ruin a day, can't I?'

'Go on,' she said, giving his shoulder a playful push. 'You'd make somebody a wonderful mother.'

Josh was remonstrating cheerfully when Ashworth came in, his body language severe. 'Well, I'm glad somebody's happy,' he said, scowling at the glass wall and scratching at his beard.

Holly said chirpily, 'I was with Malc last night . . . and something came up.' Josh sniggered, and Holly aimed a light kick at his ankle. 'He's offered to stay a couple of weeks and poke around a bit on the Regent case. He can go places Newton wouldn't let us go.'

After Ashworth considered the implications of this, he brightened and said, 'Good girl,' then lowered himself into his chair. 'Now all we need to decide is where we want him to poke.'

Josh started tittering again, and Holly had to bite her lip to crush a giggle.

Ashworth sat there looking baffled. 'Whatever's the matter with you two?'

* * *

Once again the spade hit the hard earth. The hole was now a foot deep but still the soil was rock solid. Stones jangled against the metal shovel as PC Tony York tossed more dirt on to the pile behind him.

'Bloody shit job,' he muttered. 'Why do I always get the bloody shitty jobs?'

He pushed the spade in again, a little to the left, but this time it didn't feel quite right; the soil was too soft, too loose, as if it had been disturbed recently.

With his inquisitiveness aroused, PC York threw the spade to one side and bent down, burrowing at the hole with his gloved hands. Before long, his fingers made contact with a smooth surface. He pulled off the gloves and dug furiously around the object until he could see it was a box made from thick cardboard.

The flap at the top of the box was open. Lifting it gingerly, he peered inside. Immediately all colour drained from his face, and he fell back on his haunches, muttering a curse.

'Over here,' he called to his colleague, who was talking to Pauline Talbot at the stile. 'And radio the station for the police doctor.'

* * *

The moment Mary Newton saw her son coming along the drive, she knew something was terribly wrong. His knees were hanging out of his soiled blue jeans, and the black T-shirt which was not his own was crumpled and tattered.

The college had of course informed them that Jamie was not attending classes, which had brought loud roars of disapproval from her husband. But she had taken the news calmly, believing her son was sensible enough to embark on his own future course, which did not include computer programming. But one look at him proved she was wrong; the course he had chosen was one of self-destruction.

She did however possess far more understanding than her husband and knew that one wrong move now would mean they could lose the boy for ever. He would simply slip away unless she fought tooth and nail to maintain that tenuous link.

She heard his key turn in the lock and steeled herself for their meeting. 'Stay calm,' she whispered resolutely. 'Just stay calm.'

'Jamie.' She smiled, as he slouched into the lounge. 'I thought you were going to phone me.'

'I've had things to do.' He barely looked at her before slumping into a chair, hooking one leg over the arm.

'I've been worried about you. So has your dad.'

Jamie sneered. 'Oh yes? I bet he has.'

She sat down and kept her tone cheerful as she said, 'If you come home, he might be willing to talk about you going to art school.'

'Get real, Mum.' He jumped up, full of restless energy, and prowled around the room. 'If I come home, he'll be there day and night listing what's wrong with me.'

'Sit down, love,' Mary coaxed.

'I don't want to sit down. He does my head in — don't you understand that?'

'I know, he does mine in as well,' she said with feeling. 'But he thinks he's doing things for the best.'

'No, he doesn't. He tramples on people. He's never happy until everybody's doing just what he wants. Nothing else matters to him.'

'He's a proud man,' Mary admitted quietly.

'Bullshit. He's just got to win. That's all he cares about.'

Mary was shocked by her son's language, saddened by his hostile attitude, but she resolved to keep her thoughts hidden.

'Let me get you a cup of tea,' she said, as though this was a perfectly normal day.

Jamie grudgingly said, 'OK.' His features were set in a moody, rebellious expression which Mary hoped would not become the norm.

She almost cried while she made the tea. This was the first time since Jamie was a toddler that he hadn't greeted her with a kiss. As she fought back her tears and set about pouring the tea, she could hear him moving about in the hall.

He was back in the lounge when she entered with the tray. As soon as the tea was finished, Jamie got to his feet without so much as a smile and announced he was leaving.

Mary accompanied him to the front door.

'I'll be in touch,' was all he said.

With a heavy heart, she watched him walk away. 'We've lost you, haven't we?' she murmured. 'You've gone.'

Mary closed the front door and noticed that her handbag was not where she had left it. She always placed it on the hall table, but now it was on the floor. She picked it up and looked inside tentatively, fearful of what she might find.

Fifty-five pounds was missing from her purse.

Mary wanted to cry again, tried to cry, but the tears wouldn't come; something inside had died.

She snapped the bag shut and hugged it to herself, the ache in her chest overwhelming. 'You only had to ask, Jamie. I'd have given you the money. I'd give you anything I own.'

* * *

'The body of a newborn baby?' Holly said, hoping she had misheard the officer on the other end of the telephone.

Ashworth looked up from the report he was studying, and the computer keys fell silent beneath Josh's fingers.

'Got you, police doctor and pathologist at the scene. OK, we'll be there as soon as we can.' She put the receiver down. 'Bluebell Wood, guv. You caught the rest.'

Ashworth was on his feet. 'Yes, let's get there.'

Bluebell Wood was losing its lush summer look, and though as yet it was hardly touched by autumn the leaves on the trees looked faded and sad. The bushes and shrubs stood dismal, and it seemed a fitting place for such a gruesome find.

Alex Ferguson was at the stile, engaged in animated conversation with the uniformed police officer whose job it was to keep inquiring members of the public at bay. As Ashworth's Sierra pulled up, the doctor moved towards it.

'Chief Inspector,' he said in that formal way of his as Ashworth climbed from the car.

He nodded an acknowledgement. 'You know DS Bedford, Doctor?'

Ferguson smiled briefly at Holly as she joined them.

'Not a nice one, Chief Inspector,' he ventured. 'Newborn baby. I suspect it was stillborn, but I'll know more about that after the post-mortem. Buried a couple of feet under the surface in a cardboard box. It was a male child, not wrapped in anything, not even washed. I think he was buried just after birth — just dumped in a box and buried. The body's been here a matter of days.'

'Why would anyone do that?' Ashworth wondered sadly. He had encountered many harrowing sights in his long career, but none affected him more than those involving defenceless children.

Ferguson said, 'My guess is, the mother's little more than a child herself. If the baby had been OK, it would probably have turned up on the steps of a hospital.' The doctor let out a scornful sigh. 'The amount we spend on education . . . They seem to think if they treat children as miniature adults, that's how they'll behave. Tell children that something's fun, teach them how to do it, and let curiosity do the rest.' He cast Ashworth a disenchanted look and strode away, shaking his head. 'I've made all the arrangements,' he called from his car.

'Not a happy man,' Holly remarked.

Ashworth grunted.

'Come back, guv, you're miles away.'

'Something's just fallen into place. Shall we walk through the wood?'

Holly looked puzzled as she watched him march towards the stile. 'I thought you'd never ask,' she muttered to herself.

The officer guarding the stile was afforded an ample view of Holly's shapely legs when she hitched up her skirt to climb over. And she was still smiling about his startled expression when she caught up with Ashworth. He passed the roped-off area where the baby's body had been found without a pause and strode deeper into the wood.

Oh God, Holly thought, looks like he's on a scent.

Ashworth stopped after a hundred yards and rounded on her. 'The aldermen group — cast your mind back.'

She remembered them but was unable to make any connection.

'When we first went to Mick Wright's house about the letters,' Ashworth prompted.

'No, sorry, guv, you've lost me.'

'Ronald Curtis was telling us how intelligent and educated he was . . .'

He searched for some sign of recognition on Holly's face but found none, so went on, 'And he told us how frightened he was of the witch's curse. I remember him saying his wife was expecting a baby and he was frightened to death there was going to be something wrong with it.'

Holly looked back the way they had come. 'And you think that was Curtis's baby?'

'It's possible — don't you think?'

She looked decidedly doubtful, and Ashworth went on, 'All right, I know it's a bit far-fetched, but I read in Joyce Regent's book that, over the centuries, families affected by the curse buried their newborn babies in an attempt to appease the Devil. Or what if the baby was stillborn? Curtis could have been so devastated that he killed Joyce out of revenge. Don't forget, the man has vanished.'

'He's left his office in Bridgetown, guv, that's hardly the same thing.'

'But in the circumstances, it's something we need to look into.'

'Yes, I suppose so. His firm of solicitors should be able to tell us where he's gone.'

'After all, Holly, you don't just up and go,' Ashworth insisted. 'Not when you're a solicitor.'

'He was probably in the middle of moving when we saw him,' Holly said, ever practical.

'Why didn't he mention it, then?'

'There was no need to.' She paused and looked at him suspiciously. 'Guv, you're hoping this'll open up the Regent case again, aren't you?'

'That I am,' Ashworth replied doggedly. 'As far as I'm concerned it was never closed. Our search of Wright's house produced nothing — no murder weapon or anything else that might have connected him with the crime. Forensic evidence was nil. The case against that man is circumstantial. If I can just keep it open . . .'

'Shall we get back to the nick and make a start?'

'Yes, come on, Holly, we're wasting time.'

CHAPTER 16

When they arrived back, Superintendent Newton, shoulders straight, hands clasped behind him, was pacing to and fro in reception.

Straight away, he pounced. 'Ashworth, this newborn baby business — what's happening about it?'

Ashworth bristled, and said with exaggerated politeness, 'Holly, would you excuse me? I believe the superintendent is requesting a word.'

Newton glared at the chief inspector disparagingly and ordered him to his office.

Ashworth felt a knot of anger tighten inside his chest as he followed the strutting figure. Newton did not falter, did not speak, until they were inside the office.

Once there, he turned furiously on Ashworth. 'In future whenever we are in the presence of lower-ranking officers, you will show me the respect my rank deserves. Do you understand me?'

'While you continue to treat me as if I make the tea around here, I find it very difficult to be polite to you,' Ashworth stated in an infuriatingly reasonable manner. 'If we took this to Ken Savage, I believe you'd have a stand-off. You can't—'

'Ken Savage. Ken Savage,' Newton mocked. 'Why are you always talking about going to him? Don't you feel able to sort this out on your own, without holding on to his coat-tails?'

Ashworth was stung, but he harnessed his temper.

'With respect, you're forever hiding behind your rank of superintendent, which makes sorting out this problem virtually impossible. Now, if you'd like to stop doing that, perhaps we could sort it out some other way. I'd be in complete agreement; in fact I'd welcome it.'

Newton's face showed surprise as he stared at Ashworth's half-raised fist. 'Are you suggesting what I think you're suggesting, Ashworth?'

'I believe I am . . . Newton.'

The superintendent looked as though he had been winded, and much of his bluster seeped away. 'Well, I wouldn't have expected anything else from you,' he huffed, rounding the desk to his chair.

He sat down and motioned for Ashworth to do the same. 'I have no intention of bandying words with you along those lines, Ashworth. Now, this newborn child — I want the girl found quickly. As much publicity as we can get. Let's make youngsters realize what happens when they behave irresponsibly.'

'I don't think the mother is a young girl,' Ashworth told him.

'Nonsense, they are always young girls in these circumstances.'

'Not always,' Ashworth countered.

He started to tell Newton about Ronald Curtis, but the superintendent immediately raised a hand. 'Hold on, hold on, Curtis is a solicitor. You can't go barging in asking questions on the sort of evidence you're presenting to me. Witches' curses, indeed. I know what you're trying to do, Ashworth. You're trying to keep the Regent case open, and I forbid it.'

'I'm looking for the parents of a newborn baby. Information in my possession leads me to believe that Ronald

Curtis could help me with my inquiries,' Ashworth said flatly. 'And I intend to pursue that line.'

'Watch my lips, Ashworth. I forbid it.'

'Then I'll go to Ken Savage.'

'Oh, here we go again,' Newton said, apparently indifferent. 'You just do that.'

'With this and several other things.'

Newton's eyes narrowed. 'Such as?'

'The twenty-four-hour guard I requested for Joyce Regent.'

Certain that he had covered himself fully regarding the matter, Newton gave a humourless laugh and said nothing.

'And the fact that you deliberately withdrew mobiles from the streets, knowing full well that the burglars and car thieves would have a field day.'

Newton smiled confidently. 'Look at the crime figures, Ashworth. They're falling every day.'

'That they are, but only because you left innocent citizens defenceless so they had to set up Neighbourhood Watch schemes to protect themselves.'

'But it worked. We need the public to get more involved.'

Ashworth leapt to his feet and struck the desk top with some force. 'That wasn't the right way to bring it about.'

'It worked,' Newton repeated slowly.

'You admit it, don't you?'

That confident smile came again. 'Within these four walls, yes, I admit it, but an inquiry would be a different matter.'

'You'd lie?'

'That's not quite how I'd put it. Let's say, I'd present my case in the best possible light.'

Newton rose to face the chief inspector, but regretted the move instantly: he was a few inches shorter than Ashworth and felt at a disadvantage. He remained standing, however, and said, 'You're like a bull in a china shop, and I will break you. Not because I'm your superintendent, but because I have far more intelligence.' He leant across the desk, his colour high, and said through clenched teeth, 'I will destroy you.'

There was a quiet edge of fury in Ashworth's voice when he responded. 'That you might, but I promise you one thing, you'll know you've been in a fight. By God, you will.' He turned smartly and strode from the office.

'Leave Ronald Curtis alone,' Newton shouted after him.

* * *

Although Ashworth was not aware of it, Holly was beginning to dominate at times. She possessed a strength which matched his own and, should the occasion arise, was not afraid to exercise it.

When Ashworth stormed into CID, she despatched Josh to the canteen for three cups of tea and sat studying him while he paced about the room, tugging at his beard.

'OK, guv, shall we kick the walls in, wreck the office, or just sit down and talk about it?'

With a heavy sigh, he sank into his chair, and in a gloomy voice told her of his interview with Newton.

'And are you going to Ken Savage?'

'That I am,' he assured her. 'But that's not what's worrying me. I want to get on with the Curtis investigation, and Newton's forbidden it.'

Holly chewed her lip and pondered. 'He's forbidden you,' she said, smiling slyly, 'but not me.'

Ashworth gave her a warning look. 'Now, Holly, none of us can meddle in this until Savage gives us the go-ahead, and he'll probably faff about for days.'

'I can,' she persisted, grabbing her shoulder bag.

'Holly—'

'Look, guv,' she said, leaning on his desk, 'you're too up-front. Just cover for me. I'll take Malc and find out where Curtis has gone and if there's a baby with him. It'll be nothing to do with the police.'

'And how will you go about it?' Ashworth asked warily.

'Just trust me. You did want us to work closely together — remember?'

Ashworth would have protested, but knew it would do little good. He sighed. 'All right, but be careful.'

'Careful's my middle name,' she said, heading towards the door. 'Didn't you know?'

In the corridor she almost bumped into Josh, who had three cups balanced precariously on a tray.

'What about your tea?' he asked.

'You drink it, lover. It'll give you an excuse to visit the loo with all those lovely hunky policemen.'

He smiled ruefully. 'Bitch.'

'Are you denying you enjoy that?'

'I'm just saying you're a bitch because you're up to something and I don't know what.'

'Top secret, Josh,' she told him, chuckling saucily.

'Holly, be careful—'

'I've just told the guv'nor that careful's my middle name.'

She set off down the corridor as Josh called, 'With your sex life it has to be.'

'Now who's being bitchy?' she retorted with a grin.

* * *

Deception was an easy cloak for Malcolm Headlands to wear.

Holly found him at the hotel, and he readily agreed to help. While he shaved in the bathroom, Holly perched on the lavatory seat and outlined the information she needed.

The electric razor buzzed quietly as it moved smoothly over his contorted face. 'Right, so the first thing we find out is where this Curtis has done a runner to.' He switched off the razor and looked over his reflection in the shaving mirror. 'What did he deal with? Criminal? Civil?'

'Both,' Holly replied, while he patted on aftershave gel.

Headlands moved to the bedroom, leaving behind a fresh masculine fragrance which Holly found arousing.

'So, if I ring the practice he used to belong to, we could find out something to our advantage, as they say.' He sat on the bed and flicked through the telephone directory. 'Ah, ah,' he mused, coming upon the number. He lifted the receiver.

'They won't give you a forwarding address,' Holly said, as she settled beside him.

'I've had a lot of success with office juniors,' he told her, with a wink.

'I bet you have.'

She could hear the telephone ringing, and then the click as the receiver was picked up. A sweet, young voice said, 'Johnson, Quickson and Percival. Julie speaking. How may I help you?'

To Holly's delight, Headlands adopted a perfectly convincing upper-crust elderly voice. 'Put me through to Curtis.'

'Oh, I'm sorry, sir, but I'm afraid Mr Curtis is no longer with this practice,' the girl told him, eager to appear efficient.

'No longer with the practice? What are you talking about?' He gave the girl no time to answer, and went on, 'I am Major Hildebrand. Curtis deals with all my estate work, for God's sake.'

'I'm sure Mr Curtis would have passed everything on to his successor,' she was quick to assure him.

'Passed it on?' Headlands spluttered, causing Holly to fall about, giggling silently. 'What do you mean, passed it on? You must be aware that I'm one of your practice's best clients.'

'Yes,' the girl said with a doubtful undertone.

'Just take down my name. Major Hildebrand. Have you done that?'

Holly looked on in amazement as the now flustered girl said, 'Yes.'

'Now give me Curtis's new address,' Headlands demanded. 'The blighter's going to get a piece of my mind.'

The girl paused momentarily, obviously in a quandary. 'I really am frightfully sorry, Major, but I can't divulge that information.'

'My girl, you are the first contact potential clients have with the practice,' Headlands told her gravely. 'And I would like to say I found you very helpful when I complain to the partners about Curtis.'

The girl's indecision was almost audible. Finally, she said, 'Mr Curtis has gone to live in Morton, Major.' They could hear papers rustling. 'At 22 Riverdale Walk.'

'Good.' Headlands dropped the receiver.

'You're a con-artist,' Holly said admiringly.

'You ain't seen nothing yet, kid. Now, Morton?' he questioned.

'It's a town about fifty miles away.'

'So why would the man suddenly up and move to Morton, with a pregnant wife in tow?'

'Are you coming round to the idea that Mick might be innocent?'

Headlands lit a cigarette, exhaled slowly, and watched the smoke drift towards the ceiling. 'I don't know,' he said, 'but every good journalist will tell you nothing is as it seems. Like you've said before, the case against Wright slips into place too easily.'

He stood up and grabbed his jacket, the cigarette clamped between his teeth. 'Right, let's go and dig up the dirt in Morton.'

* * *

Despite his rather frosty manner, Chief Constable Ken Savage was a pragmatist by nature, and knew he needed to bring the feud between Ashworth and Newton to an end without either party feeling they had lost face. Not an easy task; and one which was further complicated by his liking for Ashworth, and his firm belief that Newton was something of a toady.

He visited Bridgetown Police Station at Ashworth's urgent request and listened first to the chief inspector's complaints. From there he went on to interview the superintendent who gave a completely different version of events. By the end of it all, he was left with a weighty problem to solve and the start of a headache.

He was glad to be leaving the station. On his way out, Savage popped his head round the door of CID.

'Jim, walk with me down to reception.'

Ashworth readily fell in beside him and waited for the chief constable to offer his comments. They were half-way down the stairs before Savage spoke.

'I've listened to both sides of the argument, Jim, and I'm going to take what I've gleaned and mull it over.'

That did little to quell Ashworth's impatience. 'How long's it going to take?'

'Just as long as it does, Jim,' was Savage's curt reply. 'About the dead baby. I think it's highly improbable that it was Curtis's, but in view of your arguments I think we have a right to look into the man.'

Ashworth's face brightened, only to fall again when Savage added, 'But we'll have to tread carefully, so I want to think it over. I'll let you have my decision in the morning.'

They reached reception and seeing that it was empty Savage dug into his pocket for his cigarettes. 'You've checked with the registrar's office, I take it?'

'Of course. There hasn't been a birth registered in the name of Curtis.'

'Mmm.' Savage lit the cigarette and inhaled gratefully. 'I do hear what you're saying, Jim. This aldermen group sounds like a bunch of nutters, but if I give you the go-ahead on this, I want you to use an awful lot of discretion—'

'Don't I always?'

'No, quite the reverse,' Savage replied bluntly, as he viewed the tufts of hair on Ashworth's chin. 'If it turns out you're wrong and Curtis takes umbrage, we could look bloody silly talking about witches' curses.'

'Don't worry, Ken, I'll handle it with kid gloves,' Ashworth assured him.

'You'd better.' There was an awkward pause during which Savage smoked furiously. 'Jim, I don't suppose you could come a little bit Newton's way, could you?' He caught sight of Ashworth's hostile expression. 'No, I can see that's not an option.'

Ashworth held open the door and watched the chief constable strut towards his car. Half-way there, he turned. 'Oh, by the way, Jim . . .' He let out a wheezy chuckle. 'The beard suits you.'

CHAPTER 17

The drive to Morton took no time at all. Malcolm Headlands was good company, witty and charming, and his large Volvo effortlessly ate up the miles.

They had to stop in the town centre to ask directions, but finally found Riverdale Walk on the outskirts. It was a quiet, sedate road lined with upmarket properties, all of individual design. Number twenty-two turned out to be a sprawling bungalow of red brick with a blue slate roof.

'Curtis isn't hard up,' Headlands remarked, as they parked almost opposite its front gates. 'That looks like two-hundred-grand's-worth of building to me.'

'Yes,' Holly agreed. 'So, what do we do now?'

'We wait. We don't know if anybody's in yet.'

Fifteen minutes later a man emerged from the bungalow and opened the up-and-over garage doors.

Headlands lit a cigarette. 'Is that our man?'

'Yes, that's Curtis.' Holly sank down in the seat and stared at the floor of the car. 'I don't want him to see me, Malc. He could recognize me.'

'A Bentley, eh?' Headlands was impressed. 'No little wife holding a baby and seeing him off, though.'

They watched discreetly as the car moved off. At the end of the road its brake lights glowed red and it turned left.

'Well, that didn't tell us much,' Headlands muttered, drumming his fingers on the steering-wheel. He stubbed out the cigarette in the half-full ashtray and turned to Holly. 'Follow me, I've got an idea.'

'Where are we going?' she whispered, hurrying to keep up with him.

'The house next door, to ask a few questions.' He was already opening the front gate.

Holly was unsure. 'We've got to be careful, Malc. This is an undercover operation.'

'Have a little faith.'

He considered the large detached house with its Nottingham lace curtains at every window before pressing the doorbell.

Almost immediately the door opened to reveal a plain woman with mousy brown hair. She was dressed in an expensive tweed trouser suit.

'Yes?' Her speech was cultured.

'*Baby World*,' Headlands announced with a smile. He pulled out his notepad and pen.

'I beg your pardon?' the woman said.

'*Baby World*,' Headlands repeated confidently. Then, 'You don't know what I'm talking about, do you?'

'Quite frankly, I don't, and if you don't go away I shall call the police.'

'*Baby World* is a magazine,' Headlands explained. 'We recently ran a competition to find the country's cutest baby.' He stepped back to look at the house number. 'I'm sure the winner lived at this address.'

'I think I'm a little past having babies,' she said, huffing indignantly.

Headlands gave his most charming smile. 'Oh, come on now, plenty of women in their thirties have babies.'

The woman's eyes softened, and she allowed herself a giggle. 'I'll have you know I'm forty-one.'

And then some, Holly thought bitchily.

'Whatever it is you're doing, keep it up,' Headlands enthused, 'because believe me, it's working.'

'Why, thank you.' She took to toying with her hair and attempted to look bashful.

'Could it be next door?' Headlands suggested, pointing towards the bungalow.

'I don't think so.'

The woman moved out on to the step, keeping her eyes on the reporter. 'They've not been there long. The man's a professional, drives a Bentley. The woman's very smart, always coming and going, but I haven't seen a baby.'

'No tell-tale nappies on the washing line?' he prompted.

She shook her head.

Headlands laughed. 'A thousand pounds in prize money, and I can't give it away. Look, we're intruding on your time and I apologize, but it's been nice talking to you.'

The woman's eyes followed him along the drive and were still on him as they crossed to the car.

'I don't believe you,' Holly snorted. 'That woman was nearly taking her knickers off.'

'You know what they say about old fiddles . . .'

'Yes, there's many a good tune played on them.' She grinned and gave him a sideways glance. 'I shouldn't be associating with you.'

'Go on, you can't resist me, like the rest of the female population.'

'Maybe. So, what do we do now?' She struck her forehead with the palm of her hand and tutted. 'I must stop asking that, I'm supposed to be in charge.'

The banter continued until they were back in the car.

'I want to wait for Curtis to come back,' Headlands told her. 'Or at least until we see Mrs Curtis.'

Holly stared out at the bungalow. 'I'm only here to humour Ashworth. Do you think it's possible he's right?'

'If there's one thing I've learned through poking my nose into other people's lives over the years it's that just because something looks improbable, that doesn't stop it being true.' He reached for his cigarettes on the dashboard. 'Let's examine the possibilities — either Curtis has left his wife, in which case she's sitting in Bridgetown, or . . . Look, wouldn't it be easier to go to where Curtis used to work and ask if the baby's been born?'

Holly shook her head. 'It's not that easy. They'd want to know why we were asking. They're solicitors, remember. And what could we say? We want to know if it was stillborn and they buried it in Bluebell Wood? You can't go asking people questions without good reason, Malc.'

He was pensive for a while. 'There is another possibility. Perhaps Mrs Curtis is only a little bit pregnant — three months, say. Which is why I want to hang about, see if we can get a look at her.' He lit a cigarette.

'That thought had occurred to me,' Holly admitted.

'I'd better back up a bit. We're going to draw attention to ourselves parked here.' He started the engine. 'If Curtis comes back, or if Mrs Curtis leaves the house, we'll drive past.'

He pushed the gear lever into reverse and turned to look out of the back window.

'Put your seat-belt on,' Holly reminded him as she reached for her own.

'No need, is there? We're only backing up,' Headlands said, giving her a wink. 'And anyway, there's no fuzz about.'

* * *

Ashworth spent a good deal of the afternoon on the telephone. He was impatient to get started on the Curtis lead and rang the man's former practice, asking the girl to put him through to Mr Quickson.

'Hello, Jim, it's a long time since I've heard from you.'

'Ted, I wonder if I could talk to you in confidence.'

'Yes, of course.'

'It's about Ronald Curtis.'

'Ah, Curtis . . .' Quickson sounded as if he had just smelt something nasty. 'He's no longer with us. Right out of the blue he decided to start his own practice. Left us in a hell of a mess.'

'So he departed fairly hastily then.'

'Well . . .' Quickson hesitated. 'How can I put this? He wasn't a popular man. Far too ambitious. I wasn't surprised when he decided to start up on his own.'

Ashworth mulled this over. 'Did you know that his wife was pregnant?'

'I had no idea. The man was with us for six years, and he never got close to anyone in all that time. He's an aloof sort of chap, full of drive, and quite ruthless. Do you want me to ask around?'

'No, no,' Ashworth said quickly. 'I don't really want Curtis to know we're looking into him, Ted. It's all a bit delicate.'

Quickson chuckled. 'It must be if you're hesitating. Anyway, the offer's there. If you want me to find out anything, I will.'

'No, thanks very much, Ted, but I'm being hampered by station politics.'

Ashworth replaced the receiver and sat back in his chair. If it was left up to him, he would simply ask Curtis the questions, face to face, and take whatever flak resulted from that course of action. But that would only supply Newton with more ammunition to use against him.

'Newton, Newton, Newton.' He tapped his fingers impatiently on the blotter. 'Everything leads back to that man.'

His next job was to telephone around the local hotels and compile a list of all young men between the ages of sixteen and twenty who had stayed in the area during the last two weeks.

After a couple of hours jogging memories, he had assembled a lengthy catalogue of names; no descriptions, unfortunately, but three of the names were promising for they had all given London addresses.

If only he could trace Kevin Thornton.

A wave of depression swept over Ashworth as he realized he was in no position to do that. Superintendent Newton was now calling the shots, and there was no way Ashworth could look for the lad without reopening the Regent case.

'Damn, damn, damn,' he muttered harshly.

His telephone buzzed. He grabbed the receiver. 'Ashworth.'

'My God, Jim, that was a growl. Has someone upset you? It's Ted.'

'Sorry, Ted, I was lost in thought.'

'I've done some checking around. I know you said not to, but I've been very discreet, didn't mention your name, and it seems Curtis's wife was pregnant.'

'How many months, do you know?'

'Six months, at least, and I was also told that they were worried silly about that author, Joyce Regent, moving to Bridgetown. Our receptionist said his wife used to phone Curtis up to a dozen times a day. It seems they were frightened something might be wrong with the baby.'

'That much I know, but thanks anyway. Tell me, when did they leave Bridgetown?'

'A week ago.'

'Ted, I owe you a drink.' He returned the receiver to its cradle, murmuring gleefully, 'That's about when the baby was buried. A break at last.'

* * *

'There's Curtis' car,' Headlands exclaimed, 'and it looks as if his wife's with him.'

Holly glanced at the bungalow in time to see the Bentley turn right into the drive and stop in front of the garage. Curtis and a woman got out.

'Quick, Malc, they're going in.'

He started the car and slammed it into gear. As they cruised past the bungalow, Curtis was unlocking the front door and standing back to allow the woman to enter. She was tall, well-dressed, with long black hair. And she was extremely slim.

Headlands whistled softly. 'She is most definitely not pregnant.'

'No.' Holly craned her neck as she turned round to look back.

'Meal on the way home?' he suggested.

Holly glanced at her watch. 'No, I want to see the guv'nor before he goes off duty.'

* * *

Ashworth was late home that evening. Only by an hour, but it was enough to cause distant alarm bells to start jangling inside Sarah's head. Usually she could set her watch by his arrival. Added to which, he seemed very preoccupied throughout dinner, even failing to notice how dry the overcooked steak-and-kidney pie was.

'Is everything all right, dear?' she ventured after a while.

'Yes,' he grunted, as a forkful of soggy cabbage hovered at his mouth. 'Or rather, no.'

He told her about Curtis, bringing her up to date with the investigation, and she listened attentively; but all she really heard was the name, Holly, repeated over and over again.

Ashworth's expression was glum by the time he finished, and he toyed morosely with the remaining food on his plate.

While he was out exercising the dog, Sarah tackled the washing-up. She was being silly, she reasoned, scrubbing the plates with a vengeance. Holly was simply a colleague, someone her husband worked with. Just because she had transformed herself from a plain Jane into an attractive girl over the past year didn't alter the fact that she was young enough to be his daughter. But the niggling doubt remained.

Ashworth returned after thirty minutes, hoping that he had tired the dog sufficiently to make her sleep throughout the evening. It was a hope soon dashed, for as soon as Peanuts was off the lead, she bounded up the stairs and could be heard running from bedroom to bedroom.

'Oh dear, Sarah, sometimes I wish we'd had a canary instead,' Ashworth moaned, as he climbed the stairs.

At 9.45 p.m. the telephone rang out in the hall. Peanuts stood by the lounge door, barking frantically. Sarah glanced across at Ashworth who was staring at the television screen with blank eyes, his mind miles away from the flashing picture. She pushed herself up from the chair.

'Jim, it's Holly,' she called tartly.

She returned to the lounge and listened. The clink of his whisky glass as he set it down on the telephone table irritated her beyond measure, as did the sound of his spirited laughter.

After five minutes, he came back and stood before her, contemplating deeply. He seemed very preoccupied, and Sarah felt excluded, but she kept her voice bright as she said, 'Is there anything wrong, dear?'

'No, no problem,' Ashworth replied. 'It was just something she forgot to tell me earlier on.'

* * *

Jamie had finally become accustomed to the squalor in Craig's flat, his new-found freedom effectively neutralizing its stale smells. The comfortable, spotlessly clean home he had left behind was now no more than a memory. But should the memory pull him back at any time, the image of his father would always stop him from returning.

At last he had found somewhere he belonged, a place in which he could grow. To be part of the gang, to push forward on to ever more daring pursuits, had brought him acceptance and respect. Indeed, so willing was Jamie to take the initiative in their criminal activities that Craig was finding his position as leader threatened. He had taken to goading Jamie, daring him to commit more serious offences in the hope that he would refuse and lose face.

They sat around in the room filled with smoke which hung in a haze below the already heavily stained ceiling.

'I say we do a real job,' Craig said, as he sipped lager from a can.

'The pigs are all over town,' Carl countered. 'It ain't even safe to nick a car.'

'What do you say, Jamie?' Craig asked, his eyes daring the boy to say no.

'Depends what's on your mind.' He stretched out on the beanbag and surveyed the rest of the group. 'I don't know about anybody else, but I don't see nicking a bottle of wine from an empty off-licence as a real heavy deal.'

'Big man, eh?' Craig taunted. 'What would robbing a newsagent's do for you?'

'A newsagent's?' Jamie scoffed. 'Man, that's big time.'

The room was too dark for the others to see the flush this brought to Craig's face. 'The old bag's, in the High Street,' he said. 'They reckon she's got thousands stashed away upstairs. Won't trust the bank with her money.'

Jamie yawned. 'How do we get upstairs?'

'With a shooter,' Craig said quietly.

That remark brought the response he had hoped for; the rest of the group sat up, and a silence stole over them as they waited for Jamie's response.

'Where would we get one?' he heard himself asking.

Craig grinned. 'I'll get one. You in?'

Jamie drew deeply on his cigarette. 'Yeh, I'm in.'

CHAPTER 18

Ashworth felt positively uplifted as he travelled with Holly to Morton the next day. Ken Savage had finally given his permission for discreet inquiries to be made into the Curtis' and their baby.

The interior of the car was clammy and uncomfortable, even with the windows and sunroof open, but as he drove along deserted lanes, Ashworth glanced at the fields busy with harvesters and felt a cool confidence.

'Why do you reckon Newton's all the time visiting the Regent sisters?' Holly asked.

'Covering his own backside, no doubt. He knows damn well he should have offered Joyce police protection, and now he's trying to keep the girls sweet.'

It was that information, passed on by Headlands, who was still taking time out to observe the cottage, which Holly had relayed to Ashworth the previous evening.

'Is Sarah all right?' she asked, after a while.

'I think so. Why?' He slowed behind a tractor to make sure the road was clear, and then accelerated past.

'I don't know, she sounded a bit distant.'

'I didn't notice.' They were approaching the outskirts of the town. 'Right, give me directions.'

The Bentley was standing in the driveway. Ashworth gave it an approving look as they parked.

'Well, at least the man's in,' he commented, pressing the doorbell firmly.

Curtis's face wore a surprised frown when he opened the door to them. 'Chief Inspector, what are you doing here?'

'I wonder if we might have a word, sir.'

'Yes. Come in.' He motioned them into the hall. 'In there,' he said, pointing to a door on the left.

Ashworth heard sounds coming from a room at the rear which he guessed was the kitchen.

They entered the elegant lounge which overlooked a landscaped garden. A modern mahogany desk, almost hidden under a blanket of papers, seemed at odds with Curtis's expensive reproduction furniture.

'What's this about?' Curtis asked, carefully closing the lounge door.

'You've heard about Mick Wright?' Ashworth inquired.

Curtis looked perplexed. 'Yes, of course I have. Don't tell me you've come all this way to tell me that.'

'I just wondered if you'd be representing him.'

'Ashworth,' Curtis said with a great show of patience, 'I'm no longer with Johnson, Quickson and Percival, as you no doubt know.'

'Is your wife at home?' Ashworth cut in.

'What do you mean, is my wife at home? Look, what's going on here?' The man's eyes flitted from one to the other as he struggled to comprehend.

Then Holly felt herself reddening when recognition crept across his face. He pointed an accusing finger. 'You were with somebody yesterday, watching the bungalow, and today you turn up asking about my wife.'

Ashworth could see little point in continuing with the subterfuge. 'Mr Curtis,' he said, 'when we first met, you told me your wife was expecting a baby and that you were terrified something would happen to it because of the witch's curse . . .'

Curtis went white with shock, and Holly was certain Ashworth had struck a nerve. But then the man spoke. 'Hold on a minute — the body of a newborn baby turns up in Bridgetown, and you put two and two together.' Bristling with indignation, he crossed to the door and thrust it open, calling, 'Grace, could you come in here for a minute, please?'

It was a little while before the smartly dressed woman entered, an intrigued expression animating her attractive features. She was the same woman Holly had seen the day before.

'Grace, these people are police officers,' Curtis announced. 'And this is Grace Coles.' He paused. 'She's my partner in a practice we're setting up here in Morton. At present we're working from my home because our offices are not yet ready.'

'Ronald, what is this?' she said, staring at the detectives with open amusement.

'This, Grace, is police incompetence at its highest level.' Curtis swung round to cast a livid look at Ashworth. 'My wife is six months pregnant and is, at this moment, staying with her mother in Cornwall because she wanted to be as far away from Bridgetown as possible.' He crossed to his desk and picked up a pen. 'Now, Chief Inspector, because I'm a reasonable man, I'm going to give you the address so you can check it out.'

Ashworth's feeling of relief was shattered when Curtis went on, 'And then I'm going to report this matter to your commanding officer.' He passed Ashworth the slip of paper. 'I would like you to go now, please.'

'Mr Curtis, we are sorry,' Holly said.

'Leave it,' Ashworth ordered.

Outside, Holly said, 'That was a right mess I got you into, guv.'

'No, it was my idea,' he replied reasonably. 'It was a mess I got myself into. There's no need for you to shoulder the responsibility.' He marched to the car, pinching the bridge of his nose. 'This is going to make Newton's day.'

* * *

'I can't stand anymore of it,' Tanya screamed. 'I don't want him coming here anymore.'

'Shut up,' Katie spat.

'But when he asks me questions, I'm frightened in case I make a mistake.'

'Don't be silly, we've got away with it,' Katie said, grabbing the girl's shoulders and shaking her violently. 'They've got no idea. All we've got to do is keep quiet.'

'But I can't, I can't,' Tanya shouted, stamping her foot. 'It keeps going through my mind.'

'For God's sake, shut up.'

Suddenly, with terrific force, Katie smacked Tanya across the face, sending her reeling back on to the settee.

'Don't hit me, Katie,' she whimpered. 'Please, I can't bear that.'

'Just keep quiet then. Newton only comes here to cover himself. He doesn't know anything.'

The girl was snivelling, her eyes tightly shut. 'He makes me feel uncomfortable when he stares at me.' She looked up then, and her eyes grew large as Katie started towards her, hand held aloft. 'Oh no, Katie, no.'

'Just shut up . . . Wait a minute, I've got an idea.'

Tanya was cowering, hands covering her face. As the brutal tone left Katie's voice, she peered out between her fingers.

* * *

Superintendent Newton had been in the CID office for over fifteen minutes, much to Josh's discomfort. He paced the floor, hands clasped behind his back, muttering every so often as he glanced at his watch.

'How long does it take to get here from Morton?' he asked.

Josh sighed. 'About an hour, sir,' he said, keeping his eyes on the computer screen.

Newton was consulting his watch yet again when the door flew open and a subdued Ashworth entered with Holly.

A smug look enlivened his face. 'Ashworth,' he said, 'I've been waiting for you. Ronald Curtis has been on the phone, so I know the result of your inquiry.'

'That's good.' The chief inspector sounded anything but pleased as he removed his waxed jacket.

'Yes, and he's made a formal complaint about your behaviour.' Newton smirked. 'Which I've passed on to Ken Savage.'

Ashworth scratched at his beard as the superintendent made for the door.

'Carry on, then,' he said, making no attempt to disguise the satisfaction in his voice.

The door had hardly closed before Holly exclaimed, 'Balls, you pompous little prick.'

'My sentiments entirely,' Ashworth said.

* * *

'A chance to redress the balance, Jim, old son,' Martin Dutton murmured merrily to himself.

He grinned hugely as he listened to the commotion in a corridor to his right where a group of youngsters were being taken to interview rooms for cautioning.

Picking up the telephone receiver, he dialled eagerly.

* * *

'Sorry,' Headlands said, when Holly let him into her house. 'The Curtis baby theory wasn't that good, but I did make a mess of it.'

Holly smiled. 'It wasn't your fault.'

'So Ashworth's not going to eat me?'

'No, of course he isn't,' she said, pouring him a drink. 'He's a big pussycat really, but don't tell him I said so.'

He took the glass of Scotch. 'You look thoughtful.'

'Yes, I am,' she said. 'Ashworth was here earlier.'

'Was he, indeed?'

Headlands's raised eyebrows annoyed Holly; she was in no mood for his playful innuendoes, and she said sharply, 'He only came in for a few minutes. We're trying to work more closely together. Anyway, he was in a right old state. He's certain that Mick didn't kill Joyce Regent.'

'So?' Headlands shrugged as he took a drink.

'So, I think his judgement's being clouded by a dispute he's having with the new superintendent. Even if Mick confessed, I don't think he would believe him.'

'Look, Holly, I'm not used to playing the jealous lover, but I'm fed up with talking about your boss. OK?'

He left his glass on the drinks table and curled his arms around Holly's waist. 'Let's do something more interesting,' he whispered, gently nibbling her ear.

'Not tonight, Malc,' she said, pushing him away. 'I've really had a bitch of a day.'

* * *

Martin Dutton checked the time as Ashworth strode into reception. 'Jim, I'm due off duty soon,' he said, 'but this one's too good to miss.'

'How did you know where to find me?' Ashworth asked.

'When I rang your home, and Sarah said you weren't there, I put two and two together.'

'Right, where is he then?'

'Number two, and he's a nasty little piece of work.'

Ashworth took in a breath to prepare himself before entering the interview room. The constable inside the door was leaning against the wall, cleaning his fingernails, but he stood swiftly to attention when Ashworth appeared, and said a brisk, 'Sir,' to the chief inspector's nod. The young officer had a high regard for his pugnacious superior, and when Ashworth merely tilted his head towards the door, he left the room without question.

Jamie Newton was sitting at the table, exuding an air of bored indifference. He refused to look up as Ashworth approached.

'Jamie Newton?' Ashworth asked.

'Fuck off, you stupid old cunt.'

In two strides Ashworth was at the table. He leant across it, saying harshly, 'You speak to me like that again, son, and I'll clip your ear.'

'You wouldn't dare,' Jamie sneered, rising from his chair.

'Don't tempt me,' Ashworth threw back. 'Don't tempt me. Now sit down.'

Jamie was thrown by the severity of Ashworth's command and the harsh glint in his eyes, and he sank back into the seat. Ashworth pulled up a chair and watched closely as the boy lit a cigarette.

'We nicked a bottle of wine from an off-licence. Are you going to charge me with it?'

'You know better than that,' Ashworth said, his stare unwavering. 'You're here for a caution.'

'A caution?' Jamie sniggered and held out hands which rocked with an exaggerated tremble.

'Don't be silly, son, because if you continue, I'm going to lose my temper, and if I do, you'll wish you'd never been born.'

Jamie's brag and bluster was evaporating speedily. He had been led to believe that a caution was little more than a chance to laugh at the police, but this man was not playing that game. He was becoming increasingly ill at ease under Ashworth's penetrating gaze; but even so, with his remaining bravado, Jamie drew deeply on the cigarette and blew smoke into the chief inspector's face.

'I'd like to talk to you, son,' Ashworth said, narrowing his eyes against the smoke. 'But first you've got to stop being silly.' He reached forward, took the cigarette from the boy's fingers, and stubbed it out firmly. 'Now, I don't think you're like your friends. They're all going on to spend time in a detention centre. If that doesn't straighten them out, they'll drift into a life of petty crime. But I think you're a decent lad, Jamie, and talented, from what I hear.'

The boy was taken unawares by Ashworth's complimentary remark, and he said haltingly, 'Yes, but my dad wouldn't let me go to art school.'

'I'm sure that's part of the problem. And yet you can't blame others for all your troubles. These people you're going around with . . .'

'They're my mates.'

'They're not your mates. Half of you is rebelling against your father, and the other half's trying to find a place to belong.'

When Jamie lowered his eyes, Ashworth felt he was at last making headway, so he pressed on. 'You're falling over backwards to fit in with them. They wouldn't like you for what you really are, so you've become what they want you to be. What would be the alternative? They'd laugh at you, taunt you, give you a hard time. They'd try to beat you up, perhaps, and all because you're different. You're not the only one it's happened to.' He paused, and added softly, 'I've been there, son. I know what it feels like.'

Jamie's confused eyes searched Ashworth's face for a time, but then the barriers came down again. 'You're talking to me as if I'm a kid,' he muttered moodily, 'but I'm a man.'

'I don't want to hurt your pride, or destroy your ego, but you're not.'

'I'm eighteen,' Jamie countered.

'Years have got nothing to do with the state of adulthood, Jamie, any more than terrorizing people and stealing to look big in front of your so-called friends has.'

Ashworth sat easily in the chair, his arms folded, and studied the boy for a few minutes. Eventually, he said gently, 'Nobody's going to like you until you like yourself. If you continue to play this part, you're going to become that person. And you're worth a damn sight more than that, son.'

'It's not that easy,' Jamie said despondently.

'Nothing is. Look, stop taking the easy way out. Do yourself a favour and stop running away. Learn to stand on your own two feet. Take your own decisions. Be proud of yourself.'

He leant across and placed a fatherly hand on Jamie's shoulder. But the boy seemed to resent the move and his hostility resurfaced. His mouth was set in a pout as he said, 'Aren't you supposed to be cautioning me?'

'Yes, all right, I'll caution you. This time I can keep it under wraps, but if you ever end up in here again your father will have to know.'

'Oh, I get it,' Jamie snorted. 'It's the old boys act. Anything to stop him being embarrassed.'

Ashworth sighed heavily. 'If only you knew how wrong you are, son. If only you knew how tempted . . . Oh, go on, get out.'

Martin Dutton was still waiting eagerly in reception. 'Well, Jim, how did it go?'

Ashworth leant an elbow on the desk. 'I want a cover-up on this, Martin. Just say nobody connected the name because the address given was different.'

Disappointment clouded Dutton's face. 'Everybody was relying on this to take Newton down a peg or two.'

'Well, they'll have to think again, won't they?' Ashworth snapped.

The sergeant quickly held up his hands. 'All right, Jim, all right.'

'I'm sorry, Martin, but he's a nice lad, and I couldn't use him to get back at his father.'

'You've missed a golden opportunity, Jim.'

'Perhaps, but I'm not coming down to that man's level. If I can't beat him fair and square, I'd rather go under.'

He stomped off towards the door, and as Dutton watched him run down the steps, he muttered, 'You're a good bloke, Jim, but for once I wish you weren't, and I think you're going to wish the same before long.'

CHAPTER 19

Ashworth had quite a time to ponder over his dispute with the presumptuous superintendent. For over a week little happened in CID to exercise his forever active mind. The crime rate continued to fall drastically, and his beard was coming along well; but neither of those facts afforded him much pleasure.

However, on the eve of Mick Wright's second appearance before a magistrates court, Malcolm Headlands discovered something which would turn the investigation on its head.

He was in Holly's living room, sorting through a pile of photographs, when it suddenly hit him. In a state of great excitement, he rushed into the kitchen to consult with her. She glanced at the photographs and readily agreed that he might just be on to something. Headlands spread out the three photographs on the kitchen table and Holly looked them over again and again until her enthusiasm matched his own.

The idea seemed so logical that she felt compelled to telephone Ashworth immediately. It was 10 p.m., and the chief inspector was half-way down his second glass of malt so, although very interested in their findings, he deemed himself unable to drive because of the Scotch, and felt disinclined to invite them over due to the lateness of the hour. So a sober Holly collected him in her Micra and the three of them spent a good deal of time mulling over the photographs in her kitchen.

At first, Ashworth was sceptical as he sipped, with displeasure, Holly's cheap supermarket whisky while Headlands set out to convince him. They applied various likely scenarios with Ashworth, as ever, the dominant voice, certain that his interpretation of the facts was the correct one. On one thing they did agree: this was a very important and extremely damning piece of evidence.

Ashworth took no account of the time as he pondered over this intriguing piece in the puzzle, and so Sarah was left to watch the clock. She was in a foul mood, had been since Holly called to collect her husband. He was still arriving home late two or three times a week, he didn't talk about his work as much as he used to, and now he was going out at bedtime.

Sounds of a car pulling up brought her quickly to the lounge window. They were back, and that spring of doubt flowing in her mind was fed still further as she watched Ashworth smile warmly at Holly before getting out of the car. Moreover, she noted a definite look of contentment on his face as he sauntered towards the front door.

* * *

The officer ordered Mick Wright to sit as the doors of the prison van slammed shut behind him. He moved as if in a dream, his body and mind strangely numb.

Moments earlier, an application for bail had been refused, the magistrates ordering that he be detained in custody on the charge of murder. He could still see Edith's deathly white face as she watched from the public gallery, could still hear her heart-rending sobs of despair when they said goodbye in a gloomy cell below the court.

He rested his head against the side of the van and closed his eyes, praying fervently that the chemotherapy would not work and his death would soon put an end to their ordeal.

* * *

Ashworth bypassed Newton, partly to avoid another argument, but mostly because he could not stomach the man. Clutching a folder containing the photographs as if they were the winning ticket for the national lottery jackpot, he bounded up the steps of Bridgenorton Police Station and announced his arrival at reception.

Savage seemed less than pleased to see him. In fact, he almost scowled when Ashworth entered his office.

'This is a surprise, Jim.'

'And not a pleasant one, judging by your expression.' Ashworth glanced around the roomy office with its gleaming new furniture. 'Nice,' he said.

Savage reached for his cigarette packet. Already the perfume from lemon polish applied by the cleaners was doing battle with the cigarettes he had smoked.

'Sit,' the chief constable ordered tartly, indicating a comfortable chair in front of his desk. 'This isn't about Ronald Curtis, I hope.'

'No,' Ashworth said, settling in the chair.

'Good. That was a very embarrassing incident. I had to telephone Curtis and smooth him over. I think he's willing to leave it there.'

Ashworth was not particularly interested. He said, 'That's all right, then, but if Newton had left me to handle it in my own way, there wouldn't have been a problem.'

'You're an awkward old bugger, Jim,' Savage declared, before lighting his cigarette.

'That I am, but if I could have just gone and had a quiet word with the man, there would've been no need for all the subterfuge.'

Savage inhaled thoughtfully as he eyed the folder on Ashworth's lap with suspicion. 'I'll grant you there's an element of truth in what you say. So what's the point of this visit?'

'I want the Regent case reopened.'

'What?' he spluttered, almost choking on cigarette smoke. 'What possible grounds do we have for that?'

'Ken, I want you to look at some pictures.' Ashworth opened up the folder and extracted a ten-by-eight glossy photograph. 'Tanya Regent, taken in January of this year, in London.'

Savage took the photograph and studied the image of a pretty young girl in a tight black dress.

He looked up at Ashworth questioningly, and the chief inspector passed across a second photograph. 'Tanya again. Taken yesterday.'

Placing the photographs side by side, Savage saw at once subtle differences in the girl. In the recent one, she was more or less the same but a little tubbier, a fact emphasized by her tight blue jeans and figure-hugging pink top. 'The girl's obviously filling out,' the chief constable said.

'Number three.' Ashworth slid the photograph between the other two. 'Tanya, just after she arrived in Bridgetown.'

Savage's eyes widened, and he absently stubbed out his cigarette as he stared down at the pictures. This time, Tanya was frumpy, enveloped in ill-fitting jeans and an enormous T-shirt which nevertheless did little to hide the fact that she was carrying far more weight. 'Are you saying the girl was pregnant?'

Ashworth nodded. 'It's happening all the time, isn't it? Young girls giving birth without even their parents knowing they were pregnant.'

'Oh, I'm not arguing, Jim, I think you're right.'

Ashworth's relief was almost palpable. 'So I can reopen the case?'

'Now hold on,' Savage said cautiously. 'We haven't got enough for that. You think the baby in Bluebell Wood . . . ?' He pointed to the photographs.

'Well, it has to be,' Ashworth ventured.

Savage blew out his cheeks. 'And you think Kevin Thornton was the father?'

'Yes, I do. And when Joyce Regent found out about it, she was so enraged she kicked the lad out, and in retaliation for that, he murdered her.'

The chief constable was still doubtful. 'A lot of supposition there, Jim.'

'There's a lot of supposition in the case against Wright.'

Savage sat back and considered this. 'I disagree with you there, but I'll authorize an investigation into Tanya Regent concerning the baby. If you're right, and Thornton is the father, we start looking for him. But I don't want it all over the papers that we're looking for him in connection with a murder.'

Ashworth leant across and collected the photographs. 'Can I tell Newton this?'

'No, Jim,' Savage said emphatically. 'I'll give him a call.'

* * *

They were very aware of Newton's presence downstairs as they lingered nervously in the main bedroom of the cottage.

Tanya croaked, 'I told you they'd find out.'

'Just let me think,' Katie hissed.

Newton had arrived thirty minutes earlier with news that Ashworth would be calling to ask questions of Tanya involving the dead baby, which the pathologist had confirmed was stillborn.

Since then, they had been in a state of shock, but now Katie was beginning to recover. 'Right, I'll say you've lost your voice, which isn't far from the truth, and I'll do the talking.'

'But they know,' Tanya whispered hoarsely. 'And if they ask who the father was, and we tell them, they'll start looking—'

'We'll have to tell them. They'll want to know, and they'll keep on until they find out.'

'I know, but if we tell them—'

'Don't worry.' Katie slipped a protective arm around her shoulder. 'Leave everything to me. I'm going to tell them the truth.'

Downstairs, unable to stay still, Newton paced the lounge. His anger was reaching boiling-point. Ashworth had gone over his head with this Tanya Regent business, and he had received an embarrassing call from Savage ordering him not to impede the chief inspector's investigation.

He had felt impelled to drive over straight away with a warning. The news was badly received, especially by Katie, and they had stomped off upstairs without saying a word, leaving him feeling rather foolish.

He was dithering between hall and lounge, wondering what to do, when Sathan attacked him, sinking sharp claws into his leg. As Newton, surprised and in pain, knocked the cat away, its talons snagged the blue serge of his uniform trousers. And now he kept lifting his leg to fuss at the tear with his fingers.

A car pulled up, and he hurried to the window. Ashworth and Holly were leaving the Sierra. He saw them comment on the presence of his Audi as they made their way along the front path.

Newton went to answer the insistent knock. 'Ashworth,' he barked.

'Newton.'

The two men glared at each other in silence, and hostilities seemed imminent when Holly jumped in with, 'We're here to see Tanya Regent, sir.'

'I know that. Ken Savage rang me.' His eyes remained on Ashworth's face. 'I don't know what flight of fancy you're on now, but I don't want those girls upset. They've been through enough already.'

'This is getting ridiculous,' Ashworth huffed. 'You're now standing in the way of my investigation.'

Reluctantly, Newton stepped aside and allowed them to enter.

'Where is the girl?' Ashworth demanded.

'I won't have you barging in here, upsetting them,' the superintendent uttered in a low voice.

'Newton,' Ashworth warned, close to exploding.

'It's all right.' Katie's subdued voice drifted from the stairs. 'Let's go into the lounge.'

In the room, the atmosphere was electric as they waited for Tanya. She arrived presently, dressed in a pink bathrobe. Her expression was vacant, and only her startled eyes showed any emotion.

'Sit,' Katie said gently, pointing to the settee.

The girl slumped into the seat and sat with head bowed.

Katie said to Ashworth, 'You'll have to bear with Tanya, I'm afraid. She's lost her voice, what with the shock and everything. Now, the superintendent's told me all about this, and I've decided to tell you the truth.'

Ashworth perched on the arm of a chair to face them. Holly stayed at the door, digging into her shoulder bag for notepad and pen. Newton hovered behind the settee and stared at Ashworth with loathing.

'Which is?' he asked.

An oppressive silence followed.

Katie gave a sad smile and patted Tanya's arm. 'You want to know about the baby found in Bluebell Wood?'

Ashworth nodded grimly.

'It was Tanya's. When I found out she was pregnant, I worked out when the baby would be due. She started having pains, so I sent Joyce away to London to stay with her agent . . .' The floodgates were open and Katie spoke rapidly, apparently eager for the secret to be finally out in the open. 'I knew she'd stay there as long as I wanted because she'd be enjoying herself. I've been reading all I could find on delivering babies.'

'And you coped with bringing a baby into the world, all on your own?' Holly cut in with amazement. 'But your sister could have died.'

Katie stared at her. 'It's funny the things you can cope with when you have to. I gave Tanya something, so she was out of it. Anyway, when the baby didn't cry, I knew it was dead. I waited till the early hours and took it out and buried it.'

Ashworth frowned. 'What if the baby had been alive?'

'I would've taken it to a hospital and left it where it could be found.'

'Who was the father?' Ashworth asked.

Tanya started to sob quietly. 'Steady,' Katie soothed. 'It's nearly all over.'

Ashworth cleared his throat and waited.

'Kevin Thornton was the father,' Katie said at last, looking from Ashworth to Holly. 'And don't judge her. Sharing a house with somebody perpetually half naked with a boy in tow can have a bad effect on anybody.'

'I'm not judging you or your sister,' Ashworth said assuredly. 'I'm more interested in where I can find the boy.'

'I've no idea.' Katie said. 'I've already told you that.'

'Did your mother know about the baby?' Ashworth probed.

'No, and I doubt she'd have cared if she had.'

'She didn't find out about the baby and then tell Thornton to leave?' Ashworth persisted.

'No, she didn't. How many times do you need telling? She got fed up with Thornton, that's all.'

Ashworth leant forward. 'And he wasn't here the night before your mother was attacked?'

'No, I told you, no.'

'That's enough, Ashworth,' Newton ordered brusquely. 'You're distressing the girl.'

'I've no more questions,' Ashworth said, getting to his feet. 'I'm sure we can leave the superintendent to tie up the loose ends.'

Newton watched from the window as they climbed into the Sierra. That look of resolute arrogance on Ashworth's face filled him with annoyance.

'You do realize that your sister will have to go into hospital for post-natal care.'

He was still watching Ashworth, so did not see Katie's hand clamped across Tanya's mouth in an effort to stifle her protests.

'Yes, I know that. I'll go with her and stay the whole time she's there.'

'That's good.' When he turned, Tanya appeared calmer as she huddled in a corner of the settee.

Katie said, 'Go upstairs, Tanya, I want to talk to the superintendent.'

The girl rose passively and, with head downcast, she left the room.

The door clicked shut as Katie said, 'There's something else you ought to know.'

'Yes?' The question was curt; Newton had had enough surprises for one day.

'Tanya's on drugs — heroin, mostly. Kevin started her on it, and now she's really hooked.'

Newton felt he was falling deeper and deeper into a quagmire. 'They'll find out at the hospital,' he said shortly.

'I know, that's why I'm telling you now.'

'I doubt if anything will be done about it,' Newton said, his mind racing. 'She should be charged with possession, but in the circumstances . . .'

'Ashworth wouldn't let it go. He's got a down on us.'

'You can leave Ashworth to me.'

'I hope so.' Katie studied the superintendent for sometime. 'You'll have to stop him finding Kevin as well.'

This brought a sharp look from Newton. 'I beg your pardon?'

'Stop him finding Kevin. We know who the murderer is, and I don't want this all over the newspapers again. So, just see to it.'

'You can't order me about, young lady,' Newton blustered.

Katie's eyes narrowed. 'You should have agreed to Ashworth's request for a police guard, and you didn't. Now, I'm quite happy not to cause you any problems about that, but in return I expect some favours.'

Newton's mouth hung open. 'I don't believe I'm hearing this.'

'Well, you are. Look, I don't give a stuff about the murder, but I do care about Tanya.'

'If she's taking drugs, she needs treatment,' Newton responded coldly.

'I know that,' Katie conceded, 'but after everything she's been through, it's not the most important consideration, is it? Just one more problem could be enough to push her over the edge.'

The superintendent was filled with unease at the realization that he was deliberately failing to exercise his duty. 'Are there any more shocks?'

'Yes, but only one. I went to bed with Kevin a few times. He could be very persuasive, I can tell you.'

'I'm sure that's no business of mine,' Newton said. He was beginning to feel sullied by the overwhelming sordidness of this situation.

'But Tanya knows nothing about it. You see, she thinks she's in love with Kevin. He promised to marry her when she turns sixteen.' Katie smiled grimly. 'He'll say anything to get his way.'

'He sounds a charming piece of work,' Newton huffed.

'Yes, he is, but he does have a way with girls. Tanya still believes he's coming back when this is all over. If she finds out I've had sex with him, she'll be devastated. I'm all she's got left to cling to.'

Newton considered this. 'I can see your predicament, but he has had sexual relations with a minor which is an offence.'

'In this day and age?' Katie retorted scornfully. 'You mean to say you'd go all over the country looking for him, just for that?'

He most certainly would have done, and taken great pleasure in doing so, but he was in a corner, and said hesitantly, 'Well, no, I wouldn't . . .'

'But Ashworth would?'

He nodded gravely. 'Yes.'

'Why?'

'Because he thinks Thornton was involved in your mother's murder.'

'What? But that's ridiculous.'

'I know it is, but there's little I can do to persuade him otherwise. And anyway,' Newton continued angrily, 'Thornton has committed an offence, and as a police officer Ashworth is fully entitled to pursue him.'

'All right, but I don't want Tanya hassled about the drugs.'

'I'll guarantee that,' Newton said reluctantly.

'Good. We just want to be left in peace now, to salvage what's left of our lives.'

CHAPTER 20

Ashworth did not allow the grass to grow under his feet. The moment they arrived back at CID, he contacted the Metropolitan Police with a request to detain the three young men who had stayed in Bridgetown around the time of the murder.

Then, as always when he felt the hunt was really on, he went solo, and visited the hotels where the three had stayed.

One name, Scott Rivers, began to interest him more and more. The description coaxed out of the proprietor matched exactly that of Thornton. And it came to light that although he had booked into the Lancaster Hotel for a full week, he left suddenly on the day after Joyce Regent's attack. The proprietor was able to recall this because Rivers had omitted to settle his bill.

Ashworth felt certain that this boy was of vital importance to the investigation. After all, Kevin Thornton wouldn't use his real name, not with the newspapers looking for him. And the lad did leave Bridgetown in a hurry soon after the murder. For the first time since the start of this case, he believed he was finally getting somewhere.

So preoccupied was he with his thoughts that Ashworth was standing outside Mick Wright's cottage before he even realized. His knock was answered by Edith, dressed as ever in a dowdy pinafore dress.

She looked tired, and her face clearly showed the strain, but she smiled fondly when she saw him. 'Hello, Jim.'

He smiled back. 'Hello, Edith.'

'Come in,' she said. 'I'll make you a cup of tea.'

He followed her along to the kitchen and sat down while she filled the electric kettle. 'What's the news on Mick?'

'Much the same.' She plugged in the kettle and turned to him. 'The doctors say he's responding well to the chemotherapy. They say it could prolong his life no end. Though God knows what for.'

'Now, come on, don't say that.' Ashworth reached out and put a reassuring hand on her arm. 'I'm still working on the case, don't forget. I don't want to raise your hopes too much, but there's a new lead.'

Edith's watery eyes settled on his face. 'You don't know how much it means to me and Mick to know you think he's innocent. Sometimes it seems that's the only thing that's keeping him alive.' She sniffed loudly and turned away to busy herself with the tea.

Ashworth got up and leant against the sink. 'Have you spoken to him today?'

'Yes, I ring him about three or four times every day. The screws — that's what Mick calls them,' she said with a smile, 'well, they're ever so good to him. Let him have as many calls as he likes, they do.'

'My offer to take you to see him still stands, you know,' Ashworth said, as he watched her pour the tea.

'No.' She shook her head and passed him a mug. 'He says he'd rather I didn't go, not to the prison. His hair's falling out — did you know?'

'That must be the chemotherapy,' Ashworth told her gently.

'Must be. But isn't it odd? What with everything else going on, his hair's the thing that's worrying him the most.'

Ashworth stayed for another hour, and Edith was quite cheerful by the time he took his leave.

* * *

Craig wandered the dirty back streets of Bridgenorton. He had, like Jamie, dropped out of college and now, without a positive outlet for his energies, his mind dwelt more and more on his resentment of the boy.

It could no longer be denied that the superintendent's son had slowly but surely taken over his position as leader of the gang, a fact brought home to Craig quite strongly the previous night when he'd had to force Sharon to have sex. And yet the girls were still freely available for Jamie.

Craig combed the amusement arcades and public houses where a supply of drugs could always be found, all the while asking the pushers if they could provide him with a handgun. Most shied away, but an enormous black youth selling crack-cocaine in a dingy pub gave him an address. Elated, Craig made his way there.

The shooter would redress the balance. When the others saw that Jamie hadn't the bottle to use it, but that he had, then he would quickly regain their respect.

He pulled up his collar against the chill of the night and continued along the street, allowing his jealousy of Jamie to fester in his mind.

* * *

At 9.30 p.m. the telephone in Ashworth's hall rang out shrilly. In the lounge, Sarah got up and with one eye still on the television screen made her way to the door, stepping gingerly to avoid tripping over Peanuts who was barking frantically at her heels.

'It's the station, Jim.'

Ashworth picked up his glass of malt and hurried to the telephone. 'Ashworth,' he said.

'Hello, Jim, it's Martin Dutton. I just thought I'd let you know the Met have picked up Scott Rivers. They say he's got no previous as far as they know, but these kids are always changing their names so they can't be a hundred per cent certain. They're delivering him to us in the morning.'

'That's good news, Martin. Thanks for letting me know.' He replaced the receiver and stood cradling his Scotch. Then, after a brief hesitation, he picked it up again and dialled.

Through the open doorway of the lounge, Sarah watched him punch out the digits.

* * *

The bed creaked beneath Headlands and Holly.

She was on top, and so fervent were their endeavours that the discarded quilt lay in a crumpled heap on the floor quite a way from the bed.

Holly sucked in her bottom lip, and her breathing became rapid as she quickened her movements. Headlands groaned and the bed creaked again.

Then the telephone rang.

'Shit,' Holly exclaimed, glaring at it with hatred. 'Double shit.'

'Leave it,' Headlands urged.

'No, it could be important.' She picked up the receiver, and breathlessly said, 'Hello?'

'Hello, Holly, are you all right?' There was concern in Ashworth's voice.

'Yes, guv.' She swallowed hard and smiled down at Headlands. 'You've caught me working out. I'll get my breath back in a minute.'

While Ashworth relayed the news concerning Scott Rivers, Holly gulped in air. Headlands was running his finger down her perspiration-covered stomach, causing her to wriggle about on top of him.

'That's interesting, guv,' she said, pushing away the finger. 'Malc? No, he's not here. He's deeply into something at the moment.' She had to stop and stifle a giggle. 'But I'll tell him as soon as he comes.' Or just afterwards, she thought. 'OK, guv, I'll see you in the morning.' She replaced the receiver.

'What's he want?' Headlands murmured.

'Can't it wait?' She started to move again.

Headlands let out a moan. 'A few minutes, I suppose.'

'A few minutes?' she breathed in his ear. 'You'd better be joking, lover boy.'

* * *

Scott Rivers fitted exactly the image of Kevin Thornton in Ashworth's mind. The chief inspector was standing with Holly and Headlands, and as a uniformed officer led the boy past them *en route* to the interview room, Ashworth had an opportunity to study him.

The youth was tall and slim, his light-coloured hair tied back in a pony-tail. There was a look of open animosity on his face as he slouched along, fingers tucked into the pockets of his tight jeans. Ashworth glanced at his trainers, and although they were very bulky, he guessed they could easily be size sevens.

'Yes, that could well be Thornton,' Headlands observed. 'And I'm pretty sure he was the one at the cottage just before Joyce was murdered.'

Ashworth said, 'Good, that gives us something to go on.'

Their steps sounded as they approached the interview room.

'Can I take another look at him?' the reporter asked. 'This is not something I can swear to. I did only see the back of his head.'

'By all means. That could be useful. And those photographs of yours could be a way of identification. It's funny,' Ashworth mused, 'I really couldn't tell if that lad was a girl or a boy.'

'It's easy to tell the difference, guv,' Holly cut in chirpily. 'Boys have got little—'

'Yes, all right, Holly,' Ashworth chuckled, 'but in my day, men were men. I believe it's got something to do with the way they grow our food nowadays.'

The door to the interview room was ajar and they could see Rivers slouched at the table, picking at a piece of Formica which had come adrift from its surface. He looked up and scrutinized them, his eyes flitting from face to face.

'That's the boy,' Headlands whispered. 'I'm sure of it.'

'Right, Holly, let's talk to him.' Ashworth strode into the room.

'Later, please, and lots of it,' Holly whispered to the reporter, as she closed the door on his laughing face.

The uniformed constable fell back to the door and watched as Ashworth came to a halt in front of the table. Holly straight away activated the tape recorder, intoning the necessary details. And then there was silence.

After a matter of seconds, the boy looked up into Ashworth's querulous face and gave an impertinent grin.

'Mr Rivers? Scott Rivers, is it?'

'Yeh. What's it to you?' There was a cockney twang to his speech.

'Funny name, that. It reminds me of something you'd see on the credits of a film.'

Rivers shrugged. 'It's my name.'

'Have you ever called yourself anything else?' Ashworth asked quickly.

'No. Why should I?' The reply was forthright, but Rivers appeared to be uncomfortable as he squirmed in his chair.

'I'm asking the questions, son.' He sat down opposite the boy. 'Why don't you drink your tea, it's getting cold.'

'Don't want it,' he pouted, pushing the cup to one side.

'All right, let's try something else,' Ashworth said quietly. 'Did you know Joyce Regent?'

'Regent? Joyce Regent?' The boy stared into the middle distance, made a show of struggling to remember. 'No, never heard of her.'

'Have you ever been to Witch's Cottage?'

Rivers shook his head. 'No. Don't even know where the place is.'

'But you were in Bridgetown a few days ago. You stayed at the Lancaster Hotel.'

The boy averted his eyes. 'Yeh,' he admitted with reluctance.

'So what were you doing here?'

'Nothing.'

'Nothing? That does sound odd.' Ashworth considered the boy's resentful expression. 'Look, son, I want to help you. I want to stop you getting yourself into a mess. Now, I've got a witness who can place you at Witch's Cottage the day before Joyce Regent was murdered.'

Rivers shifted his position in the chair, and alarm showed in his eyes as he gazed about the room, refusing to look directly into the chief inspector's face.

'I'm saying someone saw you there,' Ashworth went on firmly.

Rivers chewed nervously on his lower lip, then blurted, 'All right, I was there. So what? I met Joyce in London, gave her a good time, so she invited me back here. She made me stay in the hotel because of some trouble she was having.'

Ashworth leant across the table. 'Was there anybody else at the cottage?'

'Joyce said her daughters were there. I didn't see 'em, but I heard 'em about.'

'And you were in Bridgetown when the woman was murdered.'

'Leave it out,' Rivers came back. 'I didn't have nothing to do with no murder. When I left her that day, I went back to the hotel, 'cause after a night with that woman, I was knackered.'

'So you can't help us with that?' Ashworth asked, drumming his fingers on the table.

'Look, when I read in the paper that she was dead, I panicked and left, but I didn't have nothing to do with toppin' her. I was only in this dump to give her one.'

'Very eloquently put,' Ashworth observed wryly.

'You can't pin that on me,' the youth protested. 'Anyway, I thought you'd got somebody for it.'

'Yes,' Ashworth said, 'but let's try another tack.' He paused, still drumming his fingers. 'Have you ever called yourself Kevin Thornton?'

A haunted look crept into the boy's eyes, and a little of his colour seeped away. 'What you on about now? I've told you who I am.' He shot the chief inspector a vehement look and started to leave the chair.

Ashworth stood up and placed a restraining hand on the boy's shoulder. 'Sit down, son, and keep calm.' Such was his size and authority that the youth slumped back immediately.

'I ain't Kevin Thornton,' he said meekly.

'That's better.' Ashworth stared into the pale face as he resumed his seat. 'Now, say I could get someone to identify you as Thornton?'

'Who might that be?' the boy questioned warily.

In order to heighten the tension, Ashworth did not respond immediately, and in the silence that followed he could hear his watch ticking. Presently, he said, 'One of Joyce Regent's daughters.'

The corners of the youth's mouth twitched, and he visibly relaxed. 'I'd say do it, then.'

'All right, that'll be all for the moment.' Ashworth got to his feet. 'Do you want some more tea, or anything to eat?'

Holly was talking into the tape recorder, terminating the interview as the boy shook his head.

'You can't keep me here, you know.'

'I can.' He looked at Holly and nodded towards the door.

'You've got no right,' Rivers said indignantly.

'I've got every right,' Ashworth responded. 'Now, you just keep quiet.'

In the corridor, Holly turned to him. 'Did you see his face when you asked if he was Kevin Thornton? He went as white as a sheet.'

Ashworth nodded with some satisfaction. 'He's our boy. Now all we've got to do is prove it.'

'He didn't seem very bothered about the Regent girls seeing him, though.'

'I know, and that's a problem.' He scratched his beard. 'We know he was very close to Tanya, and I firmly believe he was going to bed with the other girl as well, so they're not going to give him away.'

'It won't be much use to us, then.'

'Probably not,' Ashworth agreed, 'but we can watch their reactions to each other. And there is something else we can do. There's the woman who found Joyce Regent — we could set up an identity parade.'

'OK. I'll see to it.' She frowned thoughtfully. 'Guv, what do you think happened?'

He pursed his lips. 'I think Katie Regent and Thornton are in it together. Money's a powerful motive, Holly. She could inherit Joyce's fortune, pay Thornton off, and Mick Wright takes the blame. Very neat.'

The swing doors opened at the far end of the corridor, and Martin Dutton strode towards them.

Holly said, 'One thing baffles me, guv — why did the girl need Thornton? She could have killed Joyce without him.'

'Think of the woman's injuries,' Ashworth advised. 'They were fairly horrific. I don't think a slip of a girl would have the power to inflict them.' He pointed towards the door of the interview room. 'That lad's slim, but well-muscled. And there's no doubt in my mind that the assailant was male.'

Dutton stopped beside them. 'Jim, Newton's asking for you.'

'Not now, Martin,' Ashworth snapped.

'Do you think that's wise?' the sergeant asked, after a diplomatic cough.

'Very.'

'Whatever you say, Jim.'

* * *

The prison holding Mick Wright was set in remote countryside half-way between Bridgetown and Bridgenorton. It had been chosen because of its excellent medical facilities, which were necessary for the proper treatment of his illness. But although it was an open prison, security around him was tight, a prison guard never very far away.

Wright sat on his bed in the hospital wing and studied the wall of the small cubicle. This was how he spent most of his day. He was now completely bald and had taken to wearing a woollen hat to conceal his pink and shiny pate.

Warden Ian Pettit popped his head round the door. 'Phone call for you, Mick.'

He pushed himself off the bed, adjusted his hat, and joined the warden, the two men contrasting widely as they walked through the ward, Pettit, dark-haired, tall and strong with an upright stance, and Wright, painfully thin, now stooped and walking with a shuffle.

'Look, Mick, when you've spoken to your missus, why don't we go into the television room? Or I could take you for a walk around the grounds.'

Wright appeared uninterested as they pushed through the doors into a corridor. 'I'll see,' he muttered.

They stopped by the pay-phone. 'I'll wait along the corridor,' Pettit told him. 'Give you a little bit of privacy.'

Wright picked up the receiver and shrugged. 'All right,' he said. 'But I'm hardly likely to do a Ronnie Biggs, am I?'

* * *

A protesting Katie was dragged by Holly from the side of Tanya's hospital bed and ushered into the interview room where Ashworth waited with the youth they now believed to be Kevin Thornton. With a brisk shake of the head, Katie denied ever having seen the boy before, and demanded to be taken back to Tanya.

They drove to the hospital in silence; and although Holly found the teenager sullen, rude and impossible to like, she had to admit to herself that this quite obvious devotion to Tanya was rather touching.

While Holly was out, Ashworth organized the identity parade. Josh joined forces with the uniformed division, and soon found seven youths roughly the same height and build as the lad they now openly called Thornton. With little persuasion, they all agreed to take part.

Mrs Bagshaw was contacted and, gushing down the telephone with excitement, readily consented to go along to the station. She was there in no time, dressed in a blue outfit which looked as if the price tag had only just been removed.

Ashworth was waiting with Josh in reception when she arrived. 'Mrs Bagshaw,' he said, holding open the door. 'Thanks for coming.'

'It's no trouble at all.' She glanced around, fully enjoying her moment of notoriety. 'What happens now?' she asked eagerly.

'The whole procedure is quite straightforward,' Ashworth assured her. 'The identity parade's in the yard at the back of the station.'

Ashworth shepherded her along the corridor as he said, 'This is DC Abraham.'

She smiled broadly at Josh.

'It's all very simple,' he continued. 'The line-up is in the yard, and you'll view it from a large window. Just to be on the safe side, we've instructed a number of our female officers to dress in plain clothes, and they'll be in there with you. So if the suspect is identified, he won't know by whom.'

'Yes, I understand all that.'

Ashworth opened the door to the room and ushered Mrs Bagshaw in. Four WPCs were already in there. Through the window eight young men could be seen, standing in a line. The sight seemed to draw Mrs Bagshaw like a magnet. She stood in front of the window, studying them closely.

'Take your time,' Ashworth said softly. 'There's no hurry. If you recognize him, don't point — simply tell us where he's standing.'

The minutes ticked away, and in the silence Ashworth was aware of his own breathing. Someone behind him shuffled their feet.

'Recognize anybody, Mrs Bagshaw' Josh coaxed.

The woman gave an imperceptible nod. 'Yes that's him — third in from the right.'

Ashworth's head came round so fast that his neck clicked painfully, and he frowned in discomfort as he rubbed away at it.

CHAPTER 21

The gun was an ancient revolver. But to Craig, it was the most beautiful thing he had ever seen. He gently ran his fingers over it, thrilling at the feel of cold metal.

He went about the dirty flat, striking James Bond poses, and shouting, 'Bang,' as he pulled the trigger. Every so often he would go to the kitchen table and stare down at the box of bullets.

'Right, Jamie,' he said, 'tonight we'll see how much bottle you've got.'

* * *

Ashworth marched into the CID office and slumped into his chair, annoyance showing in his every movement. Josh was in much the same mood as he followed behind.

'Any joy, guv?' Holly asked from behind her desk.

'Oh yes, an abundance of it,' Ashworth replied sharply. 'Mrs Bagshaw managed to pick somebody out.'

'Thornton?' she asked excitedly.

'No,' Ashworth growled. 'A lad who works in the butchery department at Tesco, and I've known him all his life. I don't suppose you got the Regent girl to change her mind about not knowing him?' he asked with little hope.

'Sorry, guv, she didn't say a word all the way back to the hospital.'

Ashworth sighed deeply. 'Well, we can't hold him any longer, and when we let him go, he's just going to vanish.'

Holly hesitated briefly, then said, 'I could get Malc to keep tabs on him.'

Ashworth looked up quickly. 'Would he do that?'

'Yes, I've already sounded him out.' She pointed to the telephone.

'Good girl,' he enthused. 'If we keep track of that lad, I feel he'll slip up.'

'Can you hold him for a couple of hours while I go and tell Malc?' Holly asked, making a grab for her shoulder bag.

'Surely.'

She headed for the door, beaming broadly.

Ashworth seemed baffled as he watched her go. 'If she's already cleared it with Headlands, why does she need to go and tell him?'

The reason was plainly obvious to Josh: she wasn't going to see him for a few days and would want to make up for lost time.

'Josh?' Ashworth prompted.

'I don't know, guv,' he said, reaching forward to switch on the computer. 'Who can work Holly out?'

* * *

It was becoming evident to Superintendent Newton that Ashworth was deliberately ignoring him. He had been waiting for three hours now, and that band of anger across his chest was getting tighter and tighter.

Finally, he picked up the telephone and asked Martin Dutton to get Ashworth to his office immediately. A further fifteen minutes elapsed before the chief inspector appeared, by which time Newton was furious.

But he kept his feelings covered and smiled pleasantly. 'Chief Inspector,' he said, 'take a seat.'

A suspicious Ashworth complied with the request and sat to face Newton across the desk.

The superintendent beamed. 'We haven't got off to a very good start, have we?'

Ashworth was tempted to ask the man if he was feeling all right but instead, he said, 'I think, by any standard, that's an understatement.'

'Well, I'd like to go some way towards redressing the balance.'

Ashworth's eyebrows rose.

'Now, that Thornton boy you're chasing,' he continued cheerfully. 'How's that progressing? Oh, before you answer — would you like a cup of tea?'

'No, thank you.'

Ashworth's sour expression indicated that he was finding this nice side of Newton even more difficult to stomach than the unpleasant one. With little enthusiasm he told his superior of the events which forced them to release the boy they believed to be Kevin Thornton.

Newton listened with his elbows on the desk, fingertips pressed together. 'So,' he said when Ashworth had finished, 'it really came to nothing.'

'Yes.'

Newton was pleased.

'But I'm continuing with the inquiry,' Ashworth told him.

'In the current situation, do you think that's wise?' He saw that the chief inspector was about to argue, and added quickly, 'I'm going to take you into my confidence, because I think it's important that we work closely on this one.'

Ashworth waited with an air of expectancy.

'Would you agree that the Regent girls have had a very harrowing time?'

'Yes, but I also think Katie Regent had something to do with her mother's death.'

'I disagree,' Newton said, 'and if you continue with this, I think you could ruin the younger girl's life, even push her into committing suicide. Think of the consequences of that.'

Ashworth frowned. 'And why would she do that?'

'The psychiatrist at the hospital says she's pretty near to the brink,' Newton lied. 'One more upset could push her over.'

'But why should my finding Thornton upset her so much?' Ashworth reasoned. 'Unless she knew her sister was involved in the murder.'

Newton exhaled sharply, his anger threatening to emerge. 'Tanya Regent is madly in love with Thornton, but he was also having sexual relations with her sister.'

'So?' Ashworth said, failing to see the significance. 'If my investigation comes to nothing, none of that need ever come out. I can't see what you're getting at.'

'What I'm getting at,' Newton replied impatiently, 'is that you'll be charging him for corrupting a minor.'

Ashworth laughed loudly. 'That decision would rest with you, wouldn't it? And for some reason, which is beyond me, I believe you'd no more allow that than you'd allow the girls to be charged with preventing the burial of a newborn child.'

Newton's face flushed, his rage finally erupting. 'Tanya Regent is heavily into heroin, Ashworth. She's on a knife-edge.'

'Then you should be doing something about it,' he responded brusquely. 'You should be making sure she gets treatment and doesn't have access to illegal substances.'

The superintendent looked away briefly. He agreed wholeheartedly with Ashworth's comments, and chided himself for allowing this unsavoury situation to arise.

Turning back, he said quietly, 'That's my decision, and at the moment, I don't think it's the best course of action.'

'Let it be on your conscience then.'

'Ashworth,' Newton said warningly, rapping his hand on the desk.

'No, you're trying to stop my investigation by appealing to my conscience. But you're the one who's aiding and abetting the girl's suicide, by not preventing her from taking drugs.'

'That's enough,' Newton barked. 'I've tried to be reasonable with you, but I can see it doesn't work.'

'You haven't tried to be reasonable,' Ashworth said calmly, rising from the chair. 'You've tried to cover your own backside.' He walked to the door and turned. 'But it hasn't worked.' The door slammed behind him.

'Damn you, Ashworth,' Newton muttered. 'Damn you.'

* * *

Malcolm Headlands was careful not to be seen. When the boy he now thought of as Kevin Thornton was released from the police station, he was parked opposite the entrance.

Thornton came swaggering out of the building and looked around him. He waved down a passing taxi and as he got in Headlands started up the engine of the Volvo, slipped it into first gear, and then fell in behind the black cab.

He put a cigarette to his lips and pushed in the lighter on the dashboard. 'Let's see where you're going, shall we, sunshine?'

The taxi made its way across town, weaving in and out of the light traffic. At first, Headlands thought the cab was going towards Witch's Cottage, but it took a right turn, heading away from Manor Lane and towards the railway station.

The unlit cigarette was still clamped between his teeth as Headlands pulled into the station's car park. He held back and watched the taxi pull up outside the main entrance. Thornton got out, handed the driver a banknote, and disappeared into the building.

Headlands quickly parked the Volvo and sprinted across the car park. The station doors opened automatically, and he was just in time to see Thornton heading for a platform.

The boy turned unexpectedly and caught sight of the reporter. And there was panic in his eyes as he shouldered his way towards the ticket barrier before losing himself in the crowd.

Headlands leant forward and gave his most charming smile to the girl manning the ticket office. 'Hi.'

'Hello,' she said, smiling back. 'What can I do for you?'

'The lad who's just bought a ticket . . . you couldn't tell me where he's going, could you?'

'Sorry, I can't give you that information,' she said, looking beyond him at the queue of impatient commuters.

'I'm from Bridgetown CID.' He made a play of searching his inside pocket for a warrant card.

'Come on,' a man shouted from behind. 'We'll miss the train.'

The girl was flustered, and she said quickly, 'He bought a ticket to Morton.'

Headlands blew her a kiss as he crossed to check the departure board. The train for Morton was not due to leave for another thirty minutes. Good, he'd have plenty of time to get there by road.

Hurrying back to his car, Headlands thought how interesting it was that Kevin Thornton should choose to stay so near to Bridgetown.

* * *

Sarah had come to dread the ringing of the telephone; for some reason, it seemed to activate the dog. At the first ring, the Jack Russell would growl and bark, and run circles around Sarah's feet while she tried to get to it.

It was ringing now, and she muttered wearily, picking a way around the dog as she fought to get into the hall. Then, as always when the receiver was lifted and the ringing stopped, Peanuts yawned and padded off back to the lounge.

'Hello?' she said.

'Hello, is Jim at home?' a female voice asked.

Straight away, Sarah was suspicious. 'No, he's not. I'm Mrs Ashworth, can I help?'

There was a long pause. 'This is Edith Wright.'

'Oh, hello, Mrs Wright,' she replied, connecting the name at once to the recent murder. 'Can I take a message?'

Edith hesitated again. 'Well, it's just that Jim's been coming to see me. I know he's not coming tonight, and I just wanted to tell him not to bother tomorrow because my sister'll be here.'

'He's been going to see you in the evenings, has he?' Sarah asked hopefully.

'Yes, he's been a real godsend. I don't know what I'd have done without him. He's such a kind man.'

'I know,' Sarah said, smiling. 'I'll pass the message on, Mrs Wright.'

She replaced the receiver and stared down at it, sighing warmly. What a beautiful man her husband was. How could she ever have suspected that he and Holly . . . ?

The dog darted from the lounge, barking profusely.

'Don't you start again,' Sarah warned with a broad grin.

* * *

Headlands was sitting in the Volvo at Morton Railway Station when Thornton emerged from the building in a rush of travellers. A train thundered over a bridge to the left, its noise fading into the distance as the boy hung about, peering around furtively, presumably checking to see if anyone from the train was following.

'You're looking in the wrong place, kid,' Headlands muttered, sinking down in his seat as Thornton made his way to the street.

Now he had to make a quick decision. Should he follow on foot, or tail him by car?

He chose the latter and let out a relieved sigh when he spotted Thornton getting into a cab as he eased the Volvo out of the parking space.

Keeping close behind, Headlands followed the vehicle as it crawled along the side streets of the market town. Soon, the area became quite seedy: small run-down houses and littered streets. The reporter smelt what he guessed to be a cattle market, and with nostrils wrinkled, he wound up the car window.

The taxi drew up outside a small hotel called the Royalist. An ancient sign depicting the name swayed in the breeze, its paint peeling to match that on the windows and doors of the establishment. From his position outside, Headlands could see Thornton signing the register, so he pulled the car round to the building's rear and parked.

As he locked it, the aroma from the distant cattle market mingled with several unappetizing smells from the kitchen, and he made a mental note to avoid the hotel's cuisine as he approached the main entrance, carrying a holdall containing his clothes.

The hotel's foyer was no more inviting than its exterior; but the tall, leggy brunette behind the reception desk was. She was talking on the telephone, her back towards the reporter, and he turned the register around swiftly to study it.

The last name was Jason O'Brien. He had been given room number twelve. A man of many names, Headlands thought dryly, turning the register back as the girl finished her call.

She gazed at him approvingly and flashed a radiant smile. 'Hello.'

'I'd like a room, please,' Headlands said, his eyes flirting with hers. 'Number eleven, if possible.'

'Yes, that's vacant. Would you like to sign in?'

While he did so, she took in his designer clothes, his suave appearance, noted the expensive pen. 'You don't look like the type who normally stays at a place like this,' she remarked.

'And you don't look like a girl who should be working here.'

'It's a job,' she confided. 'Not many about in this dump. The room's twenty pounds a day. Payment in advance.'

Headlands gave a low whistle. 'They charge, don't they?'

He took out his wallet and handed her a twenty-pound note. With a smile, she gave him the keys, her eyes flirting again.

'What time do you get off?' he asked, leaning against the desk.

'Ten o'clock.'

'How about a drink then?'

'You are a stranger, aren't you?' she laughed. 'By that time, everything's closing down here.'

'Not in my room,' he intoned. 'Everything's just hotting up by then.'

Her eyes sparkled. 'I'll think about it.'

'You know where I am,' he said, picking up his holdall and making for the stairs.

He had propositioned the girl for two reasons. Firstly, if he was to keep tabs on Rivers-cum-Thornton-cum-O'Brien, he would need eyes and ears in this place. And secondly . . . well, those long, long legs and that shapely body had fired his interest.

'The things you have to do to get the job done,' he murmured happily under his breath.

* * *

Ashworth arrived home early, just as Sarah had expected. At the sound of his key in the lock, she went into the hall to find the dog sprawled on her back, tiny tail wagging frantically, while Ashworth knelt, stroking her stomach.

'Mrs Wright rang,' she said, going on to give him the message.

'Oh, good.'

'Why didn't you tell me you were going to see her in the evenings?' she scolded lightly.

'I'm sorry, Sarah, I didn't think you'd miss me for an hour.'

He seemed rather preoccupied, and the dog stood up and watched him curiously, head cocked to one side.

Sarah made a face. 'Didn't you notice your dinner was burnt every evening?'

'I did think it was well done, yes.'

'Well, you'll just have to take the dog out. The one day I allow for you being late, you're early, so dinner won't be ready for another hour.'

'An hour? Oh well, I'd better get the lead.'

'Yes, Jim,' Sarah smiled, shaking her head as she headed back to the kitchen.

CHAPTER 22

Getting even with Jamie was now an obsession with Craig. That single notion dominated his thoughts whatever he was doing. A sneer now distorted his lips as he watched Jamie in the dimly lit flat.

The boy was between Sharon and Laurie; they were reclining on beanbags, backs against the wall. Jamie was kissing and fondling the girls in turn, unmindful of the others. Rod and Carl were laughing at some shared joke at the other end of the room.

Craig sauntered over and sat beside Sharon, placing an arm around her shoulders, and squeezing her thigh. 'How about giving me some?' he grinned.

'Get off.' His hand was pushed away.

Viciously, he grabbed the front of her T-shirt. 'I want it,' he snarled. 'Get your knickers off.'

'Leave it, Craig.'

All talk ceased at the malice in Jamie's tone.

Craig scrambled to his feet. 'What did you say?'

'I said, leave it,' Jamie replied, pushing himself up off the beanbag.

'You don't tell me,' Craig declared, shoving Jamie hard on the shoulder and sending him staggering backwards. 'You think you're a hard man, yeh?' he taunted, pushing the boy again.

'Leave it,' Jamie warned.

'Leave it, leave it,' Craig mocked, jostling him around the room. 'What you gonna do if I don't?'

Jamie looked around at the others. From their expressions, he could see he was losing face. He needed to do something, and quickly. After a moment's thought, he clenched his fist and prepared to spring at the tormenting Craig. But the wily boy swayed out of reach of the blow and dug inside his leather jacket.

Then, with a wild grin, he drew the revolver from the waistband of his jeans and brought it up into Jamie's face.

'Come on then, hard man,' he growled.

The girls screamed.

Jamie was paralysed with dread as he watched the gun's hammer being pulled back. He wanted to run from the room, but he couldn't move, was glued to the spot, his shaking legs threatening to collapse.

For one split second he was conscious of the fearful anticipation of the others. And he saw clearly every detail of the gun's barrel as the hammer shot forward.

It landed with a metallic click on to the empty chamber.

Jamie exhaled slowly, while Craig laughed at the terror still showing in his deathly white face. He twirled the gun round with dexterity so that the handle was towards the boy.

'This is the gun we're going to use when we do the newsagent's, hard man,' he jeered. 'Have you got the bottle to carry it?'

Jamie felt all eyes upon him, and he tried to grin. 'We don't need a gun for that old lady,' he said, fighting to keep the tremor from his voice.

'You haven't got the bottle to carry it,' Craig reproached as he pushed the gun into Jamie's face.

'Tosser, tosser,' Carl shouted, with Rod quickly taking up the chant.

'Take it,' Laurie urged.

Jamie turned to her and saw doubt in her eyes, so he pushed away his apprehension and reached forward to grip the butt of the gun. 'We'll need a car.'

'Closer to the time, we'll nick one,' Craig told him. 'In the meantime, we watch the newsagent's.'

'Right,' Jamie agreed.

'And if the old girl gives us any bother, we blow her away,' Craig said, his challenging eyes never leaving Jamie's face.

* * *

Newton found he could not sleep.

Dressed in his pyjamas, he stood before the bay window in his bedroom, looking out at the night sky. He was bothered by the fact that his son had not yet come to heel. But what really ate away at his mind was the mess he found himself in with Katie Regent.

Tanya had been released from hospital, and the two sisters were now back at Witch's Cottage. He rang them on their return to check that they were all right and was met with a tirade when he stated that they were still looking for Kevin Thornton.

He had tried to console Katie with the joke that Ashworth couldn't find a needle in a haystack, but the mention of the chief inspector's name seemed only to incense them still further.

After that, regretting his attempt to make light of things, Newton warned sternly about Tanya's drug habit, advising them to seek help. But Katie made it clear that if there was any further probing about drugs, any scandal about Kevin Thornton, or if Ashworth was not kept off their backs then he, Newton, would be in trouble.

'Damn Ashworth,' the superintendent muttered. 'He's the root of all my problems.'

He looked towards his sleeping wife and sneered. Such was his feeling of superiority, that Newton felt a slight distaste for everyone. And his wife was no exception.

* * *

Malcolm Headlands would have little trouble getting to sleep; already his eyes were heavy.

Beth, the hotel's receptionist, had willingly succumbed to his charms. But, although passionate, he had found her a little lethargic after the adventurous Holly. Still naked, he stretched out on the bed and watched the girl's pubic hair vanish as she pulled on her pants.

Slipping into her bra, she crossed to the bed. 'Do me up.'

Headlands ran his fingers over the smooth skin of her back and fastened the clasp.

'I come on duty at nine, so if the boy goes out after that, I'll let you know.'

'You work long hours,' he remarked. Then, grinning, 'But it doesn't affect your energy.'

Beth laughed and finished dressing. 'I've never met an undercover policeman before,' she said excitedly.

'There're a lot of us about, you just don't spot us.'

She pulled on her jacket and was suddenly demure as she gazed down at him. 'I don't do this for everybody, you know.'

Only men, Headlands supposed. 'I know that,' he said.

She bent forward to kiss him; and although he was eager for her to leave, Headlands ran his fingers through her hair, prolonging the kiss.

Finally their lips parted. 'I'd better be off,' she said, making for the door. 'I'll see you in the morning.' She blew him a kiss, and the reporter winked back.

As soon as the door was closed, he sat up and began to take stock. Earlier in the evening the youth had gone out, with Headlands following close behind. He had wandered about aimlessly for a while, and then picked up a young girl who couldn't have been more than fourteen years old, reinforcing the reporter's belief that the boy was Thornton. As he followed them back to the hotel, he couldn't help thinking how scrawny the girl looked.

Headlands got off the bed and reached for a glass on the bedside table. He positioned the rim on the dividing wall between the two rooms and pressed his ear to its base. Magnified sounds of lovemaking came to him.

'Rather you than me, kid,' he said, wiping the glass rim with a corner of the sheet as he imagined the girl's naked body.

Pouring himself a large whisky, he decided it was time to ring Holly, report in, tell her how much she was missed.

He tried to look unsullied.

* * *

Mick Wright had planned his escape down to the last detail. All he needed now was a large slice of luck.

The day was pleasantly warm as he wandered away from the large group of prisoners watching a cricket match between the prison wardens and a local team from the nearby town.

'Where are you going, Mick?' the warden Pettit's voice challenged him from behind.

Wright turned. 'Just to the toilet,' he said.

Pettit's eyes strayed briefly back to the match, and then considered the prisoner's grey face. 'You'll come straight back?'

'Course I will,' Wright shrugged. 'Where else have I got to go?'

'OK.' Pettit's attention returned to the game when a cheer went up as a six was hit.

Wright casually strolled to the main building. Arriving at the doors to the hospital wing, he glanced back. No one was watching him, and he was now out of sight of the match. As fast as his impaired lungs would allow, Wright sidled around the building complex. He had to pause for breath now and then, but never dared stop for more than a few seconds.

Presently, he stealthily approached the kitchen yard. He peered around the corner and ducked back quickly as the kitchen door opened and a worker descended the steps with a plastic refuse sack. Fighting to provide air for his lungs, he listened to sounds of the dustbin lid hitting the ground, and the crackling of the sack as it was shoved inside. Finally, the worker's footsteps were heard on the cobbled yard, and the door closed.

Wright's heart was pounding; he imagined he could feel it hitting the tumour, causing it to spread with increased vigour. Several minutes passed before he found the courage to move.

Cautiously, he eased around the corner. The yard was now empty but for a large white van parked by a loading bay.

With a loping run, Wright covered the twenty or so yards to the vehicle, and fumbled with the handle on its rear doors, but it refused to budge. Panic swept over him, and with a mumbled curse, he pressed down harder, and was rewarded with the sound of grating metal as the doors came open.

Eagerly pushing aside white bags filled with dirty laundry, he climbed in amongst them. The doors were hardly closed when voices could be heard in the loading bay.

Huddling down nervously between the sacks, he listened while the laundry man chatted with another for some moments before climbing into the driver's seat. Peering up, he could see the man's head and shoulders through a small glass window in the partition between them.

The van's interior smelt overwhelmingly of soiled clothing, and Wright longed to cough but resisted. The driver started the engine and cruised slowly towards the main entrance. Then, after what seemed like an eternity, the vehicle came to a halt before the barrier.

Wright held his breath while a guard walked around the van, his shoes crunching on gravel. 'OK,' he said, banging on the van's bonnet. 'Take care, now.'

'Just two hours, that's all I need,' Wright mouthed. 'Don't let them miss me for a couple of hours.'

The barrier lifted, and the van passed through.

* * *

'He's just handed his key in,' Beth's voice informed Headlands, as he lifted the receiver.

'Right.' Replacing it swiftly, he grabbed his jacket and raced to the door. On the stairs, he collided with a couple coming up from reception.

'Here, what's your game?' the man snorted belligerently, as Headlands pushed past without a word.

In the foyer, Beth indicated from the reception desk that Thornton had turned right outside the hotel.

The boy was still in sight when Headlands hit the street. He was sauntering along towards the main thoroughfare. Headlands hurried along, closing the gap between them, and when he was within, twenty yards he slowed his step, not wanting to get too close.

The High Street was packed with shoppers and workers on their lunch break; and the reporter was glad of the cover they afforded him. He mingled with the crowd until the boy left the main shopping area.

Soon, the shops gave way to banks and building societies. There were few people around now, and twice the boy looked back, but Headlands ducked his head and stared at the pavement.

Immediately past a Memorial garden, the boy stopped outside a large office block and glanced back. This time he saw the reporter and recognition showed clearly in his expression before he hurried up the steps and disappeared into the building.

Headlands only went close enough to establish that it was the Jobcentre, and then he wandered back into the Memorial garden. Keeping the doors of the Jobcentre in view, he perused the names of all those who had given their lives in the last war.

And he waited.

* * *

The van slowed after about fifteen minutes.

From his position among the sacks, Wright glanced out of the rear windows to gauge where they were and was relieved to see open countryside. The driver pulled up in an area where a number of cars and heavy goods vehicles were parked.

Several minutes elapsed before Wright moved; and when he did, his face creased in pain as cramp crept steadily up his legs.

Crawling clumsily to the door, he looked out of the window. Although his view was restricted, the fact that no one could be seen in the vicinity made him bold enough to leave the van.

He opened the door and climbed out on shaky legs to the smell of fried food. Keeping to the rear of the vehicle, he looked about him and smiled.

The transport café was one he had often used and was no more than five miles from Bridgetown.

* * *

Headlands smoked a cigarette as he sat on the bench.

It was thirty minutes since the boy had disappeared into the building, and as yet he had not re-emerged. The reporter was beginning to worry.

'It's taking you a long time to sign on, lad,' he said to himself, as he walked towards the building.

The steps leading up to double swing doors were littered with cigarette ends and food wrappers. Headlands mounted them at a run, and the minute he was inside, he knew he had made a mistake. There was a rear exit.

Even before he scrutinized the two lines of people waiting to sign on, he was sure that Thornton had used it to dodge him. Muttering expletives under his breath, he approached the desk for 'New Signings'. It was staffed by a tall black girl, the silky ebony of her skin highlighted by her short white dress.

Headlands gave her a smile and winked. 'I was supposed to meet a young lad here who's registering for work,' he said. 'About half an hour ago, but I went to the wrong department.'

'I've only had one signing in the last half an hour,' the girl told him.

'Tall, slim, fair-haired lad, was he?' Headlands probed. 'With his hair in a pony-tail?'

'Yes, that's right.' Her eyes were sparkling; she was obviously taken with the reporter.

'What name did he give? Kevin Thornton?'

She shook her head. 'No.'

'Look, I'll let you into a secret . . .' Headlands leant towards her, lowering his voice. 'I'm his probation officer. He's a naughty lad, and he's going to get his knuckles rapped. What name's he using now?'

The girl picked up a form from the desk. 'Jason O'Brien.'

Headlands could see that the Royalist Hotel had been given as the address.

'What's he done?'

'Nothing for you to worry your pretty head about.'

He was about to walk away, but stopped. Headlands was a man who, even in a crisis, found it difficult to resist an attractive face. Turning back to the girl, he said, 'Do you fancy a drink sometime?'

'I might,' she replied, smiling shyly.

'Phone number?' he asked.

She held out a card. 'You can get me here between nine and five.'

He pocketed the card and backed away, still holding the girl's eyes with his own. 'Got you.'

Hurrying down the back stairs, he glanced at his watch. The kid's had forty-five minutes, he thought anxiously. If he's not back at the hotel, he could be anywhere by now.

CHAPTER 23

There was a long queue at the bus stop, and Mick Wright felt ill at ease as he joined it. Not many days ago, his blurred photograph had appeared in the newspapers; and being so near to Bridgetown, there was always a chance that someone might recognize him.

At last a green single-decker bus rounded the bend and crawled towards them. Those in the queue became restless.

'Always late, ain't they?' the woman in front of him grumbled.

Wright grunted.

The bus came to a halt with a squeal of brakes, and the people boarded slowly, most of them paying their fares, with only the odd few possessing passes.

Finally, Wright stepped on to the platform to find the driver scrutinizing him oddly. 'Fare,' the man said, gazing steadily at this passenger who appeared to be dead on his feet.

'The stop before Bridgetown — how much?' Wright asked, digging into his pocket.

'Sixty-seven pence.'

He dropped the money into the machine, and while the driver issued his ticket, Wright cast furtive glances around the passengers. Then he settled into the front seat, satisfied that they were all strangers. No one seemed to recognize him, anyway.

* * *

Headlands ran most of the way back to his hotel and arrived breathless.

'Is he back?' he asked Beth.

'No.'

'Damn.' Placing his hands on the desk, he breathed deeply. 'I've lost the little creep.'

'The girl's still in the room,' Beth said helpfully. 'She might know where he's gone.'

He smiled. 'I knew there was a reason I loved you . . . apart from your body.'

Now fully recovered, Headlands bounded up the stairs, and knocked on the door to room number twelve.

'What you want?' the girl asked.

'Open up,' Headlands called, banging on the door.

'Bleedin' hell,' she moaned in a high-pitched voice. The door was opened, and she stood there in bra and pants, a cigarette dangling from her mouth. 'What you want?'

Headlands pushed her back into the room, and as she staggered he rushed in, kicking the door shut behind him.

The girl's eyes were wide with fear, and the cigarette fell from her fingers to lie smouldering on the cheap carpet. 'You ain't going to rape me, are ya?'

'You're praying for a miracle, girl,' Headlands quipped as his eyes flicked over her thin body. 'Jason O'Brien — where is he?'

She bent down to retrieve her cigarette, eyeing him dubiously. 'You filth?'

'Where is he?' Headlands asked, more forceful now.

It was obvious that the girl assumed he was the police for she straight away relaxed. She was used to such visits, so felt quite safe. Her eyes narrowed as she drew on the cigarette. 'Said he was going up to Newcastle.'

'Newcastle? What for?'

'I dunno. Told me to wait here. Said he'd be back the day after tomorrow. Him and me are together.'

'How sweet,' Headlands replied tauntingly. 'What time's he coming back?'

'I dunno.' She stubbed out the cigarette and lazily pulled on her dressing gown.

'What time?' he persisted.

'You ain't got nothing on me.'

'Don't bet on it.' He stabbed a finger. 'I could make a lot of things up.'

She sighed. 'Early morning. Said he wants to pick his Giro up, and then we leave. Moves all over the country, Jason does.'

* * *

When he got off the bus, Wright waited until it was out of sight and then set off across the fields. He dared not go through the town for fear of recognition.

Every hundred yards or so, he needed to stop and get his breath. But, worried that his absence might have been noticed, he pushed on, ever fearful that the police could even now be waiting at his destination.

Gasping, and sometimes stumbling, he pressed forward. His watch told him it was now one and a half hours since his escape. And although he was sweating, Mick Wright felt very cold.

* * *

It was Craig's turn to watch the newsagent's. He loitered across the street, smoking a cigarette.

Over the last two days a pattern had emerged. The lunch-time trade died off around 2 p.m.; and by three there was no one in the shop apart from Ma. At three fifteen on the dot, she would disappear into the back and return some five minutes later with a cup of tea.

That was when Craig planned to strike — when Ma was in the kitchen. They would go in, turn the sign to CLOSED, and lock the door. Then they'd have the old girl cornered in the accommodation at the rear of the premises.

Only one thing was worrying him: Jamie was showing no signs of bottling out, and if he did go through with it, his status with the others could only rise.

Craig flicked the filter-tip into the gutter and grinned. Hatred for Jamie had so distorted his mind that half of him wanted the boy to refuse, while the rest of him wanted Jamie there . . . wanted to badly damage the old woman and blame it on him.

* * *

Malcolm Headlands was unsure of his next step.

He had lost Thornton for a couple of days, that much was certain. But should he ring Ashworth and Holly to let them know? If he did, he'd have no excuse for staying in Morton; he could go back to Bridgetown and return when Thornton was due back.

His mind kept flitting to the girl at the Jobcentre. Every time he closed his eyes, he saw her naked, a slight sheen on her smooth skin, unashamed lust distorting her features.

Beth was a problem. He felt his little fling with her was yet to run its course, so he couldn't bring the girl to the hotel before 10 p.m. He would have to take her out.

Headlands felt a slight pang of guilt as he dug into his pocket for her telephone number. Thornton could be anywhere by now. He could even be back in Bridgetown. The girl might have lied about Newcastle. Headlands shrugged. Why should he return to Bridgetown? Once released by the police, he couldn't get away fast enough.

Still he hesitated. But then he thought again about the white dress, and the dark body it concealed.

First things first, he thought, reaching for the telephone.

* * *

'There it is,' Wright exclaimed breathlessly, as he stopped in a small copse.

His heart was beating wildly, and he leant against a tree, gasping for air. With tired, watery eyes, he observed for a full five minutes, needing to be sure the police were not in the area.

Then, unable to contain himself any longer, he set off on the last two hundred and fifty yards.

Now he could sort this out. Now he could find some peace.

* * *

Holly was sitting at her desk, doodling on a blotter. Her drawing was fast taking the shape of a male sex organ when the telephone rang.

'DS Bedford,' she said absently, still admiring her handiwork. Then, with some urgency, 'Guv, Mick Wright's escaped from prison.'

Ashworth looked up sharply. 'When?'

'How long ago?' Holly asked. She listened. 'It could have been as long as two hours, guv.'

Ashworth's chair scraped on the floor as he stood up. 'Right, let's move,' he said, already heading for the door.

'Are we going to Witch's Cottage?' Holly questioned, hurrying behind.

'That we are,' he confirmed. 'If Wright's mind's gone, he might head there with the intention of harming the girls.'

* * *

Mick Wright felt quite calm now; it was as if he had drawn on a hidden reserve of energy.

His step was sure as he walked down the path and approached the front door.

* * *

In all the time she had known her chief inspector, Holly had never before seen him drive so fast. He stared with determination at the road ahead, his hands gripping the steering-wheel at ten to two, and with great skill drove at high speed along the dual carriageway. He took the slip road to Witch's Cottage at fifty, the roundabout at the top at thirty.

Holly had no idea of the speed he used along the narrow lanes for her eyes were tightly shut. 'My God, you can drive, guv,' she spluttered, as the car screeched to a halt outside the cottage.

Ashworth made no comment as he swiftly released his seat-belt and climbed out. Holly hastened after him, and he was already knocking on the front door when she caught up.

There was no response, so he banged harder. 'Open up — Bridgetown CID.'

No sound came from within the cottage.

In desperation, he lifted the latch. It yielded beneath his grip and the door swung open. The hall was deserted. No sound, apart from the loud ticking of the clock.

'Right, Holly, we're going in,' he said, crossing the threshold cautiously.

'Guv, search warrants—' She stopped the minute she was inside.

They could both smell it — the sickly, pungent stench of blood.

'We stay together,' Ashworth ordered. He made his way to the lounge, carefully pushing open the door.

It was empty. He looked around at the furniture. Everything seemed to be in order.

'Kitchen,' he said.

They crossed to it quickly. Again, nothing was disturbed.

'Upstairs,' he grunted.

'Hold on, guv, look.' Holly was pointing to the work top beside the oven and hob.

Ashworth's eyes followed her finger. 'What?'

'There,' she said, indicating the wooden block which housed the kitchen knives. There were six slots in the block. But only five were occupied.

'It looks like the carving knife's missing,' she said.

At that moment something sharp pierced the flesh at the back of Ashworth's neck, and it took all of his self-discipline to swallow a shout of fear.

As he spun round, the cat released its hold and landed lightly on the floor. Hatred gleamed in its eyes as it scurried off towards the lounge.

'That blasted cat,' he scowled. 'Right, let's look upstairs.'

The old staircase groaned beneath their weight.

On the landing, Holly suddenly gripped his arm. 'I'm sorry, guv,' she blurted, 'but there's something up here that's not natural.'

'I feel it, too,' he said, patting her hand, 'but we've got to move on.'

The main bedroom showed no signs of disturbance. And yet it was there that the malignant presence first felt on the landing was at its strongest. Ashworth was suddenly gripped by a powerful notion that something in the house meant them harm.

The entrance to the second bedroom was along the landing, set back in an alcove, and he headed for it, hardly able to keep his step steady.

One look at the door was enough to tell them that something was wrong. It hung on one hinge, the wood above the handle badly splintered as if someone had kicked it in.

Ashworth sensed that they were about to discover something horrific. He took in a large breath and steeled himself before peering in.

Mick Wright was slumped half on the bed, half on the floor, his sightless eyes staring up at the ceiling.

Very carefully, they entered the room. Holly gasped when she saw the body, and staggered back to the door, but Ashworth ventured on, his gorge rising.

Wright was obviously dead. The missing carving knife lay red beside the corpse.

He leant closer. There were at least three stab wounds on the body: one in the chest, and two in the left side. Wright's face held a look of mild surprise.

Ashworth backed away. 'Right, Holly, we've got a lot to do. Ring the station, and get things moving.'

'OK, guv.' They were back on the landing. 'Where are the girls?'

'I don't know,' Ashworth replied, gripping his forehead. 'There are so many questions. Who on earth could have done this?'

On the ground floor, bright sunlight beckoned them through the open front door. Eager to be outside, they hurried towards it.

But then Holly faltered. 'What's that, guv? I thought I heard something.'

Ashworth strained his ears. 'I can't hear anything.'

'Must be my imagination,' she said, shaking her head.

They carried on to the door.

'There it is again,' Holly exclaimed, stopping in her tracks. 'It sounds like an animal whimpering.'

Ashworth cocked his head, and this time he heard it. He looked around wildly for its source. 'The cupboard under the stairs,' he said. 'Stay here.'

But Holly moved with him, loath to be alone.

A shaft of light cut through the gloom in the understairs cupboard as Ashworth swung open the door. Tanya, her eyes wide and petrified, was crouched in the corner. Beside her stood Katie, dazed and staring blankly into space.

CHAPTER 24

The back of a Volvo estate provided more than sufficient room for unrestricted lovemaking. And Donna, from the Jobcentre, was proving to be far from inhibited. It was only 8 p.m., but already they had enjoyed two sensuous bouts while parked in a deserted spot.

Donna was reclining on a multicoloured car rug, the white dress pulled up, her legs open and raised at the knees. She quite obviously enjoyed having Headlands's eyes on her.

'Malc, why can't we go back to your hotel?' she purred. Then, giggling, 'We can strip off . . . really have some fun.'

He thought of Beth behind the reception desk, labouring away until 10 p.m. Glancing at his watch, he said: 'Yes, great idea, but let me take you for a meal first. Give me time to get my strength back,' he added with a smile.

'Oh, if you're not up to it . . .' she teased.

He was about to make a suggestive retort when the mobile phone buzzed.

Straight away, his mind went into overdrive. For most of his adult life, Headlands had been on the dodge from one thing or another, so he automatically went through those who had his telephone number. Holly's face kept looming in his imagination.

Reluctantly, he scrambled towards the front seat, fastening his trousers at the same time. He retrieved the telephone and said, 'Headlands,' in what he hoped was a businesslike tone.

Holly's voice sprang in his ear. 'Malc, what took you so long?'

'I was resting,' he said, quite truthfully.

'Where are you? I rang the hotel, and they said you were out.'

'It's a long story.' He glanced back at Donna and gave her a sly wink.

Holly laughed. 'God, sometimes I just don't know what you're talking about. Look,' she said, changing the subject, 'Mick Wright's dead. We found him at Witch's Cottage. It's not clear yet, but we think the Regent girls killed him. Maybe you should get back here for the story.'

Headlands was alert. The pleasures of the flesh were one thing, but an exclusive story meant a large pay-cheque. 'Any more details?' he wanted to know.

'As I said, we haven't got a clear picture yet. And we're not being helped by that prat Newton. He's having the girls questioned by officers from Bridgenorton nick because he thinks Ashworth's got it in for them.'

'And how's the big fella taking that?'

Holly sighed. 'At the last count, he's issued fifteen threats against Newton's life. Are you coming back?'

'Of course, this is a big story.' He was already thinking up excuses to pacify Donna.

'Is that the only reason?' Holly asked, subdued.

In his mind's eye, Headlands could see her pouting. 'Of course not,' he said brightly.

'Say it then,' she coaxed.

'Say what?' he asked, turning to smile weakly at Donna.

'That you're coming back to see me,' Holly prompted. 'Come on, I've been hanging around the station most of the day.'

With his back to the girl, and cupping a hand around the telephone, he mumbled, 'I'm coming back to see you.'

Holly was appeased, and Headlands went on to say he would travel back immediately, expecting to arrive in about forty-five minutes.

Pushing the telephone's aerial back, he turned to Donna. 'Sorry,' he said, 'I'll have to take a rain-check on the meal. Duty calls.'

The girl sighed as she reached for her pants. Struggling into them, she asked, 'Was that your wife?'

'No, my boss.'

'You sound on friendly terms.'

'The probation service is strapped for cash,' he blithely told her.

'What do you mean?' she asked, smoothing down her dress.

He grinned. 'What do you think she hands round, come bonus time?'

* * *

It was 9 p.m. and Ashworth was pacing the CID office. 'What's keeping them?'

Holly was watching him from her desk. 'They've started the interviews, guv. As soon as they're through, they'll let us know.'

'My own nick. My own nick . . .' Ashworth grumbled for the umpteenth time. 'And I've been sidelined.'

Holly cast an irritated glance at the ceiling, and pinched the bridge of *her* nose, before saying, 'We should know the result any time now.'

Quite a while ago, Josh had gauged the situation and retired to the canteen. Holly was beginning to wish she had gone with him.

'That's not the point, Holly. This is my investigation . . .'

She knew that his incessant complaining would go on until the Bridgenorton detectives had concluded their interviews with the Regent girls, so she closed her ears to it. As she watched Ashworth storming about, she couldn't help thinking that his beard lent him a buccaneering look, and she smiled at the thought.

Ashworth suddenly stopped and glared at her. 'Is something funny, Holly?'

'Look, guv,' she flared, getting to her feet. 'This is not my fault. OK?'

'All right, all right. Point taken.' Slightly abashed, he went and sat in his chair.

For the next ten minutes he said nothing, simply sat there, tapping a pen on the desk top. And just when Holly felt the repetitive sound would make her scream, there came a knock on the door.

'Come in,' Ashworth called eagerly.

Inspector Eric Hamp, from Bridgenorton Station, lumbered in. His bulk matched that of Ashworth's, but he possessed neither the chief inspector's grace of movement, nor his smart appearance. Hamp's old grey suit was crumpled, his shirt less than white.

'Sit down, Eric,' Ashworth said.

As he pulled up a chair, Hamp ran an impatient hand through his thick grey hair. 'None of this is my doing, Jim,' he said. 'I didn't ask to be brought in on this.'

'Yes, I know that,' Ashworth responded irritably. 'Just give me the results of the interview.'

'Well, the older girl did all the talking. Her sister's been struck dumb, but she did agree, nod of the head and all that.'

'So, what was said?' Ashworth persisted.

Hamp inhaled deeply and leant forward. 'Their story is that Wright came bursting into the cottage, threatening to kill them. He forced them back into the kitchen, ranting and raving the whole time. The eldest girl managed to grab the knife, and they escaped up the stairs and into the second bedroom, locking the door behind them. Then Wright kicked the door in—'

'That doesn't ring true at all,' Ashworth interrupted. 'The man was terminally ill. He wouldn't have had the strength.'

'Come on, Jim, you know as well as I do, anybody with a couple of screws loose will find the strength from somewhere.'

Ashworth shook his head in disagreement as Hamp went on, 'When Wright got into the bedroom, he attacked the youngest girl, got his hands round her throat, and was just about choking the life out of her when her sister stabbed him four times.'

Ashworth still looked sceptical.

'Forensic and the post-mortem were rushed through today, and they bear it out,' the inspector continued. 'The youngest girl has marks on her throat consistent with somebody trying to strangle her. All the blood found on the girls belonged to Wright. The stab wounds he suffered tally with the story. It's cut and dried, Jim.'

Ashworth thought for a few moments. 'What happens to the girls now?'

Hamp shrugged. 'Bottom line, it's down to Newton, but I can't see them being charged with anything. It's a classic case of self-defence.'

The chief inspector gave a hollow laugh. 'And where are they now?'

'I wanted them to go to hospital,' Hamp said, looking sheepish, 'but they wouldn't have it. The police doctor had a look at the youngest and couldn't find anything wrong. Then Newton stepped in, and had them whisked off to a hotel, well away from the press.'

Ashworth looked at the inspector with narrowed eyes. 'Would you say those two girls were on anything?'

Hamp considered this. 'Funny you should ask that. The youngest was definitely out of it. I've seen enough junkies to know that, and I'd say her sister had something going round her veins as well.'

'So that means they were taking drugs inside the nick,' Ashworth concluded.

'Could be,' Hamp said, clearly uncomfortable. 'Look, I'll be honest with you, Jim, I think they were given too much freedom in there. Allowed to shower by themselves. They sent out for a change of clothes, and no check was taken on their possessions. But I just thought Newton was displaying some sensitivity.'

Ashworth snorted.

'I'm sorry, Jim.' As the inspector got to his feet, he seemed about to expound further but instead, he headed for the door.

'What was time of death?' Ashworth asked.

'Around four p.m., as far as they can tell.'

He left Ashworth staring down at his desk, too absorbed in his thoughts for goodbyes. Holly followed him out and closed the door.

'What's that round his face?' Hamp asked incredulously. 'Jim hates beards.'

'Politics?' Holly suggested.

'I thought so. It's as plain as the nose on his face. Can't you talk some sense into him?'

'How long have you known Jim Ashworth?'

'About twenty years.'

Holly's eyebrows rose meaningfully.

'Yes, I take your point. When Jim's in that mood, there's no reasoning with him. But if he's playing station politics with Newton, he's going to come a cropper.'

'I think he already has.'

'Good luck, then,' Hamp said, making for the swing doors. 'You'll need it.'

As the inspector approached the doors, they opened to reveal Malcolm Headlands. The two men exchanged nods as Holly's face broke into a smile.

'Hi, lover,' the reporter said, sliding a hand over her backside.

'Get off, not here,' she chided, pushing his hand away.

'What's shaking, then?'

He listened in silence as Holly went through all that had happened and whistled appreciatively when she finished. 'That's one hell of a story,' he said. 'It hasn't broken yet?'

'No,' Holly assured him. 'The rest of the press won't get it till the morning.'

'Great.'

'Where's Thornton?'

Headlands, busy calculating how much the story would be worth, said absently, 'Oh, I lost him. Only temporarily, though. But surely he's out of the frame now.'

'My lord and master isn't accepting the facts as others are presenting them,' Holly said pointedly.

'Ah . . . and what sort of mood's he in?'

'Are you a good fighter? Really able to take care of yourself?'

'As bad as that, eh?'

'Worse — I'm just trying to bolster your confidence. Anyway, I'm off to the canteen. The guv'nor's in his office.'

'Holly . . .'

'Don't worry, I'll have all the facts for you. You can phone your story in from my place.'

Headlands hesitated before knocking on the door of CID.

'Come in.' The growl in Ashworth's voice did not make the summons inviting. He was still at his desk. 'Ah, you've heard the news, no doubt,' he snarled, motioning the reporter to sit.

'Yes, Holly filled me in. It does seem to disprove your theory about Thornton.'

'No, it doesn't,' Ashworth retorted angrily. 'You've kept tabs on him?'

'I lost him,' Headlands was reluctant to admit. 'But I know he's coming back to Morton the day after tomorrow.'

'What time did you lose him?'

'Two p.m.'

'And Wright was killed at four p.m. So, he would've had time to get back here.'

'Yes, I suppose he would,' Headlands agreed. 'But why should he?' He took a surreptitious glance at his watch, eager to get the story winging its way to London.

'How certain are you that the boy is Thornton?'

'Ninety-nine per cent. Every time he sees me he looks frightened to death.'

'And the first time he really saw you was here at the station,' Ashworth surmised. 'He obviously thinks you're the police, and he's running scared.'

'He could know I'm the press,' Headlands countered.

Ashworth discarded the theory with a quick shake of his head. 'Are you going to keep watching him?'

'Yes, because if he is Thornton, there's a story in there somewhere,' the reporter said, consulting his watch again.

'Good man. And you'll keep me informed?'

Headlands smiled hopefully. 'Same terms as before? If a story breaks, I get it first?'

Ashworth nodded.

'OK, fine then.' He started to rise from the chair. 'Look, if I'm going to meet my deadline—'

'Yes, yes,' Ashworth said, dismissing him with a brisk wave of the hand.

* * *

Sarah could not help noticing how preoccupied her husband was when he arrived home at 10 p.m. She had already taken Peanuts out, and the dog, having settled for the night, gave Ashworth a particularly half-hearted welcome before slinking off back to bed.

They sat in the lounge, with Sarah listening carefully to the facts of the case. She watched him pour the drinks, noticing with dismay the large amount of whisky in his glass, and the distinct lack of soda. A storm was obviously brewing at the station.

To her mind, the Mick Wright case seemed clear cut; and as she was aware of her husband's dispute with Superintendent Newton, she wondered if this might be affecting his judgement. However, she felt it would be unwise to broach the subject.

'Kevin Thornton has got something to do with this,' he insisted. 'I'm certain of it.'

Sarah sighed, and sipped her sherry. 'Yes, dear,' she said.

* * *

It was 3 a.m., and Headlands was driving back to Morton.

As the Volvo approached a bend, he pressed his foot on the brake pedal, and winced. Then, past the bend, he touched the accelerator and this time cried out in pain.

Holly was the cause of his discomfort.

He had telephoned his newspaper from her house and, after agreeing a fee, had passed on the details. Even now, the story of Mick Wright's death would be rolling off the presses. That had taken until two 2 a.m., by which time, he was not only ready, but eager to sample a female body.

It was then that things started to go wrong. And Headlands could only blame his generous nature for the resulting unpleasantness.

On account of the extreme length of time he had spent on her telephone, he offered Holly twenty pounds towards the bill. She tried to refuse it, but Headlands insisted, taking out his wallet to give her the note.

Unfortunately, he pulled out Donna's card along with his wallet, and Holly picked it up from the carpet, studying it suspiciously.

His explanation was simple: she was just a girl from the employment service, enlisted to help in keeping tabs on Thornton. However, the '7 p.m.' and yesterday's date he had scribbled on the back was harder to explain away, and it was then that Headlands overestimated just how far his charm could carry him.

He was attempting to pacify Holly, believing that his very closeness would drive all thoughts from her mind, when she brought up her knee with considerable force and aimed it at his testicles.

Such was Headlands's inability to tell moral right from wrong, the only worry on his mind was whether the blow would render him incapable of satisfying the amorous female population of Morton.

CHAPTER 25

At first light, the media blitz descended on Bridgetown Police Station, and by nine a.m. the building was almost in a state of siege.

But as soon as the reporters realized that Headlands had already published the full story, they accepted with resignation the prepared statement, which would perhaps fill a column on page three, and drifted back to London.

The television people showed a little more interest, staying to record interviews with Superintendent Newton; but there was little point in staying, and they were soon loading their vans.

Ashworth watched them from his vantage point high up in the CID office. He was alone, for Holly and Josh, all too aware of his foul mood and the reason for it, had elected to help the uniformed division investigate a series of break-ins. Feeling the need to be alone to lick his wounds, Ashworth had not objected. In the solitude of the office, depression gathered and settled upon him.

Without knocking, Newton threw open the door. 'Ashworth,' he called from the doorway, 'I've spoken with the chief constable, and he's congratulated me on my handling of the case.'

'Bully for you.' The chief inspector deliberately made his reply impertinent.

Newton merely smiled. 'I believe he'll be getting in touch with you later.'

Ashworth turned from the window, swallowing his anger. 'What is it you want from me?'

The superintendent's smile now bordered on a smirk. 'I remember you once told me I'd know I'd been in a fight. Well, I don't feel as if I have.'

Jamie Newton's caution drifted into Ashworth's mind. 'Perhaps it's not over yet,' he remarked calmly. 'There might just be something I could tell Ken Savage which might alter his opinion.'

'And what might that be?' Newton asked, guardedly.

It was Ashworth's turn to smile. 'You'll have to wait and see. I never play all my cards at the start.'

'You're bluffing, Ashworth.' But despite the confident tone, Newton appeared nervous.

'Wait and see.'

'I shall, and let me assure you, there'll be some changes around here . . . starting from today.'

With that, Newton puffed up his chest and closed the door.

* * *

The incessant ring of the telephone cut into Headlands's sleep. He turned over in bed and reached for it, grimacing as his injury was brought painfully to his attention.

'Hello,' he snapped.

'Malc, it's Beth.'

'Beth, I'm sorry, you woke me up . . .' He yawned. 'I didn't get in till late, and I'm bushed.'

'Listen, the girl who was with O'Brien has just checked out.' Her voice was an urgent whisper.

'And was the boy with her?' he asked hurriedly.

'No, she was by herself, but she did take all of their luggage, such as it was.'

'Good girl.' Headlands thought quickly. 'One of them should be back tomorrow to collect the Giro, so don't worry about it.'

'Shall I see you when I finish tonight?' she asked after a pause.

The reporter hesitated. 'Well, it's difficult. Last night I had to tackle a gang of ram-raiders we'd been after for sometime. I arrested them, but I collected a kick in the balls along the way.'

'Oh God, Malc, are you all right?'

'Yes, sore, but apart from that, fine.'

She giggled. 'Perhaps it might help if I massage you with baby lotion.'

Headlands, quick to see the possibilities of that offer, said, 'It could. Look, I'm not ruling anything out. You have to be tough in the police force.'

* * *

Ashworth had lunch in the police canteen, hoping that the hurly-burly of the place would take his mind off things. But as he listened to the clatter of trays, plates and cutlery, the inane chatter forever present at busy meal times, his resentment for Newton, and all that the man stood for, continued to consume him.

He chewed his way through a tasteless shepherd's pie while he put his thoughts in order. If he were to tell Savage about Jamie Newton, it might well alter the situation. After all, a superintendent's son brought in for caution did not look good.

What most annoyed him was the fact that the Regent case had been taken out of his hands, removed because of his refusal to accept the facts at face value. Newton, in discussions with the chief constable, had deliberately coloured the situation, had implied that Ashworth had been incompetent.

He pushed aside his plate, drained his tea, and attempted to concentrate on the present. That afternoon, he would have to visit Edith Wright and try to offer some comfort to the woman.

* * *

Craig looked at his watch. 'It's two o'clock,' he announced. 'Time we made our way to the old dear's shop.'

Heavy curtains were drawn across the windows of the flat, and a naked light-bulb hanging from the ceiling-rose glowed dimly.

'We gonna nick a car, then?' Carl asked, as he scrambled to his feet.

'No, we don't need one. Anyway, it'd only draw attention to us.'

The current of pressure which had built steadily throughout the morning now increased as they prepared to leave.

Craig crossed to an ancient chest of drawers, the only article of furniture in the room, and took out four balaclavas. The two girls looked on expectantly as they were handed out.

'The girls wait round the corner, right?' Craig told them for the umpteenth time. 'When we come out of the shop, we pass them the loot and the balaclavas, 'cause the fuzz won't be looking for girls. Then we all split up and meet back here. You all got that?'

A nod of heads.

'And the gun,' he said, reaching into the drawer. 'Jamie wants that. Don't you, Jamie?'

It was held out for the boy, and he took it without hesitation, positioned it in the waistband of his jeans, and zipped up his denim jacket. His mouth was set in a determined line.

* * *

The telephone call came at 2.45 p.m. Ashworth picked up the receiver, half expecting to hear Ken Savage's voice, and he was not disappointed.

'Jim, how are things?'

Ashworth smiled. 'I think you know the answer to that, Ken.'

Savage, who had obviously rehearsed some pointless chatter in order to pacify the chief inspector, pressed on regardless. 'Sarah's well, I hope. And that little dog . . . now, what's her name?'

'Get on with it, Ken,' Ashworth pressed. 'I'm in no mood to be smoothed over.'

The chief constable chuckled. 'Same old Jim.' He took a while to clear his throat, then said, 'I've looked into your complaints about Newton, and I've decided not to take any action.'

Above Ashworth's heavy sigh, he went on defensively, 'Look at it from my point of view. The crime figures for Bridgetown are plummeting. I'm going to look a bloody fool if I haul Newton over the coals for that . . .' He paused, expecting a heated reply, and was surprised to hear silence. 'Anyway, he has been proved right about the Regent case — you can't deny that.'

'I can,' Ashworth replied forcefully. 'There are so many pieces that just don't fit into place.'

'Don't be so bloody silly, Jim,' Savage exploded. 'You're letting your dislike for Newton stand in the way of everything. A five-year-old child could look at that case and know the correct conclusion had been reached.'

'I don't agree,' the chief inspector persisted.

'Jim, you're to leave those girls alone. Now, that's a direct order,' Savage told him harshly. A long pause followed, during which the chief constable capitulated slightly. Using a lighter tone, he asked, 'Is there anything else about Newton? I want to be even-handed about this.'

'Yes, there is, Ken,' Ashworth said, his intonation spiteful. 'Something that may make the man look less snowy white than you appear to think he is.'

'Go on then.'

Ashworth tilted back in his chair and studied the ceiling. 'Well . . .'

'Yes?' Savage prompted.

'Oh, it doesn't matter,' he said sourly, slamming down the receiver.

* * *

Ma Shallet was in her kitchen at the rear of the shop.

'Come on, come on,' she muttered at the kettle bouncing about on the single gas ring. 'You're taking for ever to boil.'

She popped a tea bag into a mug and was about to heap three sugars on top when she hesitated, straining her ears.

'I could have sworn that was the shop bell,' Ma said to herself. She shook her head and smiled whimsically. 'You're hearing things, girl.'

The kettle whistled as it boiled. Leaning on her stick, Ma hobbled over to the gas ring. 'Hold on then, hold on.'

She turned off the gas and removed the whistle, grateful for the silence. Then, with the tea made, she headed slowly back to the shop.

A small hall with a flight of stairs leading up to her living accommodation lay between the kitchen and the shop. Ma had hardly stepped into the confined space when she was grabbed from the left. A gloved hand was clamped across her mouth, stifling her startled scream.

The mug of tea slipped from her fingers, and as it crashed to the floor, Ma saw the group of men. They crowded around her, their covered faces close to her own.

And one of them shoved a gun to her neck.

* * *

Superintendent Newton had decided to visit Tanya and Katie at the hotel, so did not arrive back at the station until 5 p.m. It was then that Martin Dutton informed him of the raid on Ma's shop.

When Newton asked why Ashworth wasn't dealing with it, Dutton was slow to give a reply; but he was quick to disclose, rather maliciously, that the gang involved had already been cautioned on an earlier occasion.

No doubt at the time Newton thought it was efficiency which allowed Dutton to produce the paperwork on those cautions so quickly. Whether or not he was of the same opinion ten minutes later, when he left the station, white-faced and stiff-backed, was another matter.

* * *

Ashworth's absence was due to the amount of time he had felt obliged to spend with the distraught Edith Wright.

It was 8 p.m. when he got back to CID, and in order to avoid bumping into anyone, he used the back stairs.

His need for isolation was not due to any feelings of defeat. On the contrary, the hours spent with Edith had convinced him that Wright had not killed Joyce Regent, and now his mind was made up, his jaw set.

That was something he would prove. He had no idea how, but prove it he would, and to hell with the opposition.

He sat in the darkness, his elbows on the desk top, watching the lights of Bridgetown, while his mind raced. Every minute piece of evidence was recalled and held up for scrutiny as he searched relentlessly for that one piece which did not fit.

Quite how long he sat there, Ashworth had no idea, but eventually his meditation was disturbed as the door opened, and light from the corridor shot across the room.

In spite of his preoccupation, he could not help but smile when Holly, searching for the light switch, exclaimed, 'Shit,' as she banged her ankle on the filing cabinet.

Leaning forward noiselessly, he flicked on his desk lamp, blinking at its harsh light.

'Guv, what are you doing here?' Holly asked with surprise.

'Thinking,' he told her.

'Ah,' she said, flinging her shoulder bag on to her desk. She stood for a while, watching him. 'You've heard about the robbery at Ma's shop?'

Suddenly alert, he glanced up. 'No. Is she all right?'

'Yes. The little charmers used a gun. They walked away with two hundred pounds, but Ma's fine. After the dust had settled, she wanted to open up the shop. I really had to put my foot down with her.'

'Good old Ma,' Ashworth smiled, staring at the gloom lingering in the corners of the office.

'A quick-thinking man followed the gang, and then rang us. They're holed up in a flat in Hazeldene Road. Some armed uniformed officers are there, trying to talk them out. Actually, it's the crowd we had in here for cautioning.' She paused dramatically. 'Jamie Newton's lot.'

'So,' Ashworth mused, 'that young man's finally got himself into trouble.'

'Looks like it. Anyway, I need some sleep, guv. I'm off home.'

'Yes. Goodnight, Holly.'

She hesitated at the door. Turning back, she said, 'Guv, can I talk to you?'

'Surely.'

'I know what you're thinking about,' she said, crossing to his desk.

'Do you?'

Crouching down beside him, she said, 'Yes — Joyce Regent. But you're wrong, guv. The case is an open book. However much you hate Newton, it's not going to stop all the evidence proving that Wright committed the murder.'

'There has to be—'

'There's not,' Holly insisted. 'If you keep pushing this, you'll end up looking a proper fool, and that's something I don't want to see happen.'

'You're beginning to sound as though you know everything,' he remarked, with a warm smile.

'I had a good teacher.'

She collected her shoulder bag, retrieved her car keys from the desk drawer, and headed for the door. 'Leave it, guv — eh?'

'Goodnight, Holly,' Ashworth said in a dull tone.

Before long the door opened again, and Martin Dutton came in with two mugs of tea. 'Holly said you needed cheering up, Jim. Have you heard about Jamie Newton?' he asked, kicking the door closed behind him.

Ashworth nodded.

Dutton deposited the mugs on the chief inspector's desk and sat down. 'Jim,' he began awkwardly, 'could I have a word with you about the Regent case?'

Oh God, Ashworth thought, not again.

* * *

Newton was annoyed to find his house deserted. He needed to speak to his wife. As always in times of crisis, he blamed her for everything. After all, the alternative would be to apportion blame to himself and that, for Newton, was unthinkable.

He frequently rang the station for news of the Hazeldene Road siege, his exasperation growing with every call.

The more time that passed, the more determined Newton was that his wife should feel the sharp edge of his tongue.

* * *

Ashworth listened patiently to Martin Dutton, who was preaching much the same message as Holly had before him; but because Dutton was less tired, he took longer to say it.

Finally, Ashworth was able to go home. And the fact that he arrived there at nine thirty — the time he always took his first drink — had little to do with coincidence.

The Scotch and soda was poured while Peanuts flew around the lounge in a frenzy of welcome and while Sarah relayed news of the robbery and siege as it had appeared on the television. She was surprised when her husband displayed so little interest, but was supplied with the reason a while later.

When they were settled with their drinks, Ashworth told her of his defeat at the hands of Newton and broached his doubts over the Regent case. Sarah gave his words much thought, and then unwittingly covered much the same ground as Holly and Dutton.

But this time, Ashworth exploded. That uncharacteristic reaction was no doubt a combination of anger at being told by so many that he was wrong, and a need to relieve his frustrations — and who better to target than the person closest to him.

He stomped off upstairs with his drink and remained in his study for ten minutes. Then, calmer and rather ashamed, he made his way back downstairs. In the dining room he poured a fresh sherry for Sarah, and at the lounge, he poked the glass around the door.

'Peace offering,' he announced timidly.

Sarah laughed. 'Oh, come in, you daft thing.'

He gave her the glass, refilled his own, and settled in his favourite armchair.

'It looks as if Newton has got his comeuppance,' Sarah said conversationally. 'With his son, I mean.'

Ashworth made no comment.

'That's the difference between you two,' she continued in that same 'everything's fine' voice. 'I remember when John told you he wanted to be a writer. The look on your face . . .' She smiled at the memory. 'But after you'd talked to him, found out it was what he really wanted, you helped him in every way possible.'

The mention of his son brought a warm glow to Ashworth. 'Are you trying to take my mind off the fact that Newton bettered me?' he asked amiably.

'No, Jim, I'm saying you're a good father.'

'Newton didn't fight fair, you know. He lied, distorted the facts, went behind my back. He pulled every stroke in the book.'

Sarah let him talk, knowing it would be better out of his system.

'I could have done the same. The opportunity, the ammunition was there. I just couldn't bring myself to use it.'

Sarah crossed to her husband's chair and knelt beside it. 'Jim, my love, you went storming in from the front, because that's the only way you can live with yourself. Can't you see? That makes you worth ten of that jumped-up little twerp.'

'Perhaps.' He finished the Scotch and placed his glass on the floor. 'Oh, Newton doesn't bother me . . .' He caught Sarah's disbelieving expression and gave her a smile. 'Well, only my pride. No, it's what's happened to Edith Wright that really upsets me. In a short space of time her husband's cancer was diagnosed, then he was arrested and charged with murder, and then he suffered a violent death.' He shook his head despairingly, his large hands knotted into fists. 'Sarah, I look at that woman, and I can feel her heart breaking, and that makes me hurt. Can you understand that?'

She got to her feet and kissed his cheek tenderly. 'Yes, Jim, I can. It's one of the reasons why I love you. But you're trying to do the right thing for the wrong reason. Edith Wright's mind might be eased if she found out her husband didn't do it, but all the facts say he did.'

'Maybe you're right.'

'Are you having another drink?'

'No,' he said, 'not on an empty stomach. You go on up. I'll put the dog to bed.'

He could hear Sarah moving about upstairs as the dog trotted along behind him to the kitchen.

'In,' he commanded gently, pointing to the bed.

Peanuts bounced into it, instantly turning on to her back.

While Ashworth stroked her stomach, he mused, 'Do you know, girl, there's only one thing to do when things look this black, and that's pray.'

He had stopped stroking and the dog nudged his hand with her wet nose; and she carried on nudging until his attention was caught. Ashworth smiled down at the dog and resumed his stroking.

CHAPTER 26

It was a few minutes past midnight when a car dropped Mary Newton off.

She was hurrying down the drive when the door was flung open by her husband, his face distorted by rage.

'Where have you been?' he demanded, leaving her no time to answer. 'Have you any idea what Jamie's done?'

'He didn't have anything to do with the robbery,' Mary replied staunchly. 'He was living at the flat, but he left—'

'So he was mixing with that riff-raff — I don't believe it.'

'Yes, but he hasn't done anything, John. Aren't you pleased about that?'

'Pleased?' Newton strode into the lounge, then turned to his wife. 'Get in here.'

Mary followed meekly and stood before him. 'Don't let's argue, John. Jamie's safe. He's—'

'Oh, good, your precious son's safe.' He suddenly rounded on her. 'Did you know he was brought into the station for a caution?'

'Yes . . .'

Newton's eyes grew wide as he stared at his wife with incredulity. 'So you knew,' he muttered. 'Don't you realize how embarrassing that could have been for me? How it still might be?'

'Don't, John,' Mary pleaded.

'God, Ashworth of all people . . .'

'He tried to help Jamie. He talked to him.'

'Ashworth tried to help him?' Newton scoffed. 'I'll talk to the boy.'

'You'll talk *at* him, John. You talk at everybody.'

'Get him back here,' he ordered harshly.

'Stop it—'

'You just get him back here.'

'Jamie needs help,' she said desperately. 'He needs someone to talk him through this.'

'He needs a damned good thrashing.'

Mary started to cry, enraging her husband all the more.

'I'll sort the boy out,' he said. 'Give me ten minutes with him. Let him feel my belt.'

'Oh, for God's sake, shut up,' she screamed.

Never in the whole of their married life had Mary answered back. And it was an astonished Newton who stood speechless while she rushed to the mantelpiece, sweeping the ornaments from it with a stroke of her hand.

'I hate you,' she yelled through her tears. 'You've ruined my life, but you're not going to ruin my son's.'

She was hysterical now, and Newton grabbed her, bringing his hand heavily across her face.

'I hate you,' she cried, beating him with her fists. 'I have done for years.'

Suddenly she was still, and she stared at him, her eyes hard with a startling coldness. 'Do you know what he said, John? He said he wished Jim Ashworth was his dad.'

Newton reeled back in shock as he took in the look of triumph on her tear-stained face.

* * *

The plan Headlands had hatched the previous night was running exactly as he had hoped. He had guessed that Thornton would send his girlfriend to pick up the Giro, and he was proved right. She arrived at 8.30 a.m.

Headlands asked Beth to help; and under the misguided assumption that she was working with the police she willingly arranged for someone to take her place on reception so that she was free to follow the girl.

It was half an hour before the call came.

Unhurriedly, the reporter pushed himself off the bed and picked up the receiver. 'Yes?'

'She's gone into a block of flats in Stanwick Road,' Beth informed him.

'Good.' He reached for the *A–Z*. 'Do you know which number?'

'Yes, I followed her to the front door.'

'Wait outside. I'll be right there.' He replaced the receiver and grinned. 'Got you, kid. You could be my villa in the south of France.'

* * *

Ashworth received a telephone call before he left for work, and he felt a sense of relief on hearing that the siege in Hazeldene Road was over, and that Jamie Newton was not among those arrested. He knew perfectly well that his presence would be required at the interviews with the robbers, but he had other things to do, at a location far removed from the police station.

A light rain was falling as he climbed into the Sierra. Watching the hypnotic sway of the windscreen wipers, Ashworth started to hum cheerfully.

* * *

'Where's the guv'nor?' Holly snapped.

'I don't know,' Dutton bit back, from behind the reception desk. 'I'm not his bloomin' keeper.'

'We'd better get on with the interviews,' Josh ventured.

'But he should be here,' Holly said irritably.

'I rang his home,' Bobby Adams offered, 'and Mrs Ashworth said he'd already left.'

Holly glowered at the young constable. 'Right, we'd better get on with it, then.' And she strode off towards the interview rooms.

'What's wrong with her?' Dutton asked, his eyes fixed to the sway of her hips.

'Love life,' Josh said.

'Oh, I thought it might be monthly trouble.'

Josh smiled. 'Same thing with Holly. Once a month, her love life goes wrong.'

'Fine-looking lass,' Dutton remarked, leaning on the desk. 'But that temper . . .'

'Yes, sometimes I thank God I'm gay,' Josh admitted wryly.

'You know, she reminds me of Jim at times — better-looking, though,' Dutton added with a grin. 'Although you may not agree with that.'

Josh made a face and laughed good-naturedly.

Then a disgruntled Holly appeared at the door. 'Josh . . .'

'Coming, sir,' he muttered.

* * *

Headlands toured the block before parking the Volvo, driving past a puzzled Beth twice before he was satisfied. He climbed from the car and was promptly reminded of his little dispute with Holly. As a pain shot down his leg, he just hoped he would be up to the task ahead.

Stanwick Road was a main thoroughfare, containing heavy traffic but very few pedestrians. The traffic fumes stung his throat and nostrils as Headlands hurried towards Beth. Her face lit up when she saw him.

'How goes it, angel?'

'There're the flats, over there,' she said, pointing across the road.

Headlands studied the high-rise tower. 'The flat's on the ground floor, I take it.'

'Yes, the one with the beige curtains.'

'Do they know you're here?'

'I think so. They've both been looking out of the window.'

'Good. Give me five minutes, then knock on the door.'

Headlands was weaving through cars slowing in front of traffic lights, when Beth called, 'What shall I say when they answer?'

'They won't,' he assured her.

He darted in front of a delivery van, forcing it to stop. The vehicle's horn was sounded aggressively and Headlands disappeared around the side of the flats to the sound of the driver's shouted abuse.

* * *

Ashworth pulled the Sierra onto the grass verge opposite Witch's Cottage.

As he sat looking at the dwelling, reflecting on its violent history, a shiver ran the length of his spine. Every time he visited the place, he felt a presence which seemed to be forever growing in strength. Could Isobel Perkins really be haunting the place? A coward — physical or moral — he most definitely was not, but he still would not have relished an encounter with the dead witch.

He got out of the car, taking longer than usual to lock it, then crossed the lane, searching his pockets for the key the forensic department had retained since the investigation.

As he stepped along the garden path Ashworth tried to whistle, but found his mouth too dry. Then, chiding himself for his foolishness, he pulled the key from his pocket with a flourish and marched on.

He was about to insert it in the lock, when the door flew open, and the figure of a woman stood framed on the threshold.

* * *

Headlands was hardly in position at the rear of the flats before Thornton came out through the back window.

The boy was in a hurry; no sooner had his feet touched the ground than he bolted, tucking his T-shirt into his jeans as he ran.

Headlands had taken shelter behind a workmen's hut on the site of a half-demolished factory but, unfortunately, he mistimed the moment to break from cover. Thornton was some fifteen yards away, and when he saw the reporter, he skidded to a halt, his trainers sending up clouds of dust, and darted to his left, scrambling over piles of fallen masonry.

The reporter gave chase, cursing as sharp stones dug into his thin leather soles. Thornton swerved around a bulldozer, and glanced over his shoulder as he ran on, zigzagging his way through the machinery.

Headlands, his eyes smarting from the dust, kept up his pursuit, neither gaining nor losing ground. When he saw the boy enter the derelict factory, he slowed his pace. Inside, he could hear the sounds of the boy's trainers thumping on concrete steps.

The floor was strewn with lengths of disconnected copper and lead piping and other general debris. Headlands picked his way through it and started up the steps, every so often passing toilet blocks which still reeked of stale urine.

The footfalls above him ceased, but Headlands pushed on. He climbed four floors and found himself at the top of the structure. The roof had already been ripped off, and parts of the walls were missing.

At this height, the wind howled and tore into him as he made his way tentatively across the large area. Thornton was nowhere in sight.

Across the floor-space was a door, and Headlands passed through it, the wind billowing his clothing until he resembled the Michelin Man. Here, a large part of the floor was missing, and a single plank of wood had been thrown across the abyss. Beyond that was another large room, with stairs leading down at the far end.

'Bollocks,' Headlands groaned, as he eyed the plank. Staring down at the ground floor way below, he could see several people craning their necks to stare up at him.

There was nothing else for it. He would have to negotiate the plank.

Never a lover of heights, Headlands crossed his fingers and put out a cautious foot, his head spinning as he unwisely peered down.

With both feet now on the wooden bridge, he half closed his eyes and tried to edge forward against the buffeting wind.

* * *

'What are you doing here?' the woman asked shrilly.

'Bridgetown CID, madam,' Ashworth said, producing his warrant card. 'But more to the point — who are you?'

The woman, in her fifties and wearing a prim twinset and bedroom slippers, focused her small eyes on the card. 'I'm looking after the cat,' she said with an indignant sniff. 'I took him home with me at first. I live just round the corner, but he wouldn't settle, kept running back here.'

'Well, you can leave the locking up to me,' Ashworth said, edging past her into the hall.

'Make sure you do it properly,' the woman called, as she trudged up the path, her arms folded. 'There's a lot of crime about.'

'I'm aware of that, madam,' Ashworth remarked before closing the door.

He wandered into the kitchen where the cat was tucking into a dish of Whiskas. It looked up at his approach, and with hair on end, gave its characteristic spit.

'Behave yourself, or you're nicked,' Ashworth said mildly, as he beat a hasty retreat.

The stairs groaned their usual protests under his slow assent, but all too soon he was on the landing. Again he was greeted with that icy sensation on his face. He gave an involuntary shudder, and goose bumps prickled his skin.

'Yes, I know you're here,' he said, moving into the main bedroom.

Running his hands along the walls, he murmured, 'You're in the plaster, the brick. As long as this place stands, you'll be a part of it. You know what happened here. I just wish there was some way you could pass that on to me.'

He listened to the oppressive silence and chuckled. 'Well, I expected doors to be slamming, or windows crashing open and shut by now. Maybe even a big cat attacking me.'

The bedroom door creaked closed, its hinges grating.

'You don't frighten old Jim Ashworth,' he said loudly, trying to control his shaking legs. 'They did you a great wrong, Isobel, and for centuries you've been taking your revenge . . .' He cast nervous eyes around the empty room. 'You got Mick Wright in the end, didn't you? Have you ever stopped to think that if you could show one ounce of compassion or forgiveness, you might find some peace?'

He made himself cross to the door and open it. The black cat, teeth bared, talons drawn, howled in rage and came hurtling up the stairs towards him.

* * *

'Something's happened to him,' Holly persisted.

'Don't be silly,' Josh counselled. 'He's probably taken the morning off.'

They were in the CID office. The perpetrators of the raid on Ma's shop had been charged, and now the real reason for her concern was surfacing.

'I was trying to talk some sense into him last night,' she said, 'and I thought I had, but now it looks as if he's gone off on a tangent.'

'He's probably gone somewhere to lick his wounds,' Josh suggested.

'Knowing him, do you think that's likely?'

'No,' he admitted.

* * *

They were the six longest steps Headlands had taken in his life.

Once he reached the solid floor, he sank down on all fours, fighting for breath. Looking back, he could see the plank, still vibrating from his weight. As he had balanced high above the ground, all thoughts of catching Thornton had fled from his mind, but now they returned.

He looked towards the stairs. 'If they go right down, I've lost the son-of-a-bitch.'

Drawing in deep lungfuls of air, he got to his feet and stumbled towards them. In the distance, he could hear the wail of police sirens.

Rounding the corner, he stopped. The stairs were intact.

In his frustration, Headlands beat his fist against the remaining piece of wall again and again, repeatedly shouting, 'Bollocks.'

He quickly descended the stairs and was confronted by three men in smart suits. One of the men held up a hand for Headlands to stop, all the while surveying his expensive clothing thick with grime, his dust-covered hair.

Headlands eyed them cautiously. 'A young lad's just come down here.'

'Morton CID,' the burly man said, thrusting forward his warrant card. 'What do you think you're doing?'

'I'm from Bridgetown nick,' Headlands announced rashly.

The detectives exchanged glances.

'Look, that kid's Kevin Thornton. We've been looking for him,' he blustered. 'Why don't you ring Jim Ashworth?'

'Move,' the lead detective ordered sternly. 'And your story had better be true, because you've just disturbed a police raid. We've been after that lad for months.'

* * *

Ashworth left the cottage, dabbing a handkerchief at the lacerations on his face.

'Damned cat,' he muttered.

After securing the front door, he started along the path, and caught the ring of his car phone. Sprinting across the lane, he unlocked the Sierra and grabbed the receiver.

'Ashworth,' he snapped. 'Ah, Malc . . .' Kneeling on the front seat, he listened intently. 'I see. No, it's all right, I know where Thornton will be . . .' Then, almost to himself, 'He's got nowhere else to go.'

Once again, Headlands's voice was in his ear. 'All right, I'll clear it with the police. Put them on.'

It took him five minutes to convince the Morton detective that Headlands's story was true, and for the whole time he stood looking at Witch's Cottage.

With the call over, he smiled and said, 'Thank you, Isobel,' then got into the car and started the engine.

CHAPTER 27

Although Ashworth's step was firm as he mounted the steps to the station, his demeanour was furtive, and before pushing through the swing doors, he stopped to make sure that reception was deserted.

Martin Dutton, filling in a form at the desk, looked up. 'My God, Jim, what's happened to your face?'

'It doesn't matter,' he said, fingering the scratches on his cheekbone. 'Where's Newton?'

'At home, sorting his boy out, I think.'

'Holly and Josh?'

'In your office, worrying themselves sick about you. What's going on?'

Ashworth leant across and placed a hand on Dutton's shoulder in a conspiratorial gesture. 'The Regent girls — I need to know where they're staying.'

'The Saddler's Hotel.'

'Martin, I need to break them up, get one of them on their own.' When the sergeant made to protest, Ashworth said, 'Now, come on, I know your lads are keeping an eye on them.'

Dutton appeared apprehensive. He said, 'Jim, my old mucker, you really do push friendship to the limit.'

'Please, Martin.'

'All right.' Dutton said, sighing heavily. 'The eldest girl goes to a flat in Lancaster Road at about two o'clock every day.'

'That figures,' Ashworth mused.

Dutton shot him a puzzled glance. 'The lads think she goes there for drugs, but they daren't hang about because Newton's ordered that the girls are to be left alone. But as soon as they're out of the way, they intend to do the place.'

'It's not drugs, Martin,' Ashworth said, already backing away. 'What number is it?'

'Ten.'

'You haven't seen me,' he called.

Dutton watched the doors swinging back and forth after the chief inspector's hurried exit, and grumbled, 'This place gets more like a mental home every day.'

* * *

Mary Newton could hear their voices as she sat in the kitchen.

At first, she had cringed at her husband's strident tones drifting in from the lounge. But now, he sounded calmer, more reasonable. In fact, now it seemed to be Jamie's emotion-tinged voice dominating the discussion.

* * *

Katie spotted Ashworth and raced up the stone steps.

He had been waiting opposite the double-storey flats in Lancaster Road, and was moving before the main door slammed shut. Cursing, he ran up the steps, ducking under lines of washing that stretched across the wide causeway.

When Katie finally opened the door to his urgent knocking, the first thing he noticed was the telephone lying off the hook on the hall table.

'Cancelling your lover's visit, were you?' he asked with acrimony. 'It would have made things a lot easier if I'd got here before you'd done that.'

'What do you want?' Katie demanded angrily.

'A word,' Ashworth replied flatly.

'You've had more than one, now go away.'

'I'm going to speak to you. Now, I can do it here, or at the station,' he replied with his customary bluntness. 'If I pull you in for drugs, I can arrange lots of unpleasant things — an overnight stay, strip searches . . .'

Katie took a second to reflect on this, then reluctantly stood aside. 'You can come in, but I'm reporting this to Newton.'

When he entered the hall, Ashworth put the telephone receiver to his ear and chuckled at the dialling tone. Dropping it back in its cradle, he passed quickly through into the lounge.

Katie followed him in. 'What the hell do you want?'

'I'm looking for Thornton.'

'Well, you won't find him here.'

He wandered over to the window as Katie's voice lashed into him. 'You know your problem, Ashworth, there's nothing between your ears.'

'On the contrary,' he smiled grimly, 'there's quite a lot between my ears, and today it's been working overtime. I've picked my way through two almost perfect murders.'

'Really? Oh, why am I listening to this?'

He turned slowly, and grinned. 'Because you want to hear how much I know.'

'God.' Katie sank into a chair, making no attempt to stifle a yawn.

'You've cancelled your afternoon in bed, so what else have you got to do?' Ashworth said, perching on an arm of the settee. 'It's funny, sex drive has played an important part in this case. I suppose Joyce Regent was a pathetic character in many respects, but it wasn't her sex drive which led to her death . . . it was Kevin Thornton's.'

'Mick Wright killed Joyce — everybody knows that.'

'Oh no, but most people think he did.' He paused, then said, 'Kevin Thornton's an intelligent lad — dishonest, criminal, but clever. When he moved in with Joyce in London, things could have run their course. When she tired of him, he could have just moved on. But he couldn't keep his hands off young Tanya, and he got her pregnant. Now Tanya was madly in love with him. She would have followed him if he'd left, and that didn't fit in with his plans.

'It was the move to Bridgetown that really sealed Joyce's fate. Mick Wright was a gift, wasn't he? The poor devil had already admitted sending two threatening letters. It was Thornton, displaying the callous side to his nature, who killed the cat and stuck it on the door, knowing full well it would be attributed to Wright, who played his part by turning up at the cottage and attacking Joyce and, of course, you. I believe that's when the decision to kill Joyce was taken.'

'And Thornton was doing all this without anybody else knowing?' Katie scoffed.

'Oh, no,' Ashworth smiled. 'You were both in on it — that's the only way it could work.'

'You're out of your mind.'

Ashworth pressed on. 'After Joyce was killed, it looked like plain sailing. Fate dealt Mick Wright another lousy card — it put him at the scene of the attack. So, the man was in custody, but wouldn't live to stand trial, and everything looked rosy — until the body of Tanya's stillborn baby turned up. Then the hunt for Thornton was on again, and you knew if I kept looking, I'd find him. So Wright had to be sacrificed.

'I believe he was telephoned at the prison, and told that if he came to Witch's Cottage, the curse would be lifted.' He shrugged. 'I'll be kind to you here — perhaps you thought the escape, the journey to the cottage, would kill him. But Mick got there, so he had to be disposed of, murdered, and his death made to look like self-defence.'

'And what would I get out of all this?'

'Money,' Ashworth stated simply. 'Joyce's fortune.'

'But I stand to inherit half of that.'

'No, you don't,' Ashworth insisted.

'OK, so I'm not in the will,' Katie flared. 'It all goes to Tanya. But how would I have benefited, going around murdering people?'

Ashworth smiled. 'You would have benefited after the third murder had taken place. And that *would* have been the perfect murder.'

'The *third* murder? And who would that have been?'

'Tanya.'

Katie laughed. 'What?'

'Tanya,' Ashworth repeated firmly. 'It's already begun — pumping drugs into her. When she's sixteen she'll marry Thornton, at eighteen, she'll inherit. She'll be a registered addict, and with her surname changed, well, a junkie's death by overdose would go unnoticed.'

'And Kevin and I walk off into the sunset with a fortune,' Katie scoffed.

Ashworth said nothing, a knowing smile on his lips.

'You'd better go now.'

'Oh, I can't do that,' he said quietly.

Katie jumped up and flung open the lounge door. 'Leave.'

But he remained seated.

'Look, Ashworth, you're missing one thing in all this — you haven't got Kevin, and you're never going to find him. You'll never keep tabs on us when we leave here. If Tanya did take an overdose in another part of the country, or even abroad, well . . .'

Katie's mocking laughter told Ashworth that a nerve had been touched, proving that he was close to being right.

He got to his feet and, smiling slyly, dug a hand into the pocket of his waxed jacket. 'That's as close to an admission as I need.'

Alarm crossed Katie's face as he started to withdraw the hand. 'You haven't been taping this?'

Ashworth's expression was pained. 'Oh dear, you've been watching too much junk television. But I haven't been entirely honest with you. I received a message this morning.' He hesitated. 'I was told where I'd find Thornton.'

* * *

It was a humble Newton who opened the door to CID to find Holly ranting around the office. She was horrified that magistrates had granted bail to the gang who held up Ma's shop, and incensed that Ashworth had gone without her to interview Katie.

Newton coughed. 'A message from Ashworth,' he said. 'It seems he has the Thornton lad in a flat in Lancaster Road. He's requested back-up.'

'On our way, sir,' Holly said, motioning to Josh.

* * *

Ashworth was striding restlessly along the causeway at the flats, cursing himself for his stupidity.

While he was explaining how he knew Thornton would be in the flat, Katie had suddenly bolted into the bedroom, pulling furniture across the door before he could get to it. He tried to shoulder it open, but the door would not budge.

So, he was in a dilemma. He could persist with the door, making escape through the rear window a possibility, or he could radio for help. He chose the latter, and in minutes a mobile was positioned in a slip road behind the flats.

Ashworth's radio crackled. 'Nothing showing here, Chief Inspector,' PC Bennett informed him. 'The bedroom window's wide open, but I can't see anybody.'

'Stay in place, Alan, I'm going in.'

'Will do.'

As Ashworth started to move, Holly and Josh came bounding up the steps.

'What gives, guv?' she asked breathlessly.

'Thornton's in there,' he told her. 'Or I hope he still is. He's barricaded in the bedroom.'

They rushed inside the flat as Ashworth explained, 'I intended to disturb an assignation, but it didn't work out as I'd hoped.'

'What, you mean Katie — Thornton?' Josh asked, as they crossed the lounge.

'Spot on.'

Ashworth's weight hit the bedroom door, but it still refused to move. He took several steps back and ran at it, grunting with pain as his shoulder collided with the wood.

The door shuddered slightly, and something behind it slid back a little way across the carpet.

'It's giving, guv,' Josh shouted.

Ashworth kicked out at the door, and slowly it began to open. With each kick it moved back several inches until they could squeeze through.

Holly was the first in. 'He's gone, guv, there's only the girl.'

Ashworth looked towards the open window, its curtain billowing in the breeze.

Straight away, Katie sprang towards him, fists flying. 'You clever bastard.'

Holly went into action, aiming a karate kick at Katie's middle, and following up with an arm-lock. 'Steady, girl,' she cautioned.

As they struggled, Ashworth strode forward, pointing a finger. 'Kevin Thornton,' he said, 'I'm arresting you on suspicion of the murders of Joyce Regent and Mick Wright . . .'

Throughout the rest of the caution, Holly and Josh stood transfixed, while the person they believed to be Katie Regent screamed doubt on Ashworth's parentage.

* * *

The whole of the station was in shock by the time Thornton and Tanya were brought in.

Holly and Josh conducted the interviews, during which many of Ashworth's suspicions were borne out.

He looked up expectantly when they entered the office.

'Both charged, guv,' Josh told him.

'Good,' Ashworth mused.

Making no attempt to conceal the anger in her voice, Holly said, 'You should have told us, guv.'

'I couldn't.'

'We could have brought him in for a strip-search.'

'It wouldn't have worked.'

'Bollocks.'

Ashworth sprang to his feet. 'Holly, there's a line, and you're crossing it.'

She glared at him, then flounced to her chair, still muttering.

Resuming his seat, Ashworth said defensively, 'I guessed Thornton had rented that flat so he'd have somewhere to take his girls, and I would've liked to catch him with his trousers down, so to speak. But he spotted me, so that put paid to that.'

'You could have brought him into the station,' Holly grumbled.

'That wouldn't have given us a result. It would have proved Katie was Thornton, nothing more. I had to go in and make him think I could prove everything I was saying, and I couldn't have done that in an interview situation. If we'd brought them in, they'd have played one off against the other; and although Tanya's an accessory, I don't want her getting the twenty-five years Thornton's facing. She doesn't deserve that.'

'That thing with the names was clever, guv,' Josh said, 'but surely you didn't go in just on that?'

'You see, Josh, what always worried me about Thornton was that he couldn't be found. The press, the police, they were all looking for him. Now that suggested he was either dead, out of the country, or hiding behind another identity. That's why I was so keen on the lad Malc was chasing all over Morton — that boy was changing names every day.'

He leant back in the chair, hands clasped behind his head. 'I don't think the interplay with the names was meant to be clever, it was just convenient. Thornton had always been known by his initials, and any way you say KT, it comes out as Katie. So when the press started swarming around Joyce, he didn't need to change his name, or even his appearance overmuch. With that effeminate face, high-pitched voice, long hair, he just needed to wear those baggy clothes and he became a girl.'

'Who was Malc chasing all over Morton, then?' Holly asked.

'Oh, we've stopped sulking, have we?' Ashworth teased.

Holly allowed herself a smile as Ashworth said, 'That was unfortunate. The lad was involved in a benefit fraud, signing on all over the country, using different names. That positive reaction we got when I asked if he'd ever called himself Kevin Thornton was probably due to the fact that he couldn't remember whether he had or not. Anyway, he saw Malc here and assumed we were after him for that. He's been using Morton for sometime, and the local police were on to him.' He laughed. 'They were none too pleased when Malc fouled up their operation.' He spread his hands. 'There, does that cover everything?'

'No, it doesn't,' Holly said. 'You risked everything: job, pension, even credibility. What made you so certain that Katie was really Thornton?'

'The cat told me.'

Holly laughed. 'The cat?'

Ashworth got up and reached for his waxed jacket. 'Yes. I knew Thornton was here, and hiding behind another identity, so I went to the cottage and asked Isobel Perkins to tell me what happened . . .'

'And she got the cat to jump on your shoulder, and whisper in your ear,' Holly quipped.

'I like to think she did,' Ashworth said, suddenly pensive. 'As I was leaving, the animal attacked me . . .'

Holly was puzzled. 'It always did, guv, it couldn't stand you.'

'It couldn't stand men, Holly, but it loved women.'

She thought back to the day at the cottage when the cat wrestled playfully on her lap. 'Yes, but I still don't follow.'

'As that cat came hurtling up the stairs at me . . .' He paused, fingering the scratches on his cheek. 'It's hard to explain, but I saw clearly our first visit to the cottage, after we warned Malc off. It suddenly flashed into my mind, and I saw it as plainly as I'm seeing you. Katie was walking up the stairs . . . and the cat started spitting at her.'

'Of course,' Holly said, bringing a hand up to her forehead. 'Meaning she was a he.'

'That's right,' Ashworth said, zipping up his jacket. 'Now, the odds on total recall of such an irrelevant incident must be millions to one.' He smiled. 'No one will ever convince me I didn't receive some help.'

He left his bewildered detectives to mull over his words. In the corridor Superintendent Newton was marching quickly towards him.

'Congratulations on the case,' he said briskly.

'Thank you.'

'Ashworth, I don't think I'm ever going to get along with you, because you get my back up.'

'Well, as a policeman, I've very little respect for you, and as a man, I've even less.'

Newton's eyes narrowed. 'You have to have the last word, don't you?'

'Whenever possible,' Ashworth agreed.

'I've been home, talking to my son,' Newton said quietly, unable to look the chief inspector in the face. 'He was almost in on that newsagent raid, but he told me that something you said made him stop and think.' He did look at Ashworth then. 'And whatever our differences, that's something I must thank you for.'

'Jamie's a fine lad. I hope he makes it.'

'I shall give him all the help I can,' Newton said, almost to himself. 'Well, we'll leave it there, shall we . . . Chief Inspector?'

Ashworth inclined his head. 'For the moment . . . sir.'

Newton was about to offer a rebuke, but stopped as a spark of humour showed in his eyes.

'Now, if you don't mind,' Ashworth said, 'I'm going home to have a shave.'

THE END

ACKNOWLEDGEMENTS

I would like to thank the West Midlands Police and Mr David Seary of Her Majesty's Prison, Winson Green, Birmingham, for their kind assistance during the writing of this book.

ALSO BY BRIAN BATTISON

DETECTIVE JIM ASHWORTH SERIES
Book 1: TIED TO MURDER
Book 2: THE PRICE OF MURDER
Book 3: FLIRTING WITH MURDER
Book 4: MURDER IN THE COTTAGE

MORE BOOKS IN THE SERIES COMING SOON!

Thank you for reading this book.

If you enjoyed it please leave feedback on Amazon or Goodreads, and if there is anything we missed or you have a question about, then please get in touch. We appreciate you choosing our book.

Founded in 2014 in Shoreditch, London, we at Joffe Books pride ourselves on our history of innovative publishing. We were thrilled to be shortlisted for Independent Publisher of the Year at the British Book Awards.

www.joffebooks.com

We're very grateful to eagle-eyed readers who take the time to contact us. Please send any errors you find to corrections@joffebooks.com. We'll get them fixed ASAP.

Printed in Great Britain
by Amazon

25722616R00172